STRIFE

The Novel

Terrance Mobley

Copyright © 2020 Terrance Mobley
All rights reserved
First Edition

PAGE PUBLISHING, INC.
Conneaut Lake, PA

First originally published by Page Publishing 2020

ISBN 978-1-68348-525-4 (pbk)
ISBN 978-1-68348-526-1 (digital)

Printed in the United States of America

Contents

Acknowledgments 5

Strife 7

Prologue 9

The Road to Oblivion 13

Coming Storm 20

Boogey Man 23

Calling in the Dead 30

If Only It Was Just a Nightmare 40

Utopia 46

Broken Dreams 53

Selection 58

Last Breath 66

The Void 73

We, Not the People 80

Death Awaits You 88

Price of Knowledge..91

May Tomorrow Come..96

Secrets, Lies, and Holo-Vids..99

Bad Deal...102

Not So Friendly Rivalry...104

Liberation of Chaos..109

The Truth of Lies..118

Conception..124

Gladiator..132

Point of View..139

Old Wounds..147

Raging River..153

False Beginning...168

Turning Point...178

Shall We Begin..185

Acknowledgments

WELL, I HAVE TO SAY it has been a long road, and one I never quite thought I would get to the end of. I want to, first and foremost, thank God for so much, because without him and the talent he has given me in the form of a wonderful imagination and the heart to dream beyond the boundaries of everyday life, I could never have written this book. Next, I want to thank my buddy, my brother from another mother, and my best friend Gerald (a.k.a. Jay). Thanks for always encouraging me to believe that it was okay to let my imagination fly. To my dear friend Emily, I want to say thank you for all the love and support throughout the years. To my amazing sister Latoya, thank you for believing in me and always being there to encourage me, keeping me on the right path, and keeping me eager to see my dream come to reality. Next, I would like to thank my BFF Samantha. She has always been like a sister to me. Thank you for always reminding me that life is supposed to be fun and that my happiness is important. To my good friend Kay, thank you for your honesty and mentorship in turning my dream into the book you now hold. To Chelsea, a great friend who is proof that everyone God allows to cross our path in life holds meaning, thanks for all your help. Finally, in saving the best for last, I would like to thank Angie for so much. Without her, "Strife" would never have seen the light of day. Truly God blessed me the day he brought our lives together. Words can't even begin to explain how much you have been a blessing in my life and to the creation of this book. Through your love, support, mentorship, friendship, and heaven-sent dedication to see my dream come to life, I now present to you *Strife*.

Strife

IN THE YEAR 2126 THE United Space Coalition (USC) sits on the brink of extinction, decimated by an unrelenting, unforgiving, merciless enemy in a fifteen-year war created by the desire to expand the boundaries of its control across the stars. With total annihilation looming ever closer, desperation has forced a last-ditch effort to preserve the coalition. A colonization fleet has been launched with the hopes of starting over far from the reach of their executioner, the Demzerai.

Survive; that is the sole mission of the USC's last colony fleet. Ensure that the remnants of humanity and its Vaxian allies can rebuild and live. Yet they still dream of peace hidden away from their Demzerai executioners.

Forced to land upon the alien world of Tallagen, Colonization Fleet Epsilon has forged a new home over the last 175 cycles. Everyday citizens huddled behind the safety of the cities' barriers and holographic skies overhead, gladly embrace the illusion of utopia. However, peace is merely a word mentioned in the halls of the senate, while outside the barrier's death and the constant threat of war are as sure as the sun rises.

But now whispers of deception have begun to unfold. Greed, desperation, and the lust for power threaten to consume not only the colonies but Tallagen itself.

Prologue

FIRST LIEUTENANT NORMA CAROLA SAT monitoring the two screens at her station aboard the battlecruiser USCS *Advent*. Her nervousness added to the tension that already hung so heavily in the air from the rest of the bridge crew. Even Captain Bill Trevor, whose poise never seemed to waver even during the grueling battle at Loasan, seemed to be on edge. Although he didn't express it on his face, his pace back and forth about the bridge to double-check weapons, shields, sensors, and engineering along with his calls for constant updates from the flight deck was a clear giveaway that Captain Trevor was more than just concerned with ensuring that every station was operating at peak performance and was ready for the unexpected. Lieutenant Carola could understand his desire to ensure the *Advent* was ready.

The battle in the Loasan system had taken a severe toll on the United Space Coalition. Some two hundred and seventy human and Vaxian capital ships and well over four hundred thousand lives had been lost. The *Advent* was one of the few ships that had managed to escape the massacre when Fleet Admiral Malone signaled for all surviving ships to retreat. Admiral Malone's ship never made it out. His flagship, the carrier USCS *Rheinholt*, had been too badly damaged. There was no way the carrier had any chance in making it back through the jump gate, but he had known that when he ordered what was left of the fleet to retreat.

Once again, the USC had been defeated. It was almost always the same case when fighting the Demzerai. They held a major tactical advantage, outclassing the USC in every area of technology, from weaponry to defenses. Victories against them were far and few between. More often than not, each engagement with them ended in defeat for the USC and Loasan had proved to be no different.

Demzerai ships were capable of entering hyperspace on their own without having to depend on jump gates like the USC. Giving their ships a tactical advantage that allowed them to jump directly into a star system without warning, a common tactic of theirs. Within seconds of their arrival, they would immediately begin to unleash deadly barrages, crippling or outright destroying ships before a fleet had a chance to react. The battle at Loasan had begun the same way. The minutes that followed felt like hours as the fleet reacted, moving to close the distance to bring the Demzerai ships into weapon range. The USCS *Norwin*, a Shilow class cruiser, erupted into a miniature sun off the starboard bow as its forward shields collapsed and it took a direct hit that cut through its bow all the way to its fusion core. Any ship short of a battlecruiser was only able to sustain a few direct hits before their shields were compromised or failed altogether. Then the real slaughter would begin. Dozens of other ships were downed before the USC fleet was able to get within range to retaliate.

Ships were reduced to burning wrecks or exploded into massive balls of fire that lit up like the stars themselves as their fusion cores were breached. The Demzerai were unrelenting in the attack; their captains had no desire for prisoners. Demzerai fighters were known for intentionally targeting escape pods and lifeboats. Very rarely were there ever survivors to be found after a battle with the Demzerai. Time after time, when reserves or a rescue operation were sent in after a battle, they were met with fields of debris and burnt-out hulls. Because of this fact, Admiral Malone and his crew positioned the *Rheinholt* between the Demzerai fleet and the jump gate instead of trying to escape. With all the power they could muster, they dove full speed into the heart of the Demzerai fleet before overloading the *Rheinholt*'s core. The *Advent* managed to pass through the jump gate just as the *Rheinholt*'s explosion took out the Demzerai flagship as well as several others. Admiral Malone and his crew's brave sacrifice had paid off, allowing twenty-four ships to escape the massacre at Loasan.

STRIFE

The USCS *Advent* was lucky that day in her escape; she had taken heavy damage during the engagement at Loasan, with even heavier personnel losses. Almost a quarter of her crew had been lost. Five weeks in dry-dock at the Kippa shipyard and an influx of fresh crew members to replace those lost or those too injured to ship out had brought the *Advent* to 82 percent readiness. In reality, the *Advent* would need at least another six weeks in dry-dock to be back at 100 percent. But there just wasn't any time left. The news of the Demzerai fleets' devastating victories at the core systems of Centauri Prime, Furo, and Gammatin meant they were only a few weeks away at most from being able to attack the Sol System. The Vaxian's home system had already been lost just months ago to the Demzerai. Over sixteen billion men, women, and children had been annihilated in less than ninety-six hours. The news of the Vaxian fall sent the overwhelming message throughout the USC. The Demzerai would not stop until every piece of the USC was wiped from the galaxy. The USC was given no time to lick its wounds; it had to fight back and hold the Demzerai at bay until operation "Godspeed" was ready.

Much was being gambled on Operation *Godspeed* being successful. The hope of the United Space Coalition rested in the hands of over three million colonists aboard the seventy-two ships now slowly moving into formation above the planet Marrium. The *USCS Advent* was now tasked to escort Marrium along with the cruisers USCS *Darthom* and *Highmoors*. Together, they would form Colonization Fleet *Epsilon 218*, the USC's last effort to prevent their utter annihilation. The weight of it all was more than anyone was expected to bear. The previous colonization fleet *Charlie 217* had been destroyed by a Demzerai surprise attack on the Yinti-Two shipyard. Considering recent events, it was completely understandable that Captain Trevor along with the entire crew was on edge, especially since the survival of the USC was at stake.

Lieutenant Carola's attention was suddenly drawn back from past events by warning chimes and the steady flow of tactical information scrolling across her station's screens as the ship's sensors detected Demzerai warship arriving into the system.

"Captain! Enemy contacts, bearing Alpha four-point six-two, Yankee seven point nine," Lieutenant Carola called out with urgency, trying to mask her growing fear at the situation.

Immediately, the crew began to scramble as Captain Trevor, who was standing nearby, called for battle stations. The rest of the fleet was also beginning to mobilize as well. An attack had been anticipated by the USC and precautions were put in place to prevent a repeat of what had happened at Yinti-Two.

"Signal the colonization fleet to prepare to move out at full speed, heading Alpha four-point six-two, Yankee seven point nine on my command. Have the *Darthom* and *Highmoors* move to flank positions," Captain Trevor ordered as he watched the Demzerai warships closing in on the holo-screens in the command and control center of the bridge.

"They jumped right in between us and the jump gate, Bill," Lieutenant Captain Grutter, the XO, said as he watched the Demzerai attack force spread out. "They're moving into a "U" formation, trying to corral us and prevent us from getting to the jump gate by having us plunge straight into them."

"We have no choice, let's hope our strike fleets behind the moons can buy us the time we need," Captain Trevor said with a look of resolve on his face that expressed he was willing to do whatever it took, to get the fleet through the jump gate.

The Road to Oblivion

THE MOMENT THE MONEY WAS transferred to his account, he couldn't have cared less what the job entailed as long as he then would have the means to restore his name and obtain his revenge. That was until he found himself here, thirty-five miles outside the safety of Kansin's Barrier, about to enter an abandoned school once used to teach Feralans to speak the common dialect. Of all the jobs Marcus Johanis had undertaken, this one was the first that made him second guess if the money was really worth it. When he was first contacted by the mysterious woman simply known as Coraina, he was unsure of what to think. She was offering half the payment upfront to deliver a small artifact locked in a stasis box. The fact that the initial payment turned out to be far more than his normal exorbitant fee was all the incentive he needed—he jumped at the job. It seemed too good to be true, but he hadn't had a decent job offer in the last thirteen months. Not since the Sonjo cartel leader, Rubin Coo had screwed him over by spreading that he was responsible for taking out Anjon Gurtail, the third-largest cartel boss in Kansin. Rubin, the bastard that had hired him for the hit in the first place, and then turned around and tried to have him killed to clean up the loose ends. In less than one cycle, he had gone from being the premier go-to hitman for the crime cartels to a facking errand boy, constantly having to look over his shoulder as every wannabe hitman was looking to take him out and make a name for themselves. Collecting on the reward being offered for his head by the cartels was an obvious bonus.

He laughed at the idea. Take him out? Me, Marcus Johanis, a.k.a. Charon? A devilish smile crossed his face at the thought of all the fools he had killed for trying to earn a name off him. Fack, the whole Sonjo cartel, every one of them, would die a slow, agonizing death while knowing it was Charon who snuffed out their miserable facking lives. Especially, Rubin, he thought to himself.

The job, up until now, had gone smoothly; transportation and documentation had been arranged to get him outside the barrier without raising any suspicions. He had been given military patrol routes—times of patrols, heavily controlled areas, and com-link frequencies, allowing him to slip past unnoticed. Everything was working like clockwork just as Coraina said it would. Someone with a lot of influence had to be behind this all; access to such high-level military security information was far above any of the cartel informants. With the thought of how his bank account was going to look, he shrugged his shoulders and realized he could give a fack, so long as he got the rest of his pay.

Before long he had arrived at the coordinates, he was given to make his drop. It didn't look like much, but then again, the abandoned station had been unused for some twenty cycles. His hand went to the pistol holstered on his hip as he pushed aside the foliage that partially blocked the otherwise unobstructed entrance to the building. Inside was dark except for the occasional pen-sized beams of light that squeezed between the vegetation covering the greater portion of the building and windows. He fumbled around in a side pocket of his backpack before retrieving a light stick. With a snap, the stick began emitting a soft light that filled the immediate area, sending several ranknids scurrying into the shadows nearby. He clutched the gun at his side a little tighter, startled by their sudden movement.

"Facking scavengers…just facking scavengers that's all…relax," he muttered to himself.

Very few things unnerved him, but something about the foot-long centipede-like creatures made the hairs on the back of his neck stand up. He took a deep breath to calm his nerves before continuing on. The inside of the building was larger than it had looked from the outside. Split into two main rooms, he was in the smaller of the two. It seemed most likely to have been a reception area considering the vegetation-covered counter and cracked view screen partially hanging on the wall behind it. To the left, there was a doorway, the doors partially ripped from their hinges, hung loosely, having been violently forced open long ago.

He cautiously stepped forward, one hand on his weapon and ready to draw at the first sign of danger, the other raising the light stick to push back the seemingly endless darkness of the larger room. Desk and chairs laid scattered about, overgrown with moss and plant life. An eerie silence hung in the air, only broken by the occasional sound of a ranknid's multiple legs rapidly hitting the wooden floor in succession as they scurried away to escape the approaching light.

"Facking bugs. I don't know why you even exist, except to make my damn skin crawl," he said out loud, crushing the rear of a ranknid under his boot with a sickening crunch as it tried to dart to the safety of an overturned desk.

The bug hissed back in defiance and revealed inch-long fangs as its mandibles flexed open in the throes of death. Startled, he stepped back while slowly removing his machete from his backpack, keeping his eyes on the dying insect and judging just how close he was willing to get, before lashing out and severing the insect's head from its body with cruel satisfaction.

Suddenly, something much larger moved nearby. Cycles of training kicked in and a rush of adrenaline flooded his bloodstream. In the space of a breath, his pistol was drawn while his mind raced to comprehend how something so large had gotten so close without him noticing. A flash of metal and a slap-like blow to the back of his hand sent his pistol flying into the darkness, followed by another rapid blow to the back of his legs, which forced him to his knees. The sudden realization of a cold razor-sharp edge at rest across the back of his neck quickly put aside the idea of fighting back. Slowly, he removed his hand from the combat blade holstered on his hip along with his grip on the machete. He raised his hands in surrender as he sat back on his legs, turning slightly to the left to see his attacker that now stood fully in the light of his light stick.

The Feralan stood like a statue, her spear-like sword gripped firmly in her hand keeping her out of his reach for the moment. Turning his head to get a better view, he felt the sting of fresh blood trickle down his neck and silently cursed. He noticed the gleam coming from an identical spear-like sword in her left hand. Marcus attempted levity, "Let me guess…you're as good with your right hand as you are with your left? So, ridding you of the one held at my neck would likely still not change the current situation. I bet you give great handjobs being ambidextrous. Oh, the fun we could have," he said cheekily.

The elegant dark brown armor she wore resembled molded wood rather than the metal it actually was, providing protection to vital areas without restricting her movement. It was a deep contrast to her fiery red hair, which was tightly woven into a braid draped over her left shoulder.

"FYI, I've got to make sure I don't damage that pretty armor of yours, sweetheart," he sneered sarcastically.

A wicked smirk played across his face as he played with the thought of seeing her ample nakedness; what little fear he had felt was quickly turning into something far more sinister. Had she not held a blade ready to decapitate him, he would have been aroused at the thought of her trying to fight back as he took her before he slit her throat. He locked eyes with her, searching for any weakness to take advantage of and thus, turn this predicament around to his advantage, yet the animalistic face mask she wore concealed all but the hatred in her emerald eyes.

"Pa'tack le na ahel kuch nild," she finally spat coldly, breaking the long tense silence.

"Yeah, I am going to love facking you too, sweetheart." He smiled back maliciously.

"Actually, Marcus Johanis," she said, "you are pathetic, no better than vermin. Would you choose to prove her correct?" a unified chorus of male and female voices responded from beyond the light to his left.

Marcus turned his head to see who was speaking, cursing himself as the sting of the unrelenting Feralan blade bit into his neck again and the sensation of fresh blood began to trickle anew. He strained to see beyond the reach of the light.

"Who might you be?" Marcus growled, doing little to hide his growing agitation.

"I am the voice of many that speak for one, a simple messenger, no more, no less. I am a means to a beginning," the mysterious figured replied.

"What the fack does that mean?" Marcus shot back.

The mysterious figure spoke again, this time toward the Feralan in her native tongue, ignoring Marcus's crude question. Slowly, the Feralan warrior lifted her blade from his neck while moving to join the figure now standing just beyond the edge of the light.

Taking a moment to recover his weapons, Marcus stood and said, "Well, now that we got the pleasantries out of the way, how about we get done with what I came here for so I can collect the rest of my payment? I have quite a few people left to kill…painfully." Marcus smirked eyeing the Feralan.

Ignoring Marcus, the mysterious figure stepped forward into the light of the circle to hand the Feralan warrior a book of some sort wrapped in cloth, which she quickly secured in a leathery pouch on her waist. She turned to leave the chamber, eyeing Marcus intensely, her eyes full of hatred. She paused briefly before passing by him to utter something sharply before continuing, on disappearing into the darkness.

"Don't you go too far, sexy. I won't be long," Marcus called over his shoulder. If she did manage to get away, once he got back to Kansin, he would find a woman with fiery red hair like the Feralan and take out all his frustration on her before killing her, he figured. He smiled at the thought, yet there was still business to attend to first.

He shrugged off his backpack and cleared his mind of his murderous fantasy, for now, returning his full attention to the mysterious robed figure before him. It moved closer but seemed to glide rather than walk across the mossy floor, which made Marcus somewhat uneasy for some reason. Perhaps, it was the fact that as hard as he tried to gain a glimpse of the mysterious figure's face, it remained hidden beneath the hood it wore. Perhaps it was because the underlying male and female voices that spoke no longer sounded artificial as he had first thought.

"You have something for me, Marcus Johanis. It is why you are here," the robed figure intoned as it motioned toward his backpack.

With his original mission again at the forefront of his mind, he quickly replied, "Yeah, let's get this over with. Here's the stasis box I was told to deliver. Enjoy, I'm out of here. I got about fifteen minutes before the next military patrol comes through this area," Marcus said, handing over the box and tossing his backpack on his left shoulder.

"Marcus Johanis, I have one more offer for you."

"No thanks, I got all I need. Hire someone else. I have my own plans to attend to," Marcus said interrupting the robed figure as he turned to walk away.

"I offer you far more than you can currently comprehend, Marcus Johanis. I offer you redemption, to become greater than you are, to serve a higher purpose."

The robed figure moved closer to place a hand on his shoulder. Immediately Marcus readied his gun, pointing it directly at the head of the robed figure. "Do not even think to facking touch me! Save your facking religious babble for someone who gives a damn, understand?"

A chill fell upon the room as the robed figure slowly backed away. "I offer you one final chance. Do not allow ignorance to cloud your mind, Marcus Johanis."

Marcus fired a shot just to the left of the robed figure, intentionally missing its head by mere inches. "You don't get it, I said no!"

"Very well. Lord Harbinger Thaticus, he has made his choice. I leave you to your fate, Marcus Johanis," the robed figure proclaimed as it faded into the darkness.

Marcus backed away slowly. Not much had seemed right since the robed figure appeared but now something really felt wrong. He could sense another presence, the terrifying aura it emitted chilled the room. Nervously, his eyes searched the area within the confines of his light stick's illumination, the hair on the back of his neck standing at attention. For the first time, since he was a boy being chased through the sewers by rival gang members, he felt the prickle of true fear. Sweat beaded down his face, his breathing grew shallow and quick, and panic overtook him. He turned to run, dropping his light stick in the process but immediately halted, falling to the ground as he slammed into something large within the darkness. Petrified, he looked up and realized that what he had hoped was a wall was actually something far beyond his fragile psyche's comprehension. A giant towered over him in complete silence, its grim features hidden within the shadows cast from the dying light stick, which now laid out of his reach.

On the ground and unable to run, Marcus's survival instinct to fight kicked in and he raised his pistol, firing again and again in rapid session. He was heedless to the fact that each round ricocheted off the giant's armor, continuing to pull the trigger long after the magazine was emptied. Callously, the giant reached down with one massive three-fingered hand seizing Marcus by the wrist and lifting him from the ground effortlessly, deliberately crushing every bone within his wrist and shattering his forearm in the process. In a last-ditch show of defiance fueled by both desperation and pain, Marcus thrashed and kicked but it was to no avail. The giant remained unyielding and silent until Marcus finally fell still. Delirious with pain and exhaustion, Marcus hung as limp as a rag doll, suspended several feet from the ground. In almost complete silence. The giant drew him closer. The sounds of his heavily beating heart and ragged breathing seemed to amplify as Marcus lifted his head to stare into the giant's unblinking jet-black eyes that stared back at him through the helm. Ancient, cold, remorseless they drew him into their dark and unforgiving depths.

The unbearable silence was slowly stripping away at what remained of his sanity. It felt as if death itself was in attendance and even the creeping vermin no longer scurried about for fear of being noticed. Then, the giant spoke. His voice powerful, deep, and commanding, he intoned, "Proceed to oblivion."

Over the next few minutes, Marcus felt the life within him slowly drain away and dimly heard the cacophony of his own screams, fueled by the burning agony that ignited every nerve ending in his body, before finally there was nothingness.

Coming Storm

SERGEANT SECOND CLASS GERALD HOCK, or Cav, never really got excited about a mission until the doors opened; he preferred to just recline back into his battle-frame and allow his mind to take him somewhere else. He would tune out the background chatter coming from the pilots, Captain England, and Captain Mathers, as they talked over the com-link with the control tower prior to take off, getting weather updates and other situational awareness information for the flight.

He chuckled as he heard the voice of Lieutenant Cosby, the new navigator. He was only a second lieutenant and new to the flight crew on the dropship. This would be his first real mission. He was a young and overeager nineteen-cycle-old kid from the Ritz district of New Hope. He had the, "I had it all, but now I want to rebel and piss off my filthy rich parents" attitude; so he joined the Aviation Corps and sheared his strawberry blonde hair into the traditional "high and tight" to see the world outside the barrier.

As Cav slowly drowned out the LT's voice from his thoughts, he looked around at his fellow squad mates. All their standard data—battle-frame type, load out, name, call-sign, height, weight, vitals, and proximity—flashed up in front of him. Master Sergeant Calvin Griggs, call-sign Hammer, was the squad's leader. At the age of thirty-four cycles he was young for a master sergeant, but nonetheless was a wise and inspiring leader who genuinely cared about his troopers and took the principles of being a non-commissioned officer to heart. He was also the kind of leader who never had to raise his voice to get his point across or express his disappointment.

Directly in front of him was Sergeant Second Class Terrance Wilchcombe, call-sign Maluss. They had been like brothers from the day they met in basic training ten cycles ago. There was no one he trusted more and on more than one account, Maluss had proven just how reliable he was. He smirked because, even though he couldn't see Maluss's eyes, he knew he was checking out Corporal Yu, the crew chief, as she made her pre-flight checks with the other crew chief, Corporal Johnson. Maluss never passed up the chance to hook up with any cutie that caught his eye, and Corporal Yu was definitely that. Although her hair was tucked away in a neatly tied bun, he had a feeling when it was down, it went past her lower back. A purposely loosened lock of hair fell across her face to accent her exotic features. She was absolutely Maluss's type. He laughed to himself.

He took a glimpse to his left and there sat Sergeant Second Class Acalia Perez, call-sign Dead Shot. She was quite striking in her own right. He always found it odd, considering Acalia's blended heritage of Latin and Israeli descent, that Maluss never once made a pass at her, or even saw her in "that" way. She was the squad's sniper, and damn good at ventilating the head of a target at a thousand meters before it could take two breaths. Shooting and killing seemed instinctive for her, like she was born for it, which seemed ironic for someone so religious. She said she didn't "take lives" but instead "helped them move on to the next life."

Distracted by the ever-present commotion outside, he turned and looked through the open tailgate into the hanger. Out there, the hustle and bustle of aircrafts coming and going, technicians working on damaged aircraft, ammo handlers loading and unloading gunships, were a constant reminder of the dangers outside the barrier. His sensors locked on to an incoming MEDEVAC. The MDS-82, her flight crew, was known for going into the thick of danger to retrieve the wounded. The MDS-82 was both a blessing and a curse to those on the battlefield. The wounded were getting out, but, by the same token, death was right around the corner for some unlucky bastard.

He refocused his attention to the front of the dropship as he heard the voice of Sergeant First Class Luther Hagen, call-sign Anvil, the squad's assault battle-frame pilot and also the oldest member at thirty-five cycles old. He had experienced more than his fair share of combat throughout his sixteen cycles of military service and seen things that belonged only in the darkest of nightmares. Anvil rarely spoke, but, when he did, it was direct and to the point, just like when he laid down fire from his frame's ARG-11 Rail gun, nicknamed Boom Hammer. It fired sixty millimeter mass reactive explosive rounds at Mach 3, and nothing he knew of could withstand a hit from it. There had been rumors of creatures that could but hopefully, Cav thought, they were just that…rumors.

On a sudden whim, Cav reduced his com-link to a barely audible volume and brought up a map of the Kansin barrier expansion. Multiple key points flashed on the map, each representing areas of major enemy activity. Every few decades one of the cities would expand its barrier to make room for the growing population. Kansin was currently going through its third such expansion in less than ten cycles, something that was unheard of since the founding of the barrier cities some one hundred and seventy-five cycles ago.

Of the five barrier cities, Kansin had always been the smallest, but that had been changing over the last ten cycles. Kansin had become a favorite for those looking to get rich and enjoy a fast-paced nightlife. Several large corporations had come to Kansin after the city's first great expansion had uncovered huge mineral deposits.

He was snapped back from his thoughts by the familiar whine of the engines powering up. The flight crew suddenly jumped up from playing a game of Crescent and began quickly making their final pre-flight checks. He increased the volume of his com-link as Lieutenant Cosby's voice snapped over it, "Flight mission! Flight mission! Flight mission data received, uploading into nav computer."

Corporal Yu hit the button to raise the rear tailgate as the dropship began to rise. As the dropship cleared the barrier, he saw heavy rain and several flashes of lighting across the night sky. The drop ship's nose dipped forward as the tailgate closed, and he heard the familiar boom of the afterburners kick in.

Boogey Man

RIGHT NOW, THE THOUGHT OF never leaving the barrier city of Gordia and working on his dad's Kiyak farm really didn't seem so bad to Private First-Class Wilson. In fact, shoveling manure sounded like a blessing compared to his current reality. He had been in the service less than a cycle and, until a week ago, had never been outside the barrier for more than a few hours.

Twilight Forest was unsettling. The trees could grow up to eight hundred feet tall, with a dense and mushroom-like canopy that kept the forest below in almost total darkness. Most of the available light actually came from a fluorescent fungus that covered most of the mid and lower tree trunks, giving the illusion of constant twilight.

Every shadow seemed to hide lurking danger and it made him nervous despite his training. His platoon had come up for escort duty, replacing second platoon who had seen little action during the month they were out here; his platoon was not so lucky. By the second week, not only had they experienced several engagements with hostiles, but they had also lost three men. One of them, Private First-Class Ronald Long, Ronnie as everyone called him, had died in his arms. They had been battle buddies since being assigned to Bravo 3/77 Infantry Company almost eight months ago.

The attacks by the hostiles had become more frequent in the last few days, and the recon unit that had been attached to their company recently was overdue by thirty-five minutes. It wasn't a good sign. If something had happened to them, then just what kind of chance would he have? He spoke softly as he triggered his comlink open. "The recon is one of the elites in the Alliance Military. They are trained for extended clandestine operations deep in enemy territory. So, if something happened to these guys, I really have a bad feeling about this for us."

Suddenly the voice of Sergeant Third Class Gray came over the com-link. "Shut your mouth and keep your eyes open, Private Wilson! That goes for the rest of you too! Maintain no more than a five-meter spread between each other. These woods are thick, understood?"

Wilson mumbled a silent prayer to himself as the squad fell silent. He tried to fight the childhood fears of all the bonfire stories his grandfather would tell of the Boogey Man, who came in the night to terrify and steal children if they were bad. "Mere tales to make sure we did our chores," he reassured himself, at least he was praying so. He couldn't help but notice that his heart was beating faster. He looked over to his right and saw Corporal Tymes giving him thumbs-up as he stepped down into a draw, then disappearing into some large brush. Being the farthest man on the left side of the sweep, it was comforting to see Corporal Tymes nearby.

Tymes were as gung-ho as they came and a damn good shot. If something went bad, he was the guy to have at your side. Just then, he noticed something moved out the corner of his eye and he jumped. He snapped his assault rifle up and immediately his acquisition indicator began searching for a target as a blood-curdling howl suddenly cut through the darkness. Wilson tightened his grip on his rifle and froze mid-step, afraid to move.

"S-s-sergeant…w-w-what…was that?" Private Second-Class Mines stuttered over the com-link.

Wilson waited for a reply as he was sure the other eight were as well, but instead, he received only silence. There was a pause, and it seemed like ages to him, as he strained to hear, holding his breath, as if maybe Sergeant Gray may have been whispering.

Silence.

Corporal Siddi sprinted to Sergeant Gray's last position. The sergeant's transponder was still functioning, but his life signs indicator had gone black. Being the second-in-command, Siddi's armor had the command and control upgrades, allowing him to not only track each trooper's position like the rest of the squad but also to track their vitals. As he parted the brush, he realized why the sergeant's life sign indicator had gone black.

The remains of his throat were nothing more than a gory mess. His right arm had been ripped off of his shoulder and part of the bicep and upper arm appeared to have been…eaten. Siddi swallowed hard, tasting bile, fighting back the urge to vomit inside his helmet.

"This is Corporal Siddi. I am assuming command. Fall in on me immediately and assume defensive positions," he forced out into the com-link.

A low growl nearby followed by another howl cut through the forest. Siddi dropped into a kneeling firing position; it was taking everything he had to keep his cool. The sounds were like nothing he had ever heard and made his blood run cold in his veins. He looked at the positions of the rest of the squad in his Head-Up Display (HUD) while Private Second-Class Deering and Specialist Second Class Hansen knelt in their defensive positions nearby.

Corporal Mace stumbled and would have fallen face-first had he not been able to grab a nearby tree to regain his footing. Despite the computerized climate control within his armor, Mace was sweating. His heart was pounding so hard he was waiting for it to explode out of his chest. He was cut off from the squad and something was circling him out in the darkness. He could hear the low, throaty growls, first from his left, then moving behind him, and now it was coming from in front of him.

"Corporal Siddi, I can't get to you. I'm pinned down," Mace croaked nervously.

Siddi looked at the position of the squad; Specialist Mace was thirty-three meters northwest of them. The closest person to him was Private Mines, but before he could contact him his life sign indicator flashed red and then black. Now there were only six of them left.

Deering and Hansen were with him and Wilson and Tymes were almost back with the squad, which meant Mace was out there on his own. "Fack! We can't leave him out there alone," Siddi shouted into his com-link.

Siddi motioned to Hansen and Deering for them to move out. "Private Deering takes the rear. I'll take point, and Specialist Hansen, get on the Satcom and get us some support out here immediately. Priority alpha one! Private Wilson and Corporal Tymes double-time and catch up with us. We're going to get Mace."

"Mace hold on. We're coming for you, buddy," Siddi said reassuringly.

"Hurry please…It's close," Mace whispered, his voice heavy with fear as he stared out into the forest.

The smell of the forest seemed to intensify and sat thick in the air as the rain relentlessly continued to pour, yet through the multitude of scents, it homed in on its prey.

It had already tasted the sweetness of warm flesh and savored the hot blood of their leader. It wanted more. It moved even closer, effortlessly sliding through the undergrowth without a sound, intentionally making its presence known only when it chose and waiting for the right moment to make the next kill. It released another growl, watching as Mace jumped and swung his rifle in the direction of the sound.

"Fack you! Show yourself!" Mace yelled frantically, firing a burst into the forest.

He spun around and fired again, each of his ten-millimeter armor-piercing explosive rounds sunk deep into the tree trunks and detonated as they were designed to do deep within the target. One of the trees he struck several times, trunk exploded outwards in a shower of wood fragments as what was left of its base gave way under its massive weight.

At that moment the beast launched itself forward from the underbrush with lighting speed. Before the massive trees fell silent, it was upon him. Mace's proximity alert chimed as it closed the distance, but it was too fast and too strong to avoid. His head was jerked back, violently snapping him off his feet as instinct dictated to keep his neck from breaking. As razor-sharp canines pierced his flexible under armor sinking deep into the flesh of his throat and crushing his esophagus, Mace wished his neck had snapped.

Siddi watched Mace's life indicator turn black. He wanted to run from whatever was waiting ahead but there were still five of them armed to the teeth, he reminded himself. "Open fire on sight! You hear me damn it?" he shouted into his com-link.

"What about Mace?" Hansen panted, barely able to catch his breath as he ran to keep pace with the others.

Before anyone could answer, they came upon Mace and his attacker. They froze in mid-stride, staring at a creature that seemed to cradle the remains of Mace in its arms, his head hanging from his body by a slim piece of tendon and flesh. It showed no concern for the three-armed troopers that stood before it. It had been aware of their presence long before they were in sight. Their scents, the noises as they moved, even the beating of their hearts had betrayed them in their approach.

Yet it had made no attempt to flee or even defend itself, but instead had stayed to gorge upon its fresh kill. Without raising its head from the gaping wound in what was left of Mace's abdomen, it glared up at them, let out a throaty growl, and dug its maw deeper inside the body cavity.

"Facking kill it!" Siddi yelled as Tymes and Wilson arrived, snapping Siddi out of his dazed horror.

In unison, they opened fire, their acquisition indicators locking onto the beast. Round after round impacted and exploded on the beast's chest and torso, knocking it backwards and down. The beast now laid unmoving, a few feet from Mace's body.

"Is it dead?" Deering whispered.

"Go check, genius!" Tymes snapped back.

"It's still in one piece…There's…no blood…not one drop," Siddi said shakily with fear clearly present in his voice for the first time.

Wilson gasped as the beast slowly began to stand. Eyes the color of pure silver seemed to burn right through him. All of his grandfather's campfire stories rushed back and he shut his eyes hoping this was all a nightmare. His eyes opened and fear turned to icy terror as the beast rose to its full height and let out a monstrous howl. Muscles rippled and bulged as if its skin could barely contain them; the beast stood easily over seven feet tall, on powerful legs not shaped like a man or animal but a grotesque combination of both. Each of its muscular arms was capped with a twisted mockery of a human hand. The creation of some dark alien murder, each hand was clearly designed to rend flesh to shreds with razor-sharp talons the length of the digit it grew from extending from the three fingers and two opposable thumbs. Yet it was the middle finger that removed all doubt that death must be near. It was thicker than the others, possessing a cruel scythe-like talon twice the length and size of the finger it extended from, and it was twitching in anticipation of the slaughter to come. The head and shoulders were covered by a thick black mane that ran down its back and accented a face that would be burned into the depths of Wilson's soul for the rest of his life. Bestial, yet something in it showed intelligence—a predatory intelligence fueled with rage. Its lips curled back into something similar to a grin of satisfaction and revealed rows of vicious canines.

Tymes was the first to reopen fire as it took a step forward. Each round impacting and detonating, forcing it to step back, but it did not fall. Instead, glyphs carved into its flesh emitted an eerie cerulean glow each time the beast was struck before fading.

As the others followed suit with gunfire, another beast attacked. Hansen was the first to fall, his neck snapped with a sickly crunch as he was viciously backhanded. Tymes was not as lucky. The beast's unnaturally sharp claws cut through armor, flesh, and bone. He tried to scream from the pain, but only blood came out as he dropped to the ground.

Deering turned to face the new threat and fired, but the beast was agile and leap out of the way, leaving Deering's hail of fire to hit Siddi. His body convulsed violently as the rounds tore through and exploded deep within him, ripping him to pieces. From a tree nearby a third beast jumped and attacked Wilson. The beast struck him like a hover transport and the blow to his back sent him flying into a tree across the clearing. The world exploded into a flash of white, then all was black.

Several minutes passed before Wilson awoke to the sound of rain pouring down on his visor with the bitter iron taste of blood coating the inside of his mouth. His HUD showed that he had broken several ribs and was bleeding internally. Everything was hazy and only the stimulant from his armor kept him from blacking out again. As he drifted in and out of consciousness his mind floated back to Gordia, to the beautiful holographic skies and warm breezes. Elizabeth, his childhood love…it had been months since he had seen her in person. The memories of her beautiful face and honey blonde hair reflecting the sunlight as the two of them gazed into the horizon from the hill in the middle of her parents' wheat fields flashed before him. He closed his eyes and her laughter that he adored so much came to him like a dream, another month and they were supposed to be married.

Reality suddenly came back in a flash of pain as he was kicked hard in the side and sent airborne. Fresh blood gushed into his mouth as he landed. Slowly he pulled himself into a kneeling position and reached to pull off his helmet, which now seemed to suffocate him. He attempted to wipe the rain and blood from his eyes so that he could better focus on what stood several feet from him. It was a beast unlike the others he had seen, slightly smaller and clearly female; the flowing mane a beautiful grey with white highlights. As it approached it seemed to change; the harsh features melted away as the face became more and more feminine. When it finally stood over him, a beautiful Feralan female stared down at him, quietly observing him. Her naked body showed no signs of her previous form, save the intricate glyphs that had been carved into her upper arms, and onto her left breast.

Each breath was becoming harder than the last, and he coughed up blood as he tried not to choke. As the Feralan turned around, she muttered something sharply in a language he did not recognize. The sound of heavy footsteps in the mud advancing forced him to hug himself tightly, as he dropped back on his heels in defeat. He looked up into the night one last time wishing he was back in Gordia with Elizabeth. As the beast's hot breath passed over his head and neck, his nostrils filled with the smell of blood and the musk of wet fur. He realized he would never see her again and that the Boogey Man was very real.

Calling in the Dead

"ETA IS FIVE MINUTES. HAMMER, how do you want in?" Captain England voiced over the com-link.

Hammer was already looking at a 3-D holographic image of the area where the squad that had requested support had been, as well as noting their current positions and life sign indicators. Four of them were already dead. He noticed one of the troopers, Corporal Mace, was far from the rest of the squad; the others were moving rapidly toward his position. Griggs transposed a grid over the image and locked in a marker for Specialist Mace's location.

"Drop us there, Captain," Hammer said as he transferred the coordinates to the navigator.

"You'll have to go in hot. There's no room to set down there. That opening in the canopy isn't that big either," Captain England said as he adjusted the course to the new flight data.

"Roger that, sir. The only good landing zone is about a mile and a half away, but we need to get down there ASAP. Besides we've dropped into tighter spaces before," Hammer responded.

"Hooah! That's why they call the Twenty-Eighth the Thunderbolts!" Captain Mathers chimed in.

Hammer stood as he relayed the data to the rest of the squad, "You heard him! Get to your jump bays. We are going in hot."

Cav walked over and leaned back into his jump bay. The anticipation of what was to come helped him focus as his adrenaline began to flow. This was the part he loved the most, burning into a drop zone at over two hundred and fifty miles per hour only to activate the jump pack and kick in the thrusters at the last minute, landing with guns blazing. In fact, he was already smiling at the thought and it helped that he knew Anvil hated it.

Lieutenant Cosby's voice came over the com-link, "Three minutes to drop, stand by."

Corporal Johnson and Corporal Yu began a quick safety check to ensure each of the battle-frames were locked into their jump bays properly before sealing the inner bay doors. Finishing Cav's battle-frame check, Johnson tapped on the chest of the battle-frame, gave a thumbs-up, and stepped back into the cargo bay. As Cav's jump door slid down, he noticed Yu wave bye to Maluss. With his door sealed, a red light bathed the inside of his jump bay. He switched over to a secure link between himself and Maluss.

"Dude!" he said with disbelief.

Maluss laughed. "Just friends, bro, Ziyi's cool."

"Riiiiight, first name and you didn't tell me? Ha! I bet, should've known," Cav laughed.

"Cav, I've been wondering why the Feralans have become so hostile again. I mean, these attacks are getting worse," Maluss said with concern.

"It has to have something to do with Kansin's barrier expansion, but exactly what, I don't know. The senate keeps us in the dark so who knows? They've been making a lot of decisions that have ended up with us paying the bill over the last few cycles for the so-called betterment of mankind," Cav said with contempt in his voice.

Maluss knew where this was going, Cav was heavily into politics and no fan of the senate or the current prime minister. Cav believed people were too wrapped up in their utopian lives to see what was really happening around them. More and more, the Senate seemed swayed more by their personal agendas instead of the people…at least that's how Cav saw it. It was how a lot of people were starting to feel these days, according to Cav at least. Maluss preferred not to put too much thought into politics; he'd rather leave that headache to the senate. He was jolted out of this musing by the outer hull doors opening followed by the jump bays moving into a vertical position.

Lieutenant Cosby appeared in another virtual window next to Cav's in Maluss's vision. "Twenty seconds to drop, stand-by and God speed, Twenty-Eighth."

Dead Shot said a quick prayer over the com-link as she always did. None of them ever knew what she was saying except Maluss. She always prayed in Tagalish, the native tongue of most people from Batal. Tagalish was a combination of two ancient earth dialects, Tagalog and Russian. Maluss had picked up a few words from her as well as through a previous romance with a quartermaster but that was about it. Even though they couldn't understand her, everyone always said "Amen" at the end of the prayer, save Anvil. Anvil's faith had become a casualty of war; he had decided a long time ago to believe only in himself and his weapons.

Cav readied himself as Lieutenant Cosby called out over the com-link again, "Three…two…one…Launch!"

As he accelerated from the jump bay before the inertial damper kicked in, adrenaline rushed through him. He watched his altimeter, 9800 feet…8700 feet…6200 feet…3900 feet…1200 feet. The warning chime went off as an alarm flashed for him to activate his jump pack. No one ever activated that early except for Anvil. It was the common practice of the Twenty-Eighth to wait until after they passed the minimum safe altitude and only then max out their thrusters, inertial dampers, and jump pack to get into the fight as quickly as possible. Cav fired his maneuver thrusters only enough to ensure he would go through the opening in the forest canopy, pulse rifle ready in hand, as he prepared to land along with the others.

Maluss was the first to see the beast. It blindsided him as he landed, violently jerking him off his feet and slamming him to the ground. His frame absorbed most of the impact as he threw up his arms to block the killing blow. As he struggled against the beast, warning messages flashed in his vision but were drowned out by what he saw as he stared into the face of the beast. Silver eyes burned through him, taking him back to his childhood, hiding under his blanket and trying to drown out his mother's cries as his father beat her in a drug-induced high.

The intelligence, the rage, the hunger…Those silver eyes had given birth to a fear that was starting to overwhelm him. The beast's mouth twisted into a fiendish grin as it began salivating, tasting the kill to come.

"Get the… fack off me!" Maluss shouted, straining to push the beast off of him.

The beast growled in rage, ramming its scything talon into the battle frame's lower left side, piercing armor to the flesh deep beneath. Maluss screamed as pain shot throughout his forearm. Fear became panic as warning chimes sounded off; a structural breach warning flashed in front of him. Suddenly, the beast's ears perked up and it rolled off of him just as the phase field of Cav's blade left a shimmering wake in its place mere inches from Maluss's faceplate.

Dead Shot and Anvil opened fire as the beast disappeared into the underbrush. A howl of defiance echoed throughout the dim forest, seemingly coming from everywhere at once.

"You okay, brother?" Cav asked, helping Maluss up.

A medical data overlay appeared as Maluss stared down at the damage to his arm, flexing his hand a few times to shake off the stiffness. The medical nanites injected into his bloodstream by his battle-frame had already stopped the bleeding and begun tissue repair from the bite. His forearm would be sore for days to come.

"I'll be fine…and thanks, bro. I owe you one," Maluss groaned as he picked up his pulse rifle.

Hammer interrupted over the com-link, "I've got a live one! Barely…but he's alive. Hang in there, trooper!"

Anvil's sensors only read the rest of the squad, yet his gut told him something else was out there. He switched from night vision over to thermal vision and instantly the world became a canvas of reds, yellows, whites, blacks, blues, oranges, and greens. As he looked around, his sensors locked onto the beast who was now circling to the right of them.

"It's coming around, Hammer, moving toward you," Anvil warned as he activated his jump jets to put himself between the beast and Hammer.

"I need another few minutes to let the nanites stabilize this soldier before I can move him," Hammer replied while monitoring the nanites essential in stabilizing Deering's vitals.

He wasn't a medic, but like all battle-frame pilots, he had been trained in basic first aid. Unlike the average trooper, battle-frame pilots had the advantage of a medical assistant program incorporated into the frame instead of having to rely on a combat medic trooper. Hammer's frame had assessed Deering's injuries the moment he scanned him and programmed the injection of millions of medical nanites; however, his injuries would soon require the attention of a full medical facility if he were to live.

"There is another beast—no, make that two beasts, circling out there on our three," Dead Shot alerted the others as she quickly readied her sniper rifle.

"I got another beast over here on our six, Hammer. They're just sitting out there," Cav warned, moving to better secure his sector of fire for the coming attack.

"Maluss, you have anything in your sector?" Cav called out. "We're surrounded. I got two over here as well, using the trees for cover," Maluss said as his target acquisition sensor locked on to the nearest beast.

"Stay frosty, everyone, this trooper is almost ready to be moved. We are not sure what we are dealing with and how many there are, so keep the perimeter tight and shoot only if you have to. For now, get all the sensory data you can for the lab coats to analyze later," Hammer ordered in his normal calm and collected tone.

The beasts continued circling, using the large trees for cover as they maneuvered, looking for an opening, waiting for the command to attack the newest intruders. The beast called Arshul dug his claws deep into the trunk of the tree; he was losing his patience to a growing rage that was quickly inciting the others into a frenzy. His attention instantly moved to the figure that had slid next to him from the tree above.

Her thoughts reached into his, feeling the rage within. The raw emotions crashed against her mind like waves against the shore. As she touched his thoughts, the storm of rage calmed, and her voice became audible within his mind. "Be calm, my brother, allow the others to deal with these defilers. We must leave. The ritual must begin soon before the defiler dies."

Arshul looked down at the semi-conscious body of Wilson and could sense the life leaving him. He growled in annoyance because he knew Asla was right. He would punish the young blood of Jonan's coven for injuring the defiler to the point of death and robbing him of the chance to kill these armored defilers. As he disappeared into the depths of the forest canopy, his mind reached out to the others with one last word. "Kill!"

In unison the beasts rushed forward from all sides, their silver eyes burning with fury.

"Here they come!" Dead Shot shouted. With a quick prayer, she squeezed the trigger, watching the closest beast's head snap backward jerking it off its feet. Her bullet hitting cleanly between its eyes, she smiled as the familiar sound of weapon fire erupted all around her. This was the part where she excelled in the heat of a battle. Yet her smile quickly faded as the beast she had just shot moved into a crouching position; its head showed no sign of a bullet wound or even blood.

"Oh my god, it just got back up!" Dead Shot exclaimed in disbelief. She watched the beast defiantly stand back up with its silver eyes flaring with rage before it released a howl and charged forward.

"Magic! Faaack," Cav and Maluss sighed in unison.

Cav fired burst after burst, slowly backing up and away from the advancing horde until he stood back to back with Maluss. Each burst from his pulse rifle found a target that would not die.

"Raven One, we need an emergency evac!" Hammer hollered over the com-link as he launched a grenade, sending two beasts flying. A moment later a marker flashed on the 3-D map that appeared in his vision.

"Get your team there, Hammer. We'll be on station to pull you out," Captain England said, adjusting the drop ship's course to the new coordinates.

"Let's get to the evac site. Maluss and Cav will take point. Dead Shot, Anvil, take up the rear," Hammer ordered as he picked up Deering.

"A mile and a half straight through those things, bro. This isn't going to be easy," Cav said to Maluss as he fired another burst into the chest of a beast.

"As if it were ever easy for us, bro…Anvil, can you open the door for us?" said Maluss sarcastically as he fired another burst.

Anvil nodded in acknowledgment, stepping forward between Cav and Maluss, his back-mounted rail gun lowered into firing position over his right shoulder.

Maluss snickered, "They're about to have a really bad day."

With a half-smile of satisfaction, Anvil locked onto the closest beast, saying, "This never gets old!"

The beast's body imploded in a mist of red as the disruptor-charged round sliced through its supernatural defenses at Mach 3. The resounding sonic boom that followed a moment later was like an explosion to the hypersensitive ears of the remaining beasts, forcing them to the ground in agony.

Cav looked at Maluss. "Let's do this, brother. Go!"

In unison, they activated their jump jets, launching forward into the air believing the beasts were incapacitated. As Cav landed, he realized they were wrong. He was forced to quickly duck and tumble, activating his jump jets before he stood and barely evading the claws of a beast that attacked from the underbrush.

Hammer shortened his leap in an attempt to soften his landing; trying not to add to the injuries of the soldier he carried. This would force him to quickly fall behind, which he knew to be dangerous. That he had to stow his weapon to carry Deering made falling back even more treacherous. The beasts moved with unnatural swiftness through the forest underbrush and canopy and several of them were quickly catching up to him. He knew if he fell back much farther, the others would pull back and none of them would make it out. As he landed, two beasts dropped near him with no time to get away or draw his weapon. Without warning the ground erupted with explosions. He looked up to see Anvil spraying the area with his pulse cannon as he landed next to him.

"I got you, Hammer, keep moving!" Anvil yelled as he fired his rail gun, obliterating another of the beasts before it could recuperate.

Perched seventy feet above the forest floor, Dead Shot readied her sniper rifle as she scanned the forest below, looking to buy time for the others. Several beasts were gaining on Hammer and Anvil's position; it unnerved her at how fast these creatures could move. As she steadied her rifle, she noticed that some of the thermal signatures were different. She shifted her eyes to the rifle's scope-enhanced view, shifting its sighting to M-spectrum. The world instantly became devoid of color except for shades of gray and black, allowing her to see that the glyphs the beasts wore were burning with a white aura. She zoomed in onto a beast that had paused to scent the air. Smaller than the others, it had no glyphs carved into its flesh and it carried a weapon. She looked down into her scope and fired.

The beast's head exploded in a shower of gore. Switching back to thermal vision, Dead Shot began searching for other targets hidden among the underbrush. A split second later, another beast dropped to the floor below as another round hit true. She fired again as she opened her com-link, "Not all of them are protected by—" She was cut short by a blow that sent her flying from her perch in the canopy. Lesser branches in the lower canopy gave way to her almost one-ton bulk, tossing her to and fro, as she fought desperately to stop her fall. A proximity warning chime sounded, snapping her out of her panic, and she activated her jump jets a second too late. Her armored body slammed into the ground and everything went dark momentarily as her frame rebooted. She stood slowly, drawing her assault pistol. A red outline surrounded the pistol as she took hold of it—it was damaged.

"Be strong and courageous. Do not be afraid or terrified because of them, for the Lord, your God, goes with you. He will never leave you, nor forsake you!" she reassured herself.

In the upper corner of her vision, a 3-D image of her frame appeared, rotating to show its rearview. A red outline flashed over the main jump pack, as details of the damage scrolled next to it.

"Dead Shot, come in. What's going on?" Hammer asked, reading her elevated vitals.

"My rifle is gone, pistol useless, my main jump pack is toasted, and these things are getting close," she said, drawing her combat phase blade.

"I'll go back for Dead Shot, Hammer," Anvil said while checking his remaining ammo count.

"Cav, Maluss, hold that drop ship for us," Anvil said, launching into the air as he locked on to Dead Shot's location before launching into the air.

"We got you, buddy," Cav responded as he reloaded his pulse rifle.

"Now if someone could just come and get us," Maluss barked out sarcastically as he fired and missed a beast that was darting in and out of cover.

The tranquil peace of the three immense full moons in the cloudless night far above the raging storm was like a false barrier from the madness below. To Captain England, the soft whine of the engines was soothing. It helped him to escape Tallagen, even if it was only within the confines of his own mind. Any other night, he would have enjoyed flying so high above the clouds; at night it gave him the best view of the stars that as a child he dreamt of flying among one day as his father's father had. Yet tonight there was no peace. For months now, tranquility was often broken by the constant relay of combat chatter from the troops he delivered to battle time and time again.

"I'm turning over the stick to you," he said flatly, activating several buttons on the touch screen panel that separated him from his co-pilot Captain Mathers. "Assuming primary weapon system officer."

"Roger, I have control of the stick," Mathers responded, taking hold of the control stick with his right hand and the engine throttles with his left.

"You have the stick," England replied before looking back and up over his shoulder to the navigator station. Lieutenant Cosby was busy observing sensor readings of the storm below on one monitor, system functions on another, navigation charts on another while monitoring the com-traffic from below. He could hear the com-traffic in his own helmet and could only imagine what kind of sorcery the Twenty-Eighth could be facing that would make such an experienced battle-frame squad fall back so soon after contact. He activated another button, this time in front of him, syncing his helmet with the twin link pulse cannon turret that deployed from beneath the broad nose of the dropship.

"Two minutes to the evac site. Get ready back there. It's going to get choppy. Storm's gotten a lot worse," Captain Mathers warned, piloting the dropship into the dark storm clouds. A few moments later, the ship began to buck violently, its engines pouring out white-hot exhaust, as it powered through the unrelenting storm winds and exploded from the clouds into the heavy rain below.

Corporal Yu strapped herself into her safety harness as Corporal Johnson latched her safety line to the safety retention bar and activated a button on the panel nearby. In front of her, a hatch opened on the floor as a turret mount assault cannon rose up and locked into position just before where the tailgate ramp was lowered.

She stepped forward, grasping the firing handles to steady herself the best she could, before reaching over to activate her flight armor's internal oxygen supply. The lower half of the flight helmet quickly enclosed her nose, mouth, and lower jaw in an armored mask before the mirrored visor slid down, completing the seal. With the message "Internal Oxygen Supply Active-8 Hours Remaining," appearing in the corner of her HUD, she glanced back, giving Johnson a thumbs-up and exhaling heavily. "Ready!"

Johnson switched the internal bay lights to night operations, bathing the cargo bay with a red glow. He returned her thumbs-up and pressed the ramp release button. The tailgate doors retracted, revealing the horrible storm outside. The dark clouds swallowed the light of the three moons and the rain fell so hard it was impossible to see past the rear of the tailgate. It was complete darkness, more nightmare than night, and somewhere below was the Twenty-Eighth fighting for their lives.

If Only It Was Just a Nightmare

DARSHUL WATCHED, THOUGH HE COULD not see the flesh and blood being beneath the armored shell he could sense it. He could hear its heartbeat and taste its fear. These armored defilers were stronger than the ones he had hunted and killed in the recent past. A fall from such heights should have easily killed even one such as him, a Scarred Warrior. Yet, the defiler was very much alive and armed with a blade.

A wounded bird that can no longer fly away, he thought to himself with a fiendish smirk, revealing razor-sharp canines.

He looked to his left; his attention drawn to the sound of movement below; two of the young bloods from Jonan's coven were close. Like many from Asla's coven, he regarded those that now followed her out of fear as inferior, not worthy of the gift of being infused with a predator spirit. Only true believers in the covens were given the gifts from the Great Mother Spirit such as the glyphs of protection, which were carved into his flesh. With contempt, he watched Jonan's Young Bloods approach the defiler. He could see she was very much aware of them as she turned to face their direction and readied her blade. He growled in annoyance, thinking of how pathetic Jonan's entire coven was.

The young bloods rushed in to attack while Darshul slowly descended to the ground below. The first Young Blood launched itself at Dead Shot, attacking wildly with little control; she easily sidestepped the erratic attack and kicked the beast, sending it flying into a nearby tree. The Young Blood yelped in pain as it hit, bones breaking under the force of the impact.

Stunned, Dead Shot shifted her combat stance so that she could look in the direction of the wounded beast, amazed that it had expressed pain. It was the first time she had heard one of them acknowledge any type of anguish. She shifted again to meet the attack of the second beast but was not fast enough; it slammed into her, knocking her to the ground. For a brief moment, the beast thrashed about with her blade deep in its chest on top of her before falling still.

Quickly, she pushed the beast to the side, aware the other one was still alive. As she rolled to get up, the first beast rushed forward, its weapon held high for the killing blow. She threw up her arms in a hasty but futile defense against the coming blow, but it never came. Instead, the beast's body convulsed with each round that pierced its flesh and exploded within, tearing its torso into a gory mess that showered her. She looked behind her to see Anvil's pulse cannon barrels steaming in the rain.

"I think you have some liver on your head," Anvil said callously. "Fack you and thanks for the save," Dead Shot replied in Tagalish, standing up and removing the gore on her battle-frame. "These aren't like the others we first saw—no glyphs, smaller, and they are using weapons," she said, nudging the beast's weapon with her foot.

"We ran into a few of them up ahead but we can figure it out later," Anvil said bluntly, scanning for further threats. "How soon before your suit's nanites repair the jump pack?"

With a thought, a 3-D image of her frame's structural status appeared, rotating to the rear of the battle-frame to show the status of her jump pack. A yellow outline flashed along with data indicating it was operational, but only at 57 percent.

"It's functioning, but I won't be making long jumps anytime soon," she said.

"Here. You're better with this than a knife," Anvil grunted, drawing his assault pistol and handing it to her.

"You are *so* kind," Dead Shot replied sarcastically while she knelt down to pull her phase blade from the chest of the beast that had impaled itself upon it.

"We need to get moving now before we are completely cut off from the others by those facking things," Anvil warned.

Anvil turned, preparing to leap when the beast Darshul appeared next to him. As fast as Anvil was, Darshul was faster. With one powerful blow, Darshul tore away half the battle-frame's faceplate, along with Anvil's head, splattering blood across Dead Shot as she stood up.

Horror filled her as Anvil's frame continued to convulse in pain, still reacting to the dying nerve endings. She watched the body finally topple over and fall still, fear rapidly on the verge of overtaking her. She screamed in rage and terror, firing her weapon haphazardly. Each burst from the assault pistol did nothing more than make Darshul flinch in irritation from the impact, as he moved toward her. His silvery eyes bored into her, filling her with the terror of punishment within a demonic fiery hell to come, petrifying her with fear. With channeled hatred, Darshul lashed out with his razor-like claws, slicing through the thick armor of the battle-frame and into the soft flesh beneath. She screamed as pain shot through her side. Her frame, reacting to her frantic neural commands, activated its jump pack and sent her spinning away from her attacker. She plowed through the thick vegetation before finally falling to the ground fifty feet away. She fought to stand as her battle-frame injected her with a second dose of medical nanites along with a cocktail of pain killers and stimulants to keep her conscious. Barely able to stand, she stumbled forward through the forest with both fear and instincts driving her to activate her jump pack once again to escape.

Maluss was the first to reach the edge of the clearing, happy to finally see the dropship hovering a few feet above the ground, and with it the reality that they might actually survive. Immediately, he turned and began laying down covering fire as Hammer sprinted past him for the dropship. Cav, following closely, stopped and quickly turned to fire on a beast that was close behind.

"The motherfackers are pulling back, using trees for cover like they weren't already difficult enough to target!" Maluss shouted over the roar of their pulse rifles.

"These aren't just beasts. They're intelligent. The ones on our heels for the last half mile are carrying weapons!" Cav shouted back as he killed a creature creeping up on his left.

Hammer moved up the rear tailgate quickly, moving to seat the wounded Deering.

"Got him, Sergeant," Corporal Johnson said while moving to strap Deering in.

Acknowledging Corporal Johnson, Hammer turned to rejoin the rest of his squad as he readied his pulse rifle. He stopped short of the tailgate as Anvil's life sign indicator went black and Dead Shot's began to flash red.

"Captain England, I just lost Anvil and Dead Shot's life sign is looking bad. This is turning into a nightmare. Be ready to lift off the moment we're on board," Hammer said, racing back toward the tree line.

Dead Shot was only a few hundred feet from the dropship according to her GPS indictor, but she needed to stop and give the nanites time to control her bleeding before she passed out. She was growing weaker every second but overwhelming fear drove her on. She knew the beast was toying with her, taking its time, savoring the kill. More than once, she saw its demonic face, firing only to realize it was actually a tree or a bush. There was something in its eyes, something that had terrified her beyond reasoning.

Hammer ran up, stepping in between Cav and Maluss, as they continued to lay down suppressive fire to protect the evac site.

"We've lost Anvil and Dead Shot is out there in bad shape. These things are using magic, and we are extremely outnumbered. We need to find Dead Shot and get out of here, now," Hammer said over the com-link, pointing in the direction they needed to go.

In unison, they all fired grenades, bombarding the tree line, before leaping back into the twilight of the forest. Immediately within the underbrush that they landed in, several beasts seemingly appearing from nowhere, attacked. Hammer avoided the swing of a blade and countered, slicing the beast's arm off at the elbow with his phase blade; Maluss fired a burst from his pulse rifle, blowing the shoulder and arm off of another one. Cav, attempting to push on through the ambush, leaped forward, smashing his knee into the face of a beast, its skull giving way and caving under the impact of his armored knee as he activated his jump pack. Landing, he pushed through the densely covered forest floor to find Dead Shot collapsed on the ground with a beast attempting to tear open her chest plate.

Cav opened fire but the beast darted away, avoiding his shot only to find a second shot from Maluss's pulse rifle; its head rocked back with a wet thud before exploding outward.

"Grab her! Let's go!" Hammer shouted with urgency as he landed, firing on several of the beasts that were quickly approaching. Maluss quickly stowed his pulse rifle and picked up Dead Shot.

Giving up the offensive attack, the trio focused all of their efforts on making it to the dropship alive.

Their final leap brought them within a few meters of the tree line, unaware that the beast Katya sat above patiently, watching as the young bloods herded them toward her. She stared intently at the ship hovering in the clearing for several seconds before she turned her attention back toward the approaching defilers. She watched as Maluss raced out into the opening, the dropship descending and rotating to give him access to the rear ramp. Below her, Cav turned and opened fire along with Hammer, hoping to hold the beasts at bay long enough for Maluss to get himself and Dead Shot on the dropship.

A moment later, Hammer slapped Cav on the shoulder and shouted, "Go! I'm right behind you!"

"Okay!" Cav yelled, firing off one final burst before turning to race toward the dropship.

Like the stalwart warrior he was, Hammer held his ground, continuing to fire with deadly precision and desperately attempting to hold the line, but more of the magically protected beasts were getting dangerously close to overrunning his position. In the corner of his peripheral vision, he saw Cav only a few meters from the ramp of the dropship, it was time to leave. With renewed focus, Hammer fired one final sweeping burst along with several grenades into the forest before turning to run for the dropship. It was at that moment Katya descended upon Hammer, knocking him to the ground. With one downward motion of her scythe-like claw, she pierced through the armored head into flesh and bone, ramming it into the ground beneath.

Watching from the ramp of the dropship a wrenching pang of shock hit Cav before any warning or protest could escape his mouth.

His gaze was drawn to Katya's silver eyes, twinkling with savage satisfaction in the darkness, as she cruelly twisted her claw, stilling the death throes of Hammer's dying body. Her eyes brought back the uncontrollable and chilling fear of the night he lost his father as a teenage boy. Though Katya could not see the true face of the watching defiler hidden within his armored shell, she began to salivate, savoring the sweetness of his growing terror; a cruel smile broke across her face. She knew that her mystical stare drew forth his deepest soul-wrenching fears, and she was pleased.

Corporal Yu quickly reacted when she noticed Cav's pulse rifle slowly drop. She took hold of the turret and opened fire, but Katya leaped back, disappearing into the darkness of the forest as quickly as she had come. A moment later, several more beasts rushed howling from the tree line toward the dropship. "Sir, hostiles inbound! The remaining squad members are onboard plus one survivor from the patrol squad!" Corporal Johnson shouted over the com-link as he moved to fire into the advancing beasts along with Corporal Yu.

As the dropship rose, Cav zoomed in on Hammer's downed battle-frame. Already, several beasts were tearing into it. A renewed sense of anger and dread moved through him. Death was a common thing here on Tallagen, but to watch his mentor and friend being fed upon was more than he could bear. Targeting Hammer's battle-frame, he fired two armor-piercing grenades in rapid succession. A moment later, there were two detonations followed by an even larger and more violent explosion of Hammer's battle-frame power core. He reached out to steady himself, grabbing a safety hold as the dropship angled to clear the forest canopy and stared out into the stormy night sky. He could hear Maluss yelling at Dead Shot to hold on and the sound of a heart monitor flat-lining. All he could do was squeeze his eyes shut and hope there would be no nightmares as the tailgate finally closed.

Utopia

OF ALL THE BARRIER CITIES Senator Sullen favored, it was New Hope that captured him most of all. His job often required him to travel between the cities, so he had experienced each in detail. He stared out the window of the mag-lift, looking at the barrier generator building in the center of the city; it towered some five hundred feet above any other and he absentmindedly wondered why New Hope had secured his affection since he was a small child.

New Hope was the second largest of the barrier cities. The agricultural city of Gordia was several times larger in square miles. It wasn't the first built; that honor went to Hamina. Nor was it the grand entertainment hub. The neon-lit streets of Kansin were well known for their diverse culture, especially once the artificial sun went down. The barrier city of Batal was known for its innovations in medical research and aquatic farming. Yet despite all of this, New Hope was the center of humanity for holding model standards of utopia. It was also the home of both the senate and the prime minister.

High rises soared, decorated with immense statues built into their superstructure. Lush parks and magnificent fountains covered the cityscape. There was a serenity that melted away the stresses of life; at least, that was what the average citizen experienced. However, inside the grand walls of the senate, it was far from mundane. Constant bickering over laws and incessant arguments about reform were a common occurrence. Sometimes, he would go up to the roof and stare out into the artificial sky and wonder which was worse—the madness of constant nagging to curry political favor, or life outside the barrier. However, when the reports came back from the military detailing the horror of combat operations, the confines of the barrier seemed much more comforting.

It was hard to believe how brutal the world was outside. Over three hundred thousand colonists had died within the first six cycles of arriving on Tallagen. Alien diseases, viruses, the fauna, and of course the indigenous and intelligent races that seemed to be quite content with the extinction of the human race on Tallagen. Much of that hostility from the indigenous had to do with poor diplomacy or none at all. *Our forefathers had a true superiority complex that this place put quickly in check*, the senator thought.

The mag-lift came to a stop, jarring him back to reality. He checked his wrist PDA as the doors opened into the main hall of the senate. Two twelve-foot glass-crete doors carved with intricate designs were held in place by two large angels that framed the door. At the entrance stood two Alliance troopers in dress uniform, ceremonial katana sheathed, standing at attention. From the time he was a young boy, he had always been impressed with the burgundy and black uniforms of the army. Security seemed almost non-existent until you walked through the glass-crete doors and saw the security station, off to the side, where you were scanned. Nearby, several more Alliance troopers stood in full combat armor, four-armed with assault pistols, and the other two with assault rifles.

The prime minister isn't here today, he thought as he passed through the security checkpoint. *If he was, a strike trooper security detail would be here as well.* They were an intimidating sight to behold, clad in their power armor. Almost as much as seeing an Ares battle frame up close; which resembled an angelic knight with its large metallic wings and blazing sword. It was an impressive machine, to say the least, and simply a magnificent marvel of engineering.

The hall leading up to the inner sanctum was a mosaic of beauty. Its forty-foot, vaulted, stained glass-crete ceiling displayed a panoramic view of an earth he had never seen. Each of the support arches was an ornately sculpted angel carved directly into the wall with wings outstretched and sword held high. In the center of it all was a large fountain decorated with crystals from the Soman Desert. These unique crystals glowed from deep within when exposed to sunlight, creating a shifting array of vibrant hues as the water passed down and over them. The trees and grass that surrounded the fountain were sure to please any lover of nature. In fact, he always made a point to stop and sit at one of the benches near the fountain. It helped him collect his thoughts before going into the maelstrom of the senate. However, today he was already late and would have to forgo his normal routine.

As the doors slid open, he could hear the familiar tones of Senator Amberman speaking, "The Senate was created with a vision—to seek the best interest of the people and have members elected to speak on their behalf. However, over the last few decades, I have become witness to a cancer in this ideal. A cancer that is growing more with each new corporate law passed on behalf of some corporate lobbyist. Self-interest and greed are becoming the norm amongst you. Our young men and women are giving their lives for the greed of profit and back-handed deals. How naive do you believe me to be, Mr. Cathchel?"

Grumbling spread through the crowd as members began to protest. Sullen took his place silently, watching the reaction of the other members and that of Galum Corp's lobbyist, Mr. Cathchel. Such tension was nothing new after Amberman made a statement. He was old, around seventy-two, give or take a few cycles, and easily one of the oldest members serving in the senate. His wisdom and blunt candor were valued by many, Sullen included but had also made him quite unpopular to others. He was dedicated to serving the best interests of the people, a fact that made him very outspoken and direct, making others take heed. As Senate Leader Artres called for order, Sullen took the opportunity to view the proposal brought forth by the Galum lobbyist in his holo-viewer. Galum had been responsible for the majority of the arguments within the senate over the last decade.

After Galum's buyout of Tempest refineries eleven cycles ago, it had become the largest refinery of nulonium—the mineral required for creating the barriers and disruptor fields that protected the cities from magical intrusions and attacks. It was vital to the survival of the colonies, and a source of immense income for Galum who now controlled nearly all of the production. Galum Corporation's lobbying was the reason for Kansin's rapid expansions; now they were lobbying for another barrier city altogether. Five cycles ago, such a proposal would never have been entertained in the senate, but as Amberman stated, much had changed. Now, more and more legislation seemed to be passed in favor of agendas that held no benefits for the common citizen.

Sullen looked up as he heard the senate leader ask General Stafford for his opinion on the state of the military's ability to facilitate such an endeavor. General Stafford was a trooper through and through, and a firm believer that the government had a responsibility to the people. This ideology made him a favorite of many in the senate, especially Senator Amberman. Like the majority who had grown up in Hamina, he maintained close ties to traditional values and practices. He rose through the ranks of the military's elite strike troopers to become the top commander at the young age of fifty-two, a truly astonishing feat. The numerous awards decorating his uniform were a visible reminder of the constant war that had been necessary to survive in this harsh world, most notably the Golden Crosses of Valor that he had been awarded for the grueling offenses in the Canyon of Sorrows. A quiet man of few words, General Stafford was calm and dignified, a true professional with a stern look that projected his authority. Sullen had been given the opportunity to meet and speak with the general on many occasions after he had been assigned to the military acquisition committee. He knew to respect his advice on the state of the military and thus gave him his full attention.

General Stafford touched his holo-panel, transferring the graphs he was reviewing to the main holo-viewer in the center of the senate, as he began to speak. "Senators, I have sat here listening to you debate the creation of a new barrier city. While the grounds for it are beyond my position to opinionate on directly, I can speak as to its impact on our military forces. As you know, the military currently employs three hundred and twenty-five thousand troopers and airmen. This is a small number when compared to the task at hand, protecting over two and a half million people who are spread out over forty-five thousand square miles. The military is already stretched thin with the rapid expansion of Kansin, the renewed offensive attacks of the Feralans, and raiders attacking the coast of Batal. Currently, there are fifty-seven research and exploration teams deployed throughout the western and southern hemispheres, and now we have a new threat taxing the resources of an already strained military."

General Stafford paused to look at his aide, signaling him to display a video. Sullen, like many, looked on in shock as they watched an unknown beast begin to slaughter a squad of troopers. When the beast came into full view; the video froze, highlighting the creature, before being replaced with a holographic 3-D image of the beast, frozen in time, rotating in the center of the room. General Stafford took a moment to allow the members to settle down and continued, "Senators, I repeat, we now face a new threat. This beast is extremely dangerous and more than capable of taking down a battle-frame with ease. Intelligence is still reviewing the data and debriefing the survivors. This hazardous force has been responsible for the death of eighty-five troopers in the last two months near Kansin and will certainly require even more military assets in the expansion of Kansin. From a military point of view, we truly do not have the necessary assets to consider taking on a project as large as the establishment of a new barrier city."

Senator Harkus interjected, "General Stafford, correct me if I am wrong, but when you say assets, you mean troopers?"

Senator Amberman glared across the room toward Senator Harkus, his disdain clearly projected. Senator Harkus was a fat, pompous, waste of a seat in the senate, as far as he was concerned. He had slid through the last fifteen cycles of elections by placating the voters with what they wanted to hear along with the financial influence of the wealthy family he had married into. He was quick to support bills that furthered his capitalistic views and anything that could make him a public favorite. All else, he simply let fall to the wayside. Nonetheless, he carried a lot of support both in and out of the senate, which allowed him to use his vote as a considerable bargaining tool.

Senator Harkus spoke sarcastically, "The military always seems to need something. First, it was a more specialized ground support aircraft, so we funded the Air Corps 'next generation' gunship program and additionally authorized the purchase of five squadrons at a cost of nine billion credits. Then, it was an issue of needing a new battle-frame that could better meet current and future threats. So we authorized the accelerated testing of the Titan battle-frame that the military was so eager to put into full-scale production after its initial development phase…at a projected cost of eight hundred and fifty million additional credits. So I ask you, is the military using its inherent duties as a bargaining chip?"

The Senate was silent. General Stafford knew all too well the game played here in the inner sanctum. He knew Senator Harkus's statement was meant to antagonize him into saying something that could be twisted and used against him. He also realized not saying anything was just as dangerous, so he paused just for a moment before responding.

"Senators…the military continues to perform both its primary and implied missions with excellence while maintaining the high standards and quality of professionalism that are expected by our sons and daughters day in and day out. They freely sacrifice so much for our continued survival in this hostile world, adapting to a mission that changes constantly, whether from internal or external stimuli. Our military must be flexible and capable of adapting to change rapidly, but so must the very people we count on to support us. Anything less, and we would be asking our troopers to fight and die for a cause that their leaders do not believe in. To believe that this can be done without both change and advancement is to be either short-sighted or ignorant. As I hope you are aware, Senator Harkus, war does one of two things: it brings out the patriotism in the people, or it brings out the anti-war sentiment in the people. Either way, it is not the job of the military to decipher those feelings. We simply fight the good fight with honor. We perform the missions handed down from our leaders here, in the senate, as professionals, while maintaining the respect of the people, whether they agree with the decisions made here or not. However, recruitment has continued to decline over the last four cycles as the barrier expansions of Kansin have sparked increasing confrontations with the Feralans. Within the last six months, the media has begun to express the possibility of an all-out war with the Feralans. This type of media attention has led to a drastic decline in new recruits. So, to answer your question Senator Harkus, no. The military is not bartering in order to perform its assigned missions. Therefore, sacrifices will need to be made to ensure the young men and women we send into the fight will have a chance of coming home alive," General Stafford finished calmly, as his eyes roamed over the senate before stopping at Senator Harkus.

Immediately, the senate burst into an uproar; both positive and negative reactions to the general's statement came from all over the room. As the Senate leader fought to restore order, Sullen looked over at Senator Harkus, who had turned an interesting shade of purple from suppressed rage, and thought to himself, *Utopia?*

Broken Dreams

GERALD HAD BEEN SITTING ON the side of the highway for some time now. The farther he got away from the hospital, the more real it became. She was gone. For the last three days, he had gone to sit with her, hoping for the moment when Acalia would open her eyes, but it never came. Terrance had left just before they took her off life support. He said he couldn't bear to stand by and watch while he lost another friend. Gerald could see the anger building in Terrance, even though he tried to hide it. Unlike Gerald, Terrance was good at hiding his emotions, even when there was a raging storm within him. Only those truly close to him could ever begin to tell when something was wrong with him. Yet he was still angry at Terrance for taking the easy way out. The heart monitor beeped one final time and flat-lined. At that point, he couldn't hold back the tears anymore. He watched as Acalia's mother broke down into hysterical tears, begging Acalia to get up and talk to her. He left not too long after that, stopping only to give his condolences to the rest of her family.

    The last few days since they returned home had been some of the hardest he had ever dealt with. After speaking to Hammer's wife, now a widow, Meril, she had to be rushed to the hospital due to her emotional breakdown and almost miscarried their unborn son. He sighed. He remembered Terrance telling him that Anvil's wife didn't take it any better than Hammer's. Right now, sadness and anger were fighting to consume him. It was the reason he had pulled over to process it all. Time seemed to be non-existent as he sat there in the darkness, his thoughts muting the slight hum of the car's anti-gravity system. The steady headlights of the traffic passing by sent Gerald into a daze, deep within his thoughts. His mind was slowly drifting farther away from reality.

TERRANCE

Terrance slowly sat up; a thin sheen of sweat covered his body. The bedroom was dimly lit by the artificial moonlight that pierced the blinds. The nightmares had always been intense, but they had worsened since Acalia's passing. He glanced over at the nightstand to look at the time. He had only been asleep for forty-five minutes. "Seriously? Just go to sleep, Terrance," he whispered to himself.

Out of the corner of his eye, something stirred; he jumped and turned to see the intruder. His eyes fixated on the two silver orbs staring back at him from the darkness. A lump filled his throat and his heart began to pound like it was trying to burst from his chest. Terror struck him mute as the beast stepped forward from the shadows, the moonlight betraying its dark form for the first time as it moved slowly toward the foot of the bed. Within his psyche, the ancient and primal fear of being prey was screaming for him to run. Moonlight struck the beast's face, highlighting the rows of sharp canines as the creature's mouth turned into a twisted mimic of a smile. The creature stood before him, tasting his fear; salivating at the taste of warm flesh, it took hold of his leg.

Terrance's eyes shot wide open. Breathing heavily, cold sweat covering his body, he could hear the pounding of his heart in the stillness of the room. He sat up and looked into the corner. There was nothing. He cautiously looked around the room next, studying every shadow, reassuring himself that they were alone. He felt Ziyi begin to stir next to him. He looked down, the moonlight highlighting the soft beauty of her naked form as she pulled the covers, he had thrown off up to her chest. He slowly slid back down, curling up behind her as she snuggled into him, placing his hand to cup her lower breast and hug her close to him.

"What's wrong, angel?" she mumbled sleepily.

"Nothing," he whispered, staring into the dark corner of the bedroom for a moment. "Nothing at all…just a bad dream," he said, burying his face in her hair.

FUNERAL

Gerald hadn't spoken a word since he arrived at the cathedral. Rather than speak to anyone, he preferred to remain entrenched in his thoughts as he sat on the marble bench of the dressing chamber, staring at the coat of his dress uniform for the funeral. In fact, he had only spoken when he stopped by Calvin's home, on his way to the cathedral, to drop off the last of Calvin's things and once again give his condolences. He had said nothing else as he tried to emotionally ready himself to escort and carry the ashes of Calvin, Acalia, and Luther to their final resting place in the Veteran Memorial Cemetery. Terrance was sitting across from him in the dressing chambers, just staring blankly at the stained-glass window while he clutched the religious medallion that Acalia had given to him two cycles ago for his birthday. She told him it was a reminder that despite all he had been through, both good and bad, that God loved him, and that there was always a guardian angel watching over him and keeping him close. Terrance had never taken it off. They shared a special bond, always together, sharing everything. For him, her death meant more than the loss of a friend; it was the loss of a sibling.

Gerald noticed Terrance hadn't spoken a word either since he came into the dressing chambers. His eyes and demeanor said more than words could express. Gerald knew him well enough to know it would be better to be there for him when he was ready, rather than try to comfort him now. Besides, right now he was having a hard time coping with all of this himself; he wouldn't be much help anyway.

Gerald stood up, fastening his jacket, and took one last look in the holo-mirror before closing the armoire's doors. He looked up at the stain glass window, which was bathing the dressing chamber in various hues. The picture in the glass was of the archangel Michael triumphantly standing over a defeated devil. In its background, the gates to heaven were opened wide, with angels in clouds rejoicing in victory, blowing golden trumpets. The inscription upon it read, "Evil may win, yet its victory is fleeting in the end, the true everlasting victory will belong to the faithful and pure of heart." Gerald paused to ponder the words before turning to place a hand on Terrance's shoulder on the way out. The desolation in his eyes as he looked up said more than any words, yet his face remained blank. Gerald knew that before the end of the day he would have to be truly strong for both of them.

Major Lightfoot, the commander of the 329th Combat Frames Regiment, stood up and approached the podium. Clearing his throat, he ordered, "Command Sergeant Third Class Vance, assemble the squadron for roll call!"

Command Sergeant Third Class Vance stepped forward to stand in front of the seven troopers facing the audience.

"Parade, rest!" Vance ordered, before doing an about-face and saluting Major Lightfoot.

"Sir, the squadron is formed," Vance said, holding his salute. "Conduct roll call!" Lightfoot ordered, returning Vance's salute. "Okay, Gerald, keep it together, almost time to present the flags," Gerald told himself.

"Sound off for roll call!" Vance ordered and began calling each trooper's name, pausing for a response, before calling the next trooper.

One by one, each trooper snapped to attention, bringing their rifle to "present arms" with precisely drilled movements as their name was called, and sounding off loudly with, "Here, Command Sergeant Third Class!"

"Master Sergeant Griggs!" Vance called out, waiting for a response.

The crowd stood in silence, staring at the three small silver coffins each draped with the Flag of The Colonies. There was no response.

"Master Sergeant Calvin Griggs!" Vance called out, once again pausing for a response.

"Sergeant First Class Hagen!" Vance called out next. Again, no response came from the squad of troopers.

"Sergeant First Class Luther Hagen!" Vance called out again, his words harsh in the overwhelming silence.

Terrance closed his eyes, fighting the tears, as Vance called for Acalia next.

"Sergeant Second Class Perez!" Vance called out.

Although the pause between each call was only a few seconds, it felt like a lifetime to Terrance. His heart heavy with sorrow, he tried not to focus on the creatures that killed his friends, yet his nightmares were a constant reminder of what Acalia had faced alone. He couldn't help being angry with himself for not being there when she needed him most.

"Sergeant Second Class Acalia Perez!" Vance called once more, again no response came.

Vance did an about-face and saluted Major Lightfoot. "Sir, three troopers are absent from the formation. They have fallen in combat." "Very well. Command Sergeant Third Class Vance, let it be known that these troopers made the ultimate sacrifice in defense of mankind and the United Space Coalition. Present the flags of the fallen to their families," Major Lightfoot said, returning Vance's salute.

With the last flag given to Acalia's parents, rain began to pour down as the cleric said the final prayers for Calvin, Luther, and Acalia. There was a moment of silence before the bugler began to play the solemn notes of Taps. Its melody had become all too familiar to Gerald over the cycles, yet it always touched him the same. The pain of loss never got easier, and as the coffins slowly descended into the graves, the thoughts of what had brought them all to this moment played through his mind like broken dreams. As the last notes played, rain and tears became one.

Selection

"DID THEY START ALREADY, COMMAND Sergeant?" Gerald asked as he sat down next to Command Sergeant Archer in the uppermost row of the bay.

"No, Sergeant Second Class Landin just brought his class of cadets in," Archer said, pointing to the far side of the bay. He paused for a moment, trying to find the right words. "I heard about what happened. I'm sorry for your loss. They were all damn good troopers. I wish I could have made it to the funeral," he said remorsefully.

"Thanks, why did you want me to come here this morning, Command Sergeant?" Gerald said, changing the subject bluntly.

"Two reasons. One, I wanted you to take a look at the new Titan battle-frame, beyond just specs, since your commander and First Sergeant have deemed that the Twenty-Eighth will be one of the squads to get fielded first," Archer said, handing Gerald a holo-pad. "And two, I've already discussed it with your First Sergeant, I want to talk to you about taking over the squad. I know it's still early, only been a few weeks, but the mission must go on. The Twenty-Eighth has a long history of being one of the most elite battle-frame squads in the Alliance Military, so if you accept the position, you will get to handpick your squad."

Below, in the center of the bay, a full-size 3-D holographic image of a Gallant battle-frame appeared, next to a man wearing an armored Direct Neural Interface Pilot Suit with his helmet tucked under his right arm. He stood motionless, watching as a Titan battle-frame wearing the markings of an ace pilot came walking into the bay and onto the stage to face the audience. Gerald looked up from the holo-pad. A moment later, the chest and legs hatch opened and a female pilot wearing an unarmored Direct Neural Interface Pilot

Suit stepped out of it. Gerald couldn't help but notice how strikingly attractive she was when she removed her helmet. The skin-tight suit exposed every ample curve and her jet-black hair just touched her shoulders, contrasting vividly with her creamy complexion. Her arresting green-gray eyes captured his attention from a distance. However, what truly drew his attention was that she was wearing a Sigma Seven Elite Forces tab on her shoulder.

"Sigma Seven combat patch. I wonder if she was one of the ones that went into the Havasu Basin to pull those troopers whose drop ship was downed near that Hessaca hive," Gerald asked in a hushed voice.

A cadet turned around, clearly annoyed at Gerald and Archer for talking, as the class began.

Before the cadet could say a word, Gerald said flatly, "Cadet, you are about three seconds from testing out how good the military medical plan is. I suggest you think before you open your mouth and turn around." Glancing at Gerald's and Archer's rank insignias, the cadet turned back around, quickly turning bright red as giggles and hushed disses came from several of the nearby cadets.

"That was cold," Archer laughed. "You never took crap Cav, another reason why I think you'll make a good leader for the Twenty-Eighth."

Directing the class's attention toward the holographic image of the Gallant battle-frame, the woman began speaking. "Good morning, cadets. My name is Sergeant Second Class Angela Poison, call-sign Wraith, and I will be your primary instructor. This is Sergeant Second Class Thomas Hall, call-sign Dingo, your assistant instructor. Today, I will be giving you a block of instruction on the basic mechanical description and operation of the standard Alliance Combat Battle-Frame, the EX-121 Gallant."

The holographic image of the Gallant battle-frame resembled a giant warrior wearing a suit of full combat armor: proudly standing ready for battle, rounded chest lifted, back arched, and shoulders squared. Everything about the form inferred agility and power, even the rounded armor plating that covered the entire body. A wide upper torso supported a jump pack-like backpack with two streamlined thrusters. The large air intakes of the thrusters rose above the shoulders on both sides and angled slightly forward so as not to impede the full range of motion of the arms or head. An aerodynamic head with an opaque visor hiding the battle-frame's optics gave the machine an ominous appearance. The arms ended with armored five-finger hands; the legs ended with armored feet, complete with two squared toes equipped with retractable claws for greater stability. It was an impressive piece of technology.

"You will also be fortunate enough to be the first class to see an EX-329 Titan battle-frame up close near the end of today's instruction. That is unless you would rather do something more important, like sleep, Cadet Thomas!" Poison said, indicating to Sergeant Second Class Landin to pull Cadet Thomas to the side.

As Gerald tuned out the class, he began sifting through the list of candidates on the holo-pad once again, stopping to pull up the full records of those that caught his attention. Hammer would have wanted this, for one of them to take over instead of an outsider, he knew that much but taking over as squad leader was a huge step and one he wasn't quite sure he was ready for. He took a deep breath and began searching through the list once more. However, he always found a reason for why they were not qualified to be a part of the Twenty-Eighth. *In all honesty, no one would ever live up to the squadmates and friends I've lost*, he thought to himself.

Poison spoke directing the class's attention to the Gallant holographic image, "The battle-frame was designed from the necessity of combat operations, which required the flexibility of an infantry trooper, but with far greater survivability and firepower during the Systems War with the Demzerai. The battle-frame was just one of the technological initiatives that helped give the USC a fighting chance against the both physically and technologically superior Demzerai cloned soldiers, but that is another class by itself."

"The Gallant battle-frame stands at nine feet and four inches from the top of the jump pack intakes to the ground. Unlike older, pre-colony designs, the jump pack has been streamlined to fit like a backpack, with the air intakes and main thrusters built into it.

This, along with its height, allows for considerably easier movements through urban and forest environments. The total weight with a full combat load, to include an average pilot weight of one hundred and eighty pounds, is eighteen hundred pounds, making it almost twenty-two hundred pounds lighter than its predecessor, the Knight. The main reason for this reduction in weight is a new type of classified composite fiber material, sandwiched in between layers of diatitanium alloy, with flexible composite diatitanium mesh protecting and sealing joints, making it resistant to all but the heaviest weapon fire. Another change in the armor to add survivability is the way it is designed. Gone are the days of thick, semi-angular plates. Instead, the Gallant, like other next-generation battle-frames such as the Hades and Titan, has curved armor plates to reduce direct strikes and penetration.

"Now, onto operating the Gallant. I want you to think of the battle-frame as your body and you are the brain and nervous system of that body. All next-generation battle frame models utilize the bio-optic muscular bundle systems, or BOMBS for short," Poison continued while the 3-D model's armor vanished to show the suit's inner layers. "You can see it is designed after our own muscular structure, offering vast improvements over older systems such as hydraulics or electro-motors. BOMBS offers quicker, more precise movement, which can amplify the pilot's attributes thirty times over. However, in order for the pilot to take full advantage of this system, one must be connected directly into the frame through a Direct Neural Interface Pilot Suit or DNIPS, either unarmored like I'm wearing, or like Dingo, with carapace armor attached for field operation outside the barrier. The DNIPS allows the pilot's neural impulses to be translated directly to the battle-frame. The battle-frame's feedback and input are translated into neural impulses that the pilot's brain can process, in essence making you and the frame one being. It becomes your body. All of this is made possible by the battle-frame's cortex processing unit or CPU. Once the cockpit is closed and you are synced with the frame, the frame's sensors become your senses. You no longer see the world from the perspective of your eyes but from the enhanced view of the frame's optics. This allows you to see things like the magnetic spectrum of the world around you. The frame's sensors will enable you to hear radio waves. This can be very overwhelming. Not everyone has the mental capacity to be able to deal with such a connection. The sensory overload can cause various degrees of psychosis. In fact, 86 percent of you will not be able to handle the connection, and will not complete the six-month training program to become a Battle-Frame Pilot."

Ignoring the battle-frame operation lecture, Archer turned to Gerald. "If you'd like, I got a few suggestions for your squad. Take a look at Sergeant Second Class Joan Cadwell. She was in the Meridan Offense, a lot of combat experience. Sergeant Second Class Robert Morsen would also be a good choice too, damn good sniper." Gerald touched the holographic screen, pulling up the records of Cadwell and Morsen.

"Good choices, but not for the Twenty-Eighth. Neither one is HALO qualified." He closed their records and looked down at Hall who had taken over for the weapon segment of the lecture.

Pausing to ensure all the cadets were still awake and paying attention, Hall continued, "The Gallant's main armament is the PK-90D Collapsible Pulse Rifle, with an underslung grenade launcher mounted on the right thigh plate. Secondary armament consists of an AP-210 Assault Pistol on the left hip and a Phase Combat Knife sheathed on the left arm. Keep in mind, the weapon mountings can be changed to accommodate a left or right-handed preference."

"The PK-90D fires ten-millimeter mass reactive explosive slugs. Each slug is accelerated and fired by a magnetic pulse, in four-round bursts or single shots. It has a maximum effective range of thirty-two hundred meters and is truly devastating to both unarmored and armored targets alike. The standard loadout is four hundred and eighty rounds, in six separate eighty round magazines. The AP-210 fires fifty caliber light armor-piercing rounds in single or three-round bursts, highly effective up to five hundred fifty meters."

"Lastly, the Phase Combat Knife is quite literally the cutting edge in technology. The knife, when activated, wraps the blade in a high-frequency energy field that separates molecules as it passes through an object. This allows the blade to cut through solid matter, regardless of the structural integrity, causing massive damage," Hall said enlarging and highlighting each of the Gallant's weapons as he grabbed them from the main hologram. He gave the cadets a few minutes to study the images in further detail, before shutting the images off.

"Take fifteen. Be seated and ready to go at ten hundred hours," Poison commanded as she stood up from her computer terminal and walked over to Hall.

"I wonder what the Command Sergeant wants," Hall murmured to Poison, nodding toward Command Sergeant Archer and Gerald as they stood up and came down the stairs toward them.

"Hopefully it's not about those two guys whose asses I kicked last night," she whispered back.

"I know one thing's for sure, they now know what the word 'no' means," Hall chuckled.

"Command Sergeant, I wasn't aware you were sitting in on my classes today," Poison exclaimed as she jumped down from the stage to meet Archer and Gerald.

"Sergeant Second Class Hock, meet Sergeant Second Class Hall and Sergeant Second Class Poison," Archer said as Gerald shook their hands in turn. In the midst of shaking Poison's hand, Gerald took a moment to appreciate how beautiful she was. He had heard guys mention how hot she was before, but he had always just dismissed it as typical guy talk in the ready room. The kind of talk that was all too common whenever a new female came to a unit. She immediately became the new hotness in town.

So far, what he had heard about her was true; he wondered if the reason they called her Wraith was true as well. She had an air of sheer confidence about her, almost to the point of arrogance. In her defense, most Elite Force Troopers had the same confidence, especially aces. She had a cocky attitude because she knew what she was capable of doing. Kind of like Terrance, he thought. Looking at her, it was hard to believe that this was the same badass that kicked "Mr. I can bench press the whole gym" Stevens's butt last week. He laughed to himself, remembering the black eyes and sling Stevens still wore.

Curious, Gerald moved his attention to the Titan battle-frame on the stage. Archer walked past him and handed Poison a holo-pad. "Sergeant Hock is taking over the Twenty-Eighth and currently looking for new squad members, Sergeant Poison. I figured with your combat experience and Titan pilot training, you might be a good candidate for joining the squad. Plus, I wanted to give him a tour of the Titan since his squad will be the first to field one soon. Sergeant Hall, you and the cadets go ahead and take an early lunch,"

Archer said while turning to walk up the stairs to the stage.

"Yes, Command Sergeant," Hall replied as he snapped to the position of parade-rest before turning to head out the bay.

Gerald followed Archer up the stairs on to the stage stopping in front of the Titan to look inside before looking at the two arm-mounted assault pulse cannons. "She is a beauty…and a beast. I'd hate to be on its bad side in a fight," Gerald said as he circled the battle-frame.

"Funny, that's what they say about me," Poison snickered as she grabbed her helmet and cradled it under her arm, walking over to the Titan.

"So I have heard," Gerald jokingly replied.

"Well, the EX-329 Titan is state-of-the-art in armament and defensive capabilities. The armor is almost an inch thicker than the Hades Assault Battle-Frame, making it slightly heavier than the Hades as well. It's designed to get into the thick of the fight and provide fire support to allied forces at the same time. To do this, the Titan is armed with several impressive weapon systems," Poison said, directing Gerald's attention to the arms of the battle-frame.

"The first of these is the tri-barreled TAC-14 Assault Pulse Cannons mounted on each arm. The barrels slide forward and up, locking into place when the weapon is activated and retracting into the lower housing when not needed. Each TAC-14 can lay down a hail of twenty-millimeter mass reactive explosive slugs at twelve hundred rounds a minute. Additionally, mounted on the right shoulder is an RP-178 rocket pod. The RP-178 can carry two types of rockets, the APR-19 Anti-Personnel Rocket and the HER-57 High Explosive Rocket. Both are great for crowd control if I might add. Finally, each fist has a KG-1D Knuckle Guard which slides into place when activated for a punch. These knuckle guards project a field similar to the phase weapons around the fist, causing a chain reaction with the surface molecules of the target that result in a shaped explosion directed inward at the target. Needless to say, this creates devastating damage and a very bad day for your target."

"Really nasty up close," Gerald said, impressed.

"Another new tech addition is the Disruptor Flare. When launched into the air, the disruptor flare releases particles charged with the same disruptor energy that protects the barrier cities. These particles, though short-lived, nullify all magical energy in an area. Likewise, as with all current battle-frames, the Titan is equipped with a jump jet system, affording it excellent maneuverability," Poison said, back in lecture mode.

"I've seen the specs, but I have to admit that seeing it up close is very impressive," Gerald said, watching Poison step into the cockpit. The visor on Poison's helmet became opaque, dousing her into darkness, as her mind reached out to the suit's cortex processing unit. The suit came alive as it acknowledged her neural connection. No longer was she in darkness, but now staring down at Gerald and Archer from her giant mechanical body. She continued to connect with the cortex, no longer feeling enclosed in a ridged mechanical machine but now commanding a massive, fluid body.

"I reserved range nine, so you can show him what you and that frame of yours can do," Archer said as he extended a hand out toward the bay doors.

Gerald took a step back as the chest and legs hatches sealed; Poison turned to head out of the bay. In the back of his mind, he couldn't help but wonder…for all their technological advances, after what he had seen, would it be enough?

Last Breath

JONAN DISMOUNTED HIS STEED AS the animal pranced nervously to and fro. He paused, long enough for his escorts to join him, before quickly making his way toward the entrance in the mound. Coven Auralla, as it had been for all covens, was built underneath the base of a Sacred Vessel Tree, centered on its life root. Vessel trees were unique; they sat on a spiritual waypoint into which the life root of the tree grew. From these great trees, a veil-seer could attain many of the spiritual gifts given by the Great Mother Spirit. However deep down, he hated coming here; the spirits were unnerving to him, and deep inside, the Cainanites that Asla had created terrified him. The entrance to the coven was guarded by two Greater Wodlems who sat dormant, blending in with nearby vegetation.

Wodlems had been protectors of his people since ancient times. These plant-like creatures were grown from the seeds of a vessel tree and given life by a spiritual incantation. The Wodlems were a testament to how powerful Asla was. Not many had the ability to summon and control such creatures until they were far older than her. Truly, the Great Mother had blessed her the day she was born and cursed his people at the same time.

On the outside, Asla's coven seemed no different from any other. Walls were decorated with the history of the coven along with the Coven's sacred seal. Young children ran about playing as the adults went about their daily tasks. The sweet smell of roasting gambil filled his nostrils, no doubt for the feast that was being put on to honor the newest warriors during the Season of Renewal. The warriors of Asla's coven were some of the deadliest; this was partially due to their leader, Arshul. The twin brother of Asla, what he lacked in spiritual attunement was made up for in cunning intelligence and physical prowess. How the two had become dominant at such a young age raised many questions that none were willing to risk asking out loud; many of the original elders and more outspoken members had died recently over the last several cycles.

Jonan continued to observe Asla's coven. A group of hunters was returning with a Kiyak bull slaughtered by their deadly sword-bows. Several young children ran up and began jabbing the dead beast as if they were making the kill. The kids laughed and boasted before being playfully chased off by one of the hunters who seemed to appear from nowhere as he removed the hood of his cloak to become visible.

"Elder, they are here," Jonan's escort said, indicating to Arshul and a female Cainanite with a red mane and chestnut body fur, as they entered the main hall from one of the branching hallways. In Jonan's eyes, the Cainanite were an abomination to the Great Mother Spirit's gift and yet another testament to the power that Asla wielded. To create such creatures was a task that even the most radical among them would never attempt, much less master. Yet, the Cainanite that approached them was not like the ones of forbidden lore—ravenous beings that were consumed by the beast within them, quickly becoming beyond control. The female in front of him showed none of that savagery. Her eyes gleamed with a predatory nature, backed by an even deeper intelligence, and it made Jonan's blood run cold.

Jonan watched as those around him showed an overwhelming indifference to the creature's presence. Truly, Asla's coven had been corrupted far beyond any help. Bokar, the youngest of Jonan's escorts, was clearly trying to hide his uneasiness at the sight of the Cainanite. "Steady yourself, boy. Do not give it the satisfaction of sensing your fear," Hallen, another escort, whispered to Bokar as he moved closer to stand near Jonan.

"Elder, I was not informed that you were coming," Arshul said frostily, as he presented his palms skyward, and dipped his head briefly in respect toward Jonan.

"I sent no word of my coming as it was hastily planned. I have come on behalf of the Coven of Elders and I must speak with Asla immediately," Jonan stated.

The Cainanite stared at Jonan's escorts—first Hallen, then Finel, and finally Bokar. The icy silver eyes seemed to gleam in anticipation. "She is in the spirit chamber and will not be disturbed, Elder," Arshul said, with a hint of impudence. "In the meantime, allow us to accommodate one of your esteemed position. Please Elder, follow Ildel. She will take you to the Chamber of Elders." Arshul then turned and walked away without waiting for a response. Anger rose in Jonan at the blatant disrespect, but he quieted the thoughts of protest as the Cainanite's eyes latched onto him.

SPIRIT CHAMBER

Unlike the other chambers of the coven, the spirit chamber was not covered by mortar and brick. The floors and walls were left bare, revealing the roots and ground beneath Tallagen's surface. Several large, pulsating roots extended from the ceiling, piercing the middle of the chamber floor. In the center of the room, a lush circle of iridescent green and yellow grasses grew; some of the grass was still stained with the blood of a recent blood offering. Nearby, on an altar made of dirt, lay the source of the fresh blood—the lifeless body of Private Wilson. It was there that Asla sat in a deep trance within the dim chamber, listening to the forest, while her mind reached out to the world above. It was here, in the spirit chamber, that the coven's veil-seers would come to attune themselves with the Great Mother Spirit, seeking her guidance, entering into the veil.

The world became a mass of shifting and blurring shadows, as her spirit traveled beyond the confines of her body. She traveled the forest, occasionally touching the minds of animals along her path. She looked through the eyes of a Snare Criflix. The dog-sized arachnid suddenly dropped from its safety line in the canopy to ensnare a gambil in its netted web. She lingered in its mind long enough to feel the life leave its prey as large fangs sank deep into the soft flesh.

She began to search with more purpose, reading the intricate ebb and flow of the shifting shadows until at last, she found the clear signs of mass death. The death of so many was like a bonfire on a moonless night. She began to move toward it; waves of shadows washed over her as each soul left its physical vessel. Back in the spirit chamber, Asla smiled. She enjoyed the feeling of the waves washing over her spirit, like a gentle breeze across her skin. She basked in the sensation for a moment longer until she found the mind she sought.

DARSHUL

Darshul's eyes revealed the reason for the release of so many souls. Sitting high upon his mount, he watched as several of his hunters appeared. Their cloaks, imbedded with a spirit of the forest, moved with minds of their own, constantly shifting and warping around its wearer, sprouting branches, leaves, and changing textures to blend the wearer into their surroundings. Each hunter fired arrows with deadly precision before vanishing into the forest to attack from a new location. Darshul signaled his cavalry forward to cut off the retreat of those who tried to flee.

Jonan's coven had grown weak, and it showed in his warriors. They fought without true grace; against defilers, their blades would be a threat, but against those of his clan they were lambs ready for the slaughter. Jonan's coven had strayed away from combat, instead, seeking to become one with the Great Mother Spirit through enlightenment. With a mighty leap, his mount landed in the middle of the fray, eviscerating a male who had dared to raise a spear to attack it.

Darshul slid from his saddle as two warriors charged him; one stopped mid-stride as an arrow pierced his skull. The other warrior continued forward; blade held at a high guard. Darshul drew his cleft bladed sword-spear and, within two effortless strokes, parried the warrior's strike and removed his head without breaking his stride. All around him, death took hold as his warriors slew every male, ensuring Jonan's coven would end when the last of their life's blood returned to the Great Mother Spirit.

For the first time since Asla had entered his mind, he felt her presence. She took no precautions to hide within his thoughts; he could feel her satisfaction. As she spoke to him, he paused. "I have broken the spiritual connection of the entire coven's guardians. Ensure that you personally slay all of Jonan's offspring, as well as his mate, and return to me quickly with what I seek," Asla said, before pulling herself from Darshul's mind.

Disemboweling another attacker with a single fluid movement of his sword-spear, Darshul turned to join his warriors, herding the last of the survivors toward the living chambers.

COVEN

Hallen found himself staring at the female Cainanite Ildel, who was crouched across the room from him, and contemplating just how much power was needed to bend such a spirit to Feralan will. Truly, the ways of a veil-seer were not for him; he felt the calling of the warrior. He knew the rituals to create such beings had long been forbidden, the practices banned, and those found to be even seeking its knowledge were given a swift death. Yet, somehow the veil-seer Asla had not only attained the knowledge but had also mastered the ability to subdue these powerful spirit beasts.

He shuddered slightly from the thought of what spirits dwelled within this place. Jonan had spoken to him often of how the spirits within this coven disturbed him greatly, and that there were forces at work here that would be the death of them all.

Hallen shifted in his seat cautiously, grasping the hilt of his sword, as the Cainanite stood and stepped away from the door toward them. Bokar was not as prudent and jumped up, throwing his chair to the floor while drawing his sword. Finel stood, his sword partially drawn from its scabbard. The Cainanite paused, ignoring the armed warriors; it looked towards the door, and for the span of several breaths the room was silent, the tension thick in the air. Finally, the door opened. The Cainanite dipped its head low, keeping her eyes downward in respect as Asla entered the room. Asla paused, acknowledging Ildel, as Ildel quickly began to morph returning to her nude Feralan form. "Asla, truly the Great Mother Spirit has blessed you, child.

Yet, with such a blessing, there must be restraint guided through wisdom," Jonan said thoughtfully, as he caressed the wood-carved talisman that hung from his neck.

"Perhaps these words should be meant for your warriors as well, Elder," Asla said condescendingly; she sat at the far end of the twelve-foot table, glancing at the two readied warriors before focusing on Jonan.

Hallen eyed both Bokar and Finel, who quickly sheathed their weapons and sat down once again.

"But I am sure you did not come here to share your wisdom. Was it not mostly your warriors during our last encounter with the defilers that fell to their deaths?" Asla mocked.

Jonan locked eyes with Asla at the blatancy of her words. Within the depths of her light violet eyes, there were secrets, yet her tongue betrayed none. Hallen took note of Asla's tone and directness; he watched Ildel as she gracefully moved to stand by her mistress. She stood, coolly glancing over the room, her nude body showing no signs that would betray her mistress's plans.

"My coven has few warriors. Those I entrusted to you were slain in the recent attacks with the outsiders, along with those of the covens of Runu and Friya as well. Yet the warriors you committed to the attack lived, due to wards of protection given to them by you. I see them on the female that stands next to you now, carved into her flesh," Jonan said, anger building within him.

"Warriors?" Asla laughed. "What you and the other pathetic covens gave me were hardly warriors. In fact, I would say that in your entire coven only two are worthy of such a title—the great Hallen and the Shruid Emil. No, what you gave me was fodder. Fodder in the hopes I would embrace your coven, now that you see the power of my blessings. You fool…you still believe there can be a simple peace. You have now come to see, the Great Mother continues to bless me and those that have chosen this path I lead. What you did birthed from fear and those you gave me were mere sacrifices to the great cause of protecting the Great Mother Spirit," Asla said coldly, staring into Jonan's green eyes.

"How dare you speak to me like this? Your impertinence will not go unpunished by the Coven of Elders! You have no compassion. You seek all-out war and the death of thousands!" Jonan shouted as he stood, slamming his fist on the table.

Asla made not the slightest indication that Jonan's outburst had moved her. With a blank expression, she reached out, taking a sip from a cup nearby before speaking; she sensed the shift in the spirit realm as Jonan attempted to cast a spell and failed. "You are wrong, Elder. I seek peace…and the death of millions," she said emotionlessly.

Hallen jumped to his feet along with Bokar and Finel as the door to the chamber opened and Darshul entered nude, splattered with blood not his own, carrying a dark sack. With the coppery musk of fresh blood hanging in the air. Jonan's eyes grew wide in shock as he realized his connection to the spirit realm had been cut off. "What is this? What have you done, witch?" Jonan demanded as his three guardians drew their swords.

Asla still unmoved, replied as she stood, "I offer you the gift of being reunited with your loved ones."

Darshul stepped forward, tossing the contents of the sack upon the table. Jonan and his men, save Hallen, stepped back in horror, as the eyeless heads of Jonan's mate and four children rolled to the floor. "I had their eyes removed so they would not have to witness your shame. You see, I do have compassion despite what you may believe, Elder. Enjoy your last breath," Asla said with mock sympathy as she turned and walked toward the door, never looking back as Darshul and Ildel began to change into their Cainanite forms.

The Void

THE SCREENS WERE ALWAYS THE same, not worthy of more than a momentary glance to ensure the data from the recon satellites throughout the system was being recorded for further analysis by the appropriate department in the morning. The occasional solar flare from one of the twin suns had lost its glamour a cycle ago if it had even taken that long for him to become disinterested. Gregory Pitts had actually given up staring at the holographic screens not too long after his initial checks; coming on shift was an opportunity to focus on his thesis. The silence of the office was refreshing for a change, but also distracting.

It had been like this for the last week and he was still adjusting to the constant silence all night. Usually like clockwork two hours into his shift, Alice, one of the janitors, would show up to do her nightly cleaning. The deep-space research lab was always her last stop for the evening when cleaning the floor, and they would spend a few hours talking over coffee and whatever meal she had prepared for dinner. It had become their routine ever since he forgot his dinner at home during his internship here at the Space and Aeronautics Research Agency, or SARA, and she had offered half of hers when she overheard his stomach grumbling as she mopped.

He remembered: "Sounds like someone could use a good meal from the sound of that tummy, dear," Alice said with motherly concern.

"Huh? Oh…yeah, I sure could but I was in a rush to make it here on time. I forgot my dinner on the kitchen counter and the vending machine in the break room is broken," Gregory replied, placing his hand on his stomach to try and quiet the grumbling.

"Well, I think I can help you, that is if you like homemade beef potpie?"

"Sounds great. Are you sure you don't mind?" Gregory smiled thankfully.

"Don't be silly, dear, if I minded, I would have never offered," Alice had replied with a warm smile. "Besides, I always make too much. I'm still not used to only cooking for myself without my son and husband around."

"Oh, is your son visiting his dad for the holidays?" Gregory asked curiously.

"Oh no, my son left for basic training three days ago. My husband was killed in action during the Hallows conflict."

"I am sorry for your loss, Mrs...?"

"Wilson. Alice Wilson, but please just call me Alice. As far as my husband, it's all right now. I've had quite some time over the cycles to grieve. Besides, I know one day I will see him again and that gives me comfort. But I do worry about my son, Donald, now that he's following in his father's footsteps."

Gregory stood up. "Well, it sure is a pleasure to meet you, Alice. My name is Gregory Pitts, but please call me Greg," he said, shaking her hand.

From that point on, they spent a good part of the evening talking and getting to know each other. It turned out that she was an amazing conversationalist and well-educated on a variety of subjects in addition to being a genuinely kind lady. He had come to enjoy their nightly talks, but he understood why she wasn't here tonight. It was disheartening when the silence reminded him to look at the clock and she wasn't here.

She had just lost her only child, Donald. After a month of him missing in action, a man and woman wearing military dress uniforms showed up at her door on a Sunday morning to tell her that her son was dead. A patrol had found his body displayed like some morbid scarecrow, all carved up, by those damn savages out in the forest. Alice had called him after they left that day; at first, he had thought she had dialed him by accident because she didn't say anything for several seconds.

"Alice? Hello? Are you okay?" he had asked.

"Greg, it's my son...He's dead...," Alice croaked out through her tears.

In between her sobs, she asked him to accompany her to the viewing of the body and he, of course, agreed.

That Monday morning he picked her up and they drove in total silence for the entire twenty-minute trip to Miron Military Hospital. He had wanted to say something during the drive, but Alice's face had deterred him. It was a calm mask atop a soul assaulted by pain and tears. He remembered how he felt, walking into the morgue to view Donald's body. He could only imagine how Alice felt. Walking through the warm sand-colored hallways of the hospital before entering the cold bleached white that led to the morgue felt like a bad dream. Like the rest of the morgue, the storage room was stark white but much colder. The smell of disinfectant and formaldehyde hung heavily in the air, nauseating him. Despite the large room, he felt claustrophobic and had to take a moment to keep from turning and leaving. The walls were lined with freezer chambers. Each freezer's chamber door had a green and yellow LED light above it, along with a digital display showing a date and initials. He couldn't help but notice that the majority of them were occupied. The somber lab tech added to the gloomy atmosphere, strangely silent. He didn't say a word, making the whole setting even more morbid until finally, it was time to show Donald's body.

Not one for small talk, Gregory figured.

"Mrs. Wilson, are you ready?" the tech asked, before reaching for a freezer door.

Alice said a short prayer before replying. "Yes."

When the lab tech opened the door and slid back the sheet to reveal Donald's body, Alice collapsed into a torrent of tears. No person could have been prepared to see their child, or anyone, mutilated in such a way. Gregory would always remember that moment.

"Dear God, I hope he didn't suffer," Gregory whispered to himself. For a moment longer, Gregory sat, withdrawn inside his thoughts of that sad day, until a soft voice coming from the holo-vid brought him back to the present.

He looked up toward the large holo-vid across the room. The news was on, no surprise considering the only channel it was programmed to receive was the Colonial Network News channel. It was how he stayed in touch with what was going on in the colonies; another of his nightly routines but after about two hours the only new content was commercials for the rest of the night.

Although he was looking forward to revisiting the televised debate on "Around the Table" later, between the show's host Barry Queen, Senate analysis Monica Ow, Senator Sullen, and Senator Harkus on Bill 2062. He had missed a good portion of the debate after he noticed an anomaly that appeared and then vanished from sector eighteen-seven-nine bravo, outside the system. The satellite that detected it hadn't remained in range long enough to get any real data. So, he just logged it as miscellaneous and went back to watching the debate.

He supported the new bill being passed. Senator Harkus had a lot of valid points that he agreed with. He really didn't see what there was to debate about when it came to Bill 2062 anymore. A new city meant more room to expand, more jobs, and a better quality of life for everyone. He wasn't thrilled at the possibility of going to war but felt that the stupid savages wouldn't be happy unless they could "cleanse" the whole damn planet.

It was why he saw Senator Sullen and the rest of his party to be just like the Unity activist. Always campaigning to seek acceptance from the Feralans, to make a world where they all could co-exist. It was a flawed idea, one which only meant bending over backward in the long run, so as not to offend the Feralan.

It made the colonies look weak, in his eyes at least, and was the main reason he believed the Feralans were becoming bolder in their attacks. It was better to relocate them far away, or at least to retaliate in force and show them that the colonies were here to stay.

A warning beep drew his attention again from the debate on the holo-vid and toward one of the holographic screens to the left of his workstation. "Hmm, sector eighteen-seven-nine bravo again. DS9, what have you found this time?" he said out loud, looking at the data coming from the deep space satellite. "Whatever you detected looks to be pretty big there. Too bad it's just out of visual range. I'd like to see what it is."

In the background, he heard Barry Queen ask a question in reference to all the additional funding being used to design more military equipment rather than colonization projects. "Blame Senator Sullen's 'let's hold hands' views for that one." He snorted as he reached over to turn down the volume on the holo-vid.

The object was still at extreme range for the satellite's sensor but the reading had determined the object was composed of mostly metals. It was just over a half-mile in size and moving at around two hundred and eighty thousand miles a second. "Possibly a slow comet or really large meteorite," he speculated. "Either way, the astronomy department will be excited to see the data in the morning."

He watched the screen, hoping that the visual indicator would light up so he could take a look, but it was too far out. Gregory let out a sigh of disappointment and got up to get a cup of coffee after he tried to take a sip from his empty cup. "Well, that just blows," he said, staring down into the empty cup. He looked at the clock on the main monitor of the watch station and decided now was as good a time as any to get a fresh cup.

He walked down the hall to the break room, past the damn snack machine that was broken yet again. "With an annual budget of ten billion credits, you'd think SARA could afford to replace this piece of crap," he said out loud as if talking to someone nearby. As he walked into the break room the ceiling lights came on, illuminating the room. He made a beeline for the coffee dispenser and poured himself a fresh cup. He took a sip and smiled. Black, with just enough sugar mixed in to leave a hint of bitterness. He took a look at the digital clock under a panoramic view of the Sol system. "One forty-five a.m.," he sighed. There were still six hours to go in his shift. He turned to make the journey back to the watch station. Along the way back Alice came to mind once again, and he made a mental note to give her a call. Better yet, stop by and say hi, he thought, before his thoughts trailed off into how much longer his shift was again. When he returned to the watch station, he was greeted by several warning beeps.

At first, Greg thought one of the satellites had picked up some random object again, or maybe Nick down in IT was bored and had decided to screw around with him. It wouldn't be the first time he had played some dumb prank like this. "This is the best you could come up with at 2:00 a.m., Nick?" he said out loud, walking back to his workstation. He reached for the phone, planning to give Nick an ear full of how he should go fack himself, but instead noticed that DS9 now had a visual and that DS12 was also tracking the same large object. He touched the button to bring up the visual link on DS9.

A holographic spaceship filled the screen. He stepped back, surprised to see that the object wasn't a comet or a meteorite like he had suspected, but instead a ship of some kind. Data from DS12 began to flow across the screen in reference to the ship. Size, weight, heading, speed, and finally, type. Greg's cup shattered, spewing hot liquid onto his pants and across the floor, as it hit the ground. He took no notice as he stared at the ship type—"Demzerai: Battlecruiser: Hebra Class" flashing in bold letters. A moment later, flashing red messages reading "Data Secured. This Information is now CLASSIFIED: Theta Sierra Prime Alpha (TSPA). Deep Space Satellite 9 Cloaking Field Engaged. Deep Space Satellite 12 Cloaking Field Engaged," began scrolling across the displays before the holographic displays went offline, one by one. Only his main holographic display remained active with the message, "Security Personnel are on the way. You are to remain in place for official debriefing, Gregory Pitts."

Greg fell back into his chair, his legs giving way to the sinking feeling in his stomach. He wasn't sure what to do next. He didn't want to believe it, and if he hadn't seen it with his own eyes he never would have. "A Demzerai warship. Here. It couldn't be...Oh my God, the colonies. They have to be warned," he gasped, reaching for the phone.

"I am afraid that isn't your call, Mr. Pitts. Please come with me," said a voice from the doorway.

Gregory stood to see a man in a gray suit accompanied by what appeared to be two fully armored Colonial Security Force personnel dressed in black.

"Look, I don't know who you are, but we are all in danger. There is a Demzerai warship less than a parsec away from our system," Gregory nervously explained.

"You mean the comet you believe is a ship?" the man in gray replied calmly.

"That isn't a facking comet! It's a facking Demzerai battlecruiser! If that ship decides to come this way…Oh my god, we have to warn everyone!" Greg panicked, again picking up the phone.

"The phones have been turned off for security reasons, Mr. Pitts."

"Who are you, people? You have no right to do this!"

"You know, I was hoping you would be the smart one. Sadly, you are like all the others. Why can't any of you just accept the story? It really is simple," the man in gray replied calmly, stepping into the office to reveal the two officers drawing their sidearms.

"What story?" Greg asked, nervously eyeing the armed officers. "I…I'll say whatever you want me to say, just don't hurt me."

"I am afraid it seems we are past that point. Unfortunate, but be assured your scientific discovery will not go unfounded. Tomorrow morning's news will speak of the comet you found out there in the void."

We, Not the People

"GOOD EVENING, AND WELCOME TO C-HV news at eleven. I am Wayne Norton…"

"And I'm Amanda Bering. In tonight's breaking news, the fishing vessel *Bethony* was found after it had been reported missing three days ago. The vessel was located adrift near the coast with all eighteen crew members missing. Initial reports state all lifeboats were present and there were no indications as to what happened to the crew. Chief Wanamere of the Colonial Security Forces investigation division had the following statement:"

"The navy turned over the Bethony four hours ago after towing it back to Batal Harbor this afternoon. So far, we only have the navy's report of their initial inspection of the vessel. At this time, I am sorry, but the only thing we can confirm is that there were no survivors aboard and that there were no signs of anything that would have forced the crew to abandon their ship."

The video feed switched back to Amanda. "We will continue to follow the story, updating you as we learn more."

"Thank you, Amanda. In other news, the Senate Bill 2062 is headed for final approval. This bill to create a new barrier city will go before the Senate within the next few days and then go out for public vote soon after. If the vote is passed, this will signal a major victory for several corporations, namely Galum Corp., as they have been a major lobbyist and backer for the creation of a new barrier city. This new city would mainly be zoned for corporate expansion, manufacturing, and mining. The bill has met with a lot of opposition all across the colonies for several reasons. The main reason is due to the fact that Kansin barrier expansion is already currently causing major conflict to arise with the Feralan people. The new barrier city is expected to incite even more conflict, as it is expected to be established near several significant Feralan religious sites. Many believe it will lead to all-out war—a war that many see as unnecessary and unjust. The other reason the bill has met with a lot of opposition within the senate is that the city would be governed by a corporate board instead of an elected governing body."

"It's definitely raising a lot of tension in the senate between the parties, Wayne," Amanda added.

"It sure is, Amanda, and with mid-term elections coming up, both parties are looking to use this as an edge," Wayne replied before looking back into the camera.

"Now, onto a major phenomenon sweeping across the colonies. We're here with our very own colonial entertainment correspondent, Jamie Addision."

"Thank you, Wayne. Well, today the computer gaming company, Distance Dreams, reported that it now has over two hundred and seventy thousand subscribers to its popular Massive Multi-Player Virtual Reality Game, or MMVRG, Incursion. Having only been released a cycle and half ago, it has quickly grown, knocking out the once all-time popular fantasy MMVRG, Call of the Dragon, by rival E-Games. Unlike Call of the Dragon, Incursion has a futuristic setting in which players enter a virtual world. In this world, players become a member of one of three warring factions: The Human United Nations, parasitic humanoids called the Shadarac or the cybernetic Antox. Players take on the life of the avatar they create and then enter the virtual setting where they fully interact, living as their chosen avatar. Players can choose from over a hundred different character classes. They can be the captain of a mighty space fleet, a fighter pilot, a commander of legions of soldiers, a planetary governor, a trader, or even a normal citizen of some far-flung world, simply living a normal life other than their own. Epic space battles, planetary assaults, combat, politics, espionage, and trading—these are just some of the features the game has to offer, as well as the distinct social aspects and cultures of the three factions. The game and storyline are constantly evolving due to the actions of the thousands of players.

I am looking forward to trying it out tonight, myself. Now back to you, Wayne and Amanda."

"Thank you, Jamie. Next, when we come back, Foundation Day is right around the corner and our very own Sativa Reyes will help you find that special gift, after this break," Amanda said as the newscast transitioned to commercials.

After the commercial break, the news reporters continued to drone on, alternating news articles with video clips. Gerald switched off the holo-vid as he glanced over at the time on the nightstand; it was fifteen minutes to midnight and sleep didn't feel like it was coming anytime soon. It was so hard not to focus on what was going on behind the scenes in the senate. Every day it was becoming clearer to him that the government was moving in a direction that would sever itself from the needs of the people. He swirled the last of his Nuroc Stout before downing it and tossing the bottle into the waste disposal. He sighed, pushing the Empty Bin button on the command panel. The trash would be sent to a recycling plant where it would be broken down to a molecular level, reformed into neutral matter blocks, and then be sold to various manufacturers at a profit. *One man's trash is another man's treasure. Capitalism at work, yes, siree*, he thought to himself as he turned off the kitchen light and headed toward the bedroom.

As he walked down the hall, he noticed a light coming from the study and peeked in. Sarah was passed out on her favorite couch in the apartment, holo-pads all around her, with her datapad laid across her chest. He leaned against the door frame, smiling to himself, admiring her for a moment. It was nothing new for her to get so consumed in working on the next big story that she would fall asleep on the couch. Often times, like tonight, he would carry her to bed. She was a remarkable woman, and since the day they had said "I do," he had known he couldn't have made a better decision. She was his fantasy come true. Her Irish heritage was all too evident in her beautiful fiery red hair that only helped to magnify her enchanting green eyes. Not only was she incredibly intelligent, but she was truly a genuinely good-natured person who tried to see the good in everyone—a rare trait and in direct contrast to most of the other senate correspondents.

He picked up the holo-pads that were scattered about, placing them in a neat pile on her desk. He stopped to look at a few of them, noticing each of them dealt with Logan Summit, the CEO of Galum Corp. Logan was a part-time archeologist, interesting if not unusual, Gerald thought to himself. Gerald scanned through a few more holo-pads until Sarah stirred slightly, drawing his attention back toward her as her datapad slid from her chest onto the floor. "Let's get you to bed, sleepyhead."

ANGELA

Morning came way too soon, Angela thought, rolling over to hit the snooze for the eighth time. She squinted from the sunlight coming through the bedroom window. "Ugh…computer, 70 percent tint," she mumbled. A moment later the windows darkened, reducing the light in the room considerably. She rolled over staring at the ceiling and pushed the blankets back, letting the cool air wash over her nakedness as she stretched. She closed her eyes and settled back into the comfort of her fourteen hundred thread–count cotton sheets; there was still more of last night's party that she wanted to sleep off. She began to drift slowly back into sleep when suddenly the door to her room slid open; partially opening her eyes, she saw her best friend Mya standing in the doorway, already dressed for the gym. "So…do you plan on getting the fack up today, or am I going flirting at the gym by myself?" Mya asked, modeling her new workout outfit.

"Fack off, you know being best friends doesn't give you a license to be a pain in the ass. Besides, didn't you hook up with that guy last night? Why are you awake so early?" Angela groaned, pulling the covers back over her and throwing the pillow over her face.

Mya jumped on the bed, pulling the pillow away. "Well, I thought it was because we were drunk, but this morning he was still garbage…so I made him get up and get out. I mean, you would have thought it was his first time ever, and he was so small. It wasn't worth the trouble to take my thong off. A shame though…He was a hottie," Mya laughed as she snatched the covers off Angela.

"So you get a lame hookup and I have to pay for it on my day off? Fine, just remember, payback is a bitch. I am going to make you sweat your butt off in the gym," Angela said as she got up, tossing a pillow at Mya's head.

GERALD'S APARTMENT

"Gerald, Terrance is on the com-link. Sweetheart, I have to get going," Sarah said, sipping her coffee and using her finger to guide the holographic screen on the counter to her PDA. Gerald stopped at the entrance to the kitchen, catching a quick kiss before putting his T-shirt on. "Remember, you guys need to decide where we are having dinner tonight, and no, I don't want to go to Carl's Bar and Grill again," Sarah said, facing Terrance on the holo-viewer, before turning to kiss Gerald once more and grab her cup of coffee.

"Oh yeah, tell Terrance to decide which girl he's bringing before we leave this time," Sarah chuckled before rushing out the door.

"What's up, bro? Did you take a look at the final roster I submitted for the new squad members?" Gerald asked, pouring himself a fresh cup of coffee.

"Yeah, I did…but Poison! Seriously? Seriously!" Terrance gawked in disbelief.

"What's the big deal? I mean, she's good, no doubt about it. She meets all the qualifications and then some to be a part of the Twenty-Eighth," Gerald said as he sat down in front of the holo-viewer.

"Not knocking that she isn't, just…you know she and I went through selection for Elite Forces together, and we'll just say it's complicated," Terrance said, clearly annoyed.

"Funny, she said the same thing when I mentioned you were in the squad. It almost makes me wonder if you two facked before," Gerald laughed.

"Got jokes, do we?" Terrance said, giving Gerald the middle finger.

"So you good with Sergeant Second Class Vernon Walt joining the team? What about Sergeant Second Class Alena Tanaka? Or did you sleep with her too?" Gerald snorted, barely holding in the laughter.

"You know, if you weren't my boy, I'd tell you something right now," Terrance said sarcastically.

"Oh, I forgot to tell you. Hemsley called last night and wants to know if we can help him capture Orion Tau IV today around noon. He said the rest of the guild was going to be tied up in helping the newbies level up most of the day. So basically, he's on his own right now and needs our help while the planet is still lightly defended. He won't be able to do anything later tonight because he has to work. So I told him I would do it if he lets me harvest one of his worlds to replace my losses afterward, and he has to help us get the elder queen genome upgrade," Gerald said while moving to the living room sofa.

"Fack that! Last time I helped that dude I lost six cruisers, two battlecruisers, and my colony ship took serious damage—all because he said the planet was unguarded and then there was like four Antox players waiting for us when we jumped in the system," Terrance snapped back.

"I remember you were pissed for like two weeks," Gerald laughed. "If we do this, we can get him to help us with getting the elder queen for our hives today so we can start on getting the next tier of genetic upgrades," Gerald said, pulling up an Incursion strategy guide in a separate viewer.

"Fine! Tell him we'll do it, but I want to harvest a quarter of the planet's population as payment when we're done; otherwise, he can go at it alone," Terrance grudgingly agreed. "Oh hey, I'm heading out to the gym with Ziyi but we should be back before noon," Terrance said as Ziyi sat down next to him.

"Hi, Sergeant Hock, Terrance has to go; otherwise, Incursion won't be the only thing he won't be doing later," Ziyi said playfully.

"Okay you two, TMI, catch you later," Gerald said, closing the holo-viewer.

AMBERMAN

Senator Amberman sat at his desk reviewing the data compiled in reference to Bill 2062 on his main holo-viewer. He had long decided the bill needed to be defeated, but many in the senate saw otherwise. The passing of this bill would put the colonies in a situation primed for war if that had not already been accomplished with the Kansin expansion. It would surely destroy the fragile peace he had orchestrated over the last fourteen cycles with the Feralan people. He touched a holographic screen to his left and a 3-D map appeared of all the major Feralan covens near Kansin's latest expansion. He exhaled and reclined in his chair, looking at the many plaques and pictures scattered about his office before he settled on one. He often found himself staring at the beautifully polished wooden plaque with the hand-carved words laden in gold, "We the People." The words had been carved in High English, the native language of many of the founding senate members, and the common language throughout the colonies. He recited the words in his mind; the truth of the statement seemed lost in what he saw before him on the holographic screens.

So many lives have been lost to unnecessary bloodshed, and for what? Yes, our survival was paramount, but at what cost? he thought to himself as he increased the volume and focused on the live broadcast of Senator Harkus.

"Bill 2062 will ensure a better quality of life for every citizen. By dedicating one entire annex to major manufacturing, mining, and corporate structures, we will free up much-needed space among the other barrier cities. However, I will let Galum Corp's CEO explain further," said Senator Harkus, stepping aside to allow Logan Summit to take the podium.

"Thank you, thank you!" Logan began, waiting for the cheers to die down. "Galum Corp, along with its many corporate and industrial backers, is looking to improve the quality of your lives and the lives of your children, for generations to come. By voting 'yes' for Bill 2062, over nine hundred combined square miles will be freed within the barrier cities for new housing, quality of life improvements, and farming, without lengthy and time-consuming expansions that barely keep up with the needs of the people. In addition, we will virtually eliminate any chance for industrial pollution mishaps, preventing another incident such as the toxic chemical spill that occurred in Hamina several cycles ago. Bill 2062 will also lead to the creation of thousands of new jobs. So I ask you to demand your senate representative votes 'yes' for Bill 2062." Logan stepped out from behind the podium, smiling to the thunderous applause from the crowd.

There was no doubt in Senator Amberman's mind that Galum Corp's CEO was a powerful man; his influence spread far and wide, both in and out of the senate. He turned his attention to the holographic screen to his right, looking at a 3-D model of the beast that now had the military so concerned lately. The expansion of Kansin had been slowed considerably after three more units had been slaughtered. Sixty-seven men and women killed in less than a month. It was a shame and frightening to know that, despite all of the advanced technology they possessed, there were creatures that made it all seem insignificant. General Stafford had his staff do a very extensive study on the current state of the military and it was disheartening to see the strain this new barrier city would put on them if it was allowed to take place. A moment later, Amberman's aide Helen appeared in a small window on the main holo-viewer above the center of his desk.

"Senator, your press conference will begin in twenty minutes. We will need to make final preparations soon," she said, clearly waiting for a response.

"Very well. I will be downstairs in a few minutes. I have to make a stop first. Let Senators Lang and Sullen know I need to talk to them privately prior to the press conference," he closed the holo-viewer and stood up. He paused to take one final look at the plaque on the wall and read the words out loud, "We the People."

Death Awaits You

EMIL CROUCHED IN THE BRUSH, taking in the sight of so much death. She closed her eyes and focused, allowing her mind to search the spirit realm around the coven; all of the attackers were gone and so were any survivors if there had been any. She opened her eyes and again took in the horror before her; no honor was given to the slain; their bodies were dragged out into the open to be feasted upon by the scavengers of the forest.

As she walked among the corpses, she traced each wound with her fingertips. Every sword stroke was done with practiced precision; every arrow shot with perfect accuracy. She paused to remove an arrow embedded in the skull of one of her coven members. The arrowhead, an expertly crafted three-pronged and barbed design used to pierce thick hide or armor, had the familiar blessing of the wind upon it. Only those which followed the path of war used this blessing; it allowed the arrows to strike with the supernatural force of an Air Spirit to penetrate the strongest of defenses. She focused her mind, reaching out to detect the faint residual aura of the caster, Asla. She retrieved several more arrows, inspecting each in kind, to find the same result. There was no denying that this attack had been carried out by warriors of Asla's coven, yet as she walked further into the coven, she found no reason for the slaughter. It was not uncommon for covens to fight when differences had become too great in past times, but the victor always claimed the spoils and the dead were honored. Only warriors fought and died in such battles; to kill an entire coven was unheard of. Nothing was taken from what she could see; the food stores were untouched and the metals and minerals mined from the Great Mother had been left in their harvest bins.

As she moved deeper into the coven, it felt more and more like a tomb. Her heart was heavy with sorrow as she opened the door to her parents' dwelling. A sense of revulsion washed over her when she took in the headless bodies of her four siblings and mother sprawled about the room. Each of them had been beheaded while they were alive. For several moments she stood in the doorway, fighting the urge to vomit, as the violence committed against her family struck her like the violent winds of a summer monsoon.

She fought back the tears as she stepped into the room, the floor was still slick with blood. At last, she stood over the bodies of her mother and of her youngest sibling, Teagan. Tears streamed down her face as she kneeled and hugged Teagan's body close. Only ten cycles old, she had been a bundle of mischievous curiosity and always had her laughing. She was often called her little twin spirit; Teagan always knew when she had returned to the coven and would come running to greet her, shouting "E'Ma" Teagan's nickname for her.

Sorrow became a weight upon her till it seemed her two hearts would beat no more. She laid Teagan upon her mother's chest and looked at each of her other young sibling's lifeless bodies before slowly gathering them near her mother's body. Rohe, the eldest boy at thirty cycles, had tried to fight, no doubt to protect the others. His attacker had severed his sword arm at the elbow to disarm him before beheading him. Yarel and Narel, her twin sisters only twenty-one cycles old, were sprawled on opposite sides of the room. Their murderers having intentionally separated them before killing them; since they were newborns they had clung to each other for comfort. Her mother had fought until the last; her arms and legs bore several dark bruises where her attackers had restrained her and forced her to watch the slaughter. Emil knelt again over their gathered bodies and said a quick prayer to the Great Mother Spirit for each of them, bringing peace to their spirits as the Great Mother Spirit embraced them.

She stood covered in their blood; her sorrow turned to hatred and rage as she slowly walked back out into the open forest. The night was near, and already scavengers were gathering to feast upon the dead in the underbrush. An arrow from her sword bow felled a brave Tarskits, leaving its body to thrash about in its death throes. The armored reptile was small for its kind, only thirteen feet or so, but its presence had chased the other would-be scavengers away. A sense of urgency overcame her and she reached down, touching the soil and began to chant, allowing the blood of her family to soak into the soft earth.

She focused on the spirit realm, searching the shifting shadows until at last she found a Land Spirit and commanded it to pass through her into the natural world. A moment later her eyes, now glowing a deep purple, shot open as she felt the Spirit pass through her into the ground below. Suddenly, two hands of soil and rock broke from the ground, followed by a head, then shoulders and a torso. The Land Spirit began gathering the surrounding ground to form its massive body until at last an eight-foot giant of stone and dirt stood before her, motionless and waiting.

"Quickly, bury the dead so that they will be disgraced no more and seal the coven," Emil commanded with sorrow heavy in her voice to the silent giant. The Land Spirit turned and began walking toward the coven; each step sank deeper than the last as if wading into water. Emil watched, as one by one, sinkholes opened beneath the bodies in the area, sucking them into the depths of the Great Mother. Each body that vanished was reflected in her tears but they had become tears that promised vengeance.

Price of Knowledge

SAMANTHA SAT BACK, REMOVING HER glasses and rubbing her eyes; she had been staring at her computer's holo-screen all night and most of the morning compiling, organizing, and cataloging all the data her exploration team, Echo Four Fourteen, had collected over the last few months. It was a daunting and drawn-out task. Any sane person would have given their right hand to avoid it, no matter how strong their love for science was.

Normally, the newest member or intern got stuck with the dubious honor, but never a senior scientist. She couldn't prove it, but she was sure the reason she was getting stuck with this was that she had repeatedly shot down Lucas, the exploration team's senior male scientist, more than once in the last few weeks. Being one of six females in a group of fifty-eight people stuck together out in the middle of nowhere for six months, she had quickly become used to the constant pickup attempts. Lucas was just plain creepy though, a ghostly pale man who spent most of his time hidden away in his office. His eyes always had large bags under them as if he hardly slept, and he was easily old enough to be her father. He also gave off that eerie "stalker type" vibe. He was the kind of guy that happened to show up everywhere you were. She shivered as she remembered once stepping out from the shower and Lucas standing there with a towel and a grin. If it hadn't been for Connor coming in from guard duty to shower, she probably would have screamed.

She arched her back to relieve the stiffness in her lower back from sitting so long, which thankfully helped to take her mind off of Lucas's sickening look of pleasure when he walked in on her in the showers.

The laboratory was illuminated by the faded blue overhead lights from several of the laboratory tables in the center of the room. Like her co-workers, Samantha's personal workstation with her desk and computer was near the wall, more so out of convenience rather than a lack of space. Everyone had gone to great lengths to personalize their workstation by decorating them with various pictures of family, friends, pets, or various native species...except for Lucas. His desk was crammed with awards, degrees, plaques, and news articles featuring him or his research. *No family, just anything that helped him feel self-important,* Samantha thought to herself, looking at the rear of the lab where Lucas's office was.

"A few more weeks and I will be back in Batal, in my apartment overlooking the ocean, with nothing but my dog and my boyfriend when he isn't too busy at the hospital," she comforted herself as the door to the lab slid open.

"Hey, Doc, how are things going this afternoon?" Private Second-Class Dawkins asked, removing his helmet. Private Dawkins, or Dimples as she had nicknamed him for his smile, was one of the few soldiers she actually enjoyed spending time with. He was one of the few that didn't seem to live and breathe military life. He took a genuine interest in the world. Maybe it was his youthful age and inexperience with the outside world or the fact that he had a cute schoolboy crush on her, but he was always eager to sit down and listen to her talk about the world outside the barrier.

"I brought you something to eat, figured you could use it since I didn't see you at breakfast this morning," Dawkins said, handing her an apple and a bottle of water.

"You are a sweetheart, Dimples. I appreciate the food. I've been stuck in this lab since last night cataloging all this data and I still have a few hours to go," she sighed as she placed the fruit and water on her desk.

"Well, I'm on lab guard till this evening, or whenever the rest of second platoon gets back tonight, so I will be here to keep you company," he said, removing his assault rifle from his shoulder and pulling up a chair at the desk next to her.

"Until they get back? Where is the rest of your platoon?" she asked, taking a bite out of the apple he brought her.

"Well, I didn't get to sit in on the mission briefing, but Roman told me they were going to stake out those ancient Feralan ruins that Doctor Hallow's team found last week. There has been some enemy activity. I mean, Feralan activity, nearby the last few nights," he said disinterestedly.

"I see. So, what shall we talk about to pass the time today, Dimples?" she asked before turning around to start working again.

"Well, I would like to hear more about the world outside the barriers," he said excitedly, scooting his chair closer to the side of her desk. Samantha pulled up a 3-D holographic image of Tallagen. "Hmmm...Let me see...Well, as you know, Tallagen is Earth-like in many ways, with the exception that it is twice the size. There are four major landmasses that are called continents. Lussia is in the eastern hemisphere, which extends all the way into the northern pole region. North Jifica is in the northwestern hemisphere, along with West Jifica. Prayon is located in the southwestern hemisphere, extending down into the southern pole, along with several smaller landmasses and thousands of islands. In total, all the landmasses count for roughly 38 percent of the planet's surface area, while the other 62 percent is covered by both brackish and freshwater. The northern pole is a frozen wasteland as far as we know, while the southern pole is a giant desert that we have barely explored. Most of the western hemisphere land masses are covered in dense rain forests and mangroves, while those of the eastern hemisphere is covered in dense forest, marshes, and swamps, making for some interesting eco-systems along the way and for even more diverse fauna and plant life. In all honesty, we have only truly begun to explore the world we call home in the last eighty-five cycles, having previously only explored 15 percent of the land-masses and less than 2 percent of the oceans," Samantha said, highlighting various portions of holographic representation of Tallagen."

"Sounds cool till you start to think that everything is super large and wants to kill and eat you," Dawkins chuckled.

"You know, Dimples, only because you have such a pretty smile, I'll let that slide," Samantha half laughed, shaking her head in disbelief.

She reached over and sorted through a small container full of data crystals until she found the one she was looking for, and inserted it into her computer.

"Not everything wants to eat you. Think of nature as your body. Every cell has a purpose, and when a foreign organism enters it, especially one that is damaging to it, your body reacts to assimilate, destroy, or expel the foreign organism. Every animal and plant has a purpose in this eco-system, introduces us to it and nature adapts by doing the same. Likewise, there are different food chains throughout the eco-system, each with its own apex predator. Just because we're intelligent doesn't mean we are always at the top of the food chain, nor can you fault nature for doing what it does to survive," Samantha said as she continued working.

"So basically…it sucks to be at the bottom of the food chain, Doc?" Dawkins replied, wrenching his face in mock pain.

Samantha snickered, realizing it was simple comments like this that made him such pleasant company.

"I remember seeing those! They almost look like a dragon mixed with the giant whales from Earth I saw in science class in school! How does something that huge fly?" Dawkins pointed excitedly toward an image on the holo-screen.

Samantha smiled at his enthusiasm. "Aurora Sky Leviathans spend their entire lives airborne by naturally creating and storing a form of bio-hydrogen in large sacs throughout their bodies. They create it through a form of symbiotic photosynthesis with bacteria that live in their epidermis, skin cells to you, Dimples. This photosynthesis process is how the Leviathans also create food to nourish themselves, similar to a plant in essence, yet they are warm-blooded animals. Here's an interesting fact, they spend 70 percent of their day filtering water vapors, carbon dioxide, and other gases from the atmosphere and clouds as they seemingly swim through the air currents," Samantha explained as she watched the recent video footage she had taken of a pod of Leviathans.

"What makes them glow so beautifully at night?"

"We believe the bioluminescence colors they display may have something to do with the unique form of chlorophyll found in the bacteria that inhabit their skin cells. It is believed to be a way to recognize each other from great distances as well as a form of communication. But isn't it time for you to make your rounds? I wouldn't want you getting in trouble again for sitting here listening to me babble on," she said before cataloging the Leviathan data and continuing on to the next animal. He sat up, reaching for his rifle.

"Yeah, you're right, Doc, plus it will give me a chance to stop by operations. I am curious to know how things are going on out at the ruins. Some of the artifacts Doctor Wellers brought back were really cool. I'm looking forward to what he brings back this time," Dawkins said standing up, shouldering his rifle.

"Do you mind grabbing me a cup of java from the dining hall on your way back?" Samantha asked, realizing her cup was empty, and there were still a lot of data crystals to go through.

May Tomorrow Come

"I'VE GOT ELEVEN—NO, MAKE THAT thirteen Feralans moving into the ruins from the northwest."

"Roger that, Whisper. Maintain eyes on while we move into position," Sergeant Brooks said as he watched Sergeant Whisper settle behind a half-fallen wall on the second floor of the building across from him and then vanish as he engaged his cam-optics. "Brent, Wallace, and Hentz, secure those ruins on the eastern side. Fallon, Roman, and Newsome, hold position. I want to catch them in a crossfire. Specialist Jackman, uplink us to a satellite. I want a full overview of this area. We are not taking any chances," Brooks said as he watched the placement of each squad member in his HUD.

"Link established, signal clear, they are moving up the main road, they don't seem to be aware of us…Wait a minute. Something's going on. They just stopped," Jackman rambled over the com-link as he observed the satellite view of the ruins in his HUD.

"Patch us all in now, Jackman!" Brooks demanded as he realized he had no chance of seeing what was going on down the street from where he was hidden in the ruins.

"The Shaman is looking right at me," Whisper said as he looked up from the scope of his sniper rifle.

"There's no way she could see you from where she is, plus your cam-optics is engaged, right?" Private Roman said with disbelief.

"I am telling you; she was looking directly at me. Let me bag her and get this over with. I'm not liking this," Whisper said, looking into his scope again.

KATYA

"You sense them, do you not, Gala?" Katya questioned as she closed her eyes.

"Yes, I do veil-seer. Their defiled spirits betray them," Gala responded with disdain.

"They believe themselves hidden. I shall enjoy feeding the Great Mother Spirit their blood. Gala, Magar, and Soma, kill the defilers," Katya demanded. "Grall, bring me the two located there. They shall prove useful," Katya said, pointing in the direction of Brooks and Jackman.

"Sergeant Brooks, she just pointed in your direc—" Corporal Brent started to say before Brooks abruptly cut him off.

"I saw that. I am more concerned with why those warriors are stripping. Some kind of facking bush baby ritual? I hate them," Brooks said, zooming in on the satellite view of Soma.

The entire squad watched in disbelief as a ghostly aura of the beast they had recently seen in a warning report, rose from the naked Feralans, encompassing them like a transparent shell. Brooks, along with the others, watched in awe as the Feralans' bodies grew, contorted, and stretched, filling in the aura, until at last the ghostly forms were replaced with physical manifestations of the beast.

"Whisper, take them down!" Brooks shouted, not knowing whether it was from fear or that he realized just how much trouble they were in.

Immediately Whisper found his target locking his crosshairs on Grall's head. Selecting a deadly flechette round, he squeezed the trigger. Yet the round never struck its intended target as Grall dissipated like smoke in the wind, along with the other beasts.

"Dammit, Whisper what are you waiting for? Take the facking Shaman down!" Brooks yelled into the com-link, waiting for the telltale sound of Whisper's sniper rifle firing again, but it never came. He peered up to where Whisper hid as something dropped in the street nearby; panic took hold as the object's cam-optics field failed, revealing Whisper's decapitated head resting in his helmet.

A moment later weapon fire erupted from across the street where Fallon, Roman, and Newsome were lying in wait.

"What? How did it…!" Private Wallace yelled, followed by a blood-curdling scream. Soon even more chaotic shouting and frantic screaming erupted over the com-link.

"Sergeant Hierra, we need back up. Facking Feralans are over-running us!" Brooks shouted over the coms as he watched Private Brent's and Specialist Hentz's life-sign indicators turn black.

Specialist Roman rolled away, bringing himself into a crouching defensive position as a beast appeared from a dark mist, attacking and impaling Corporal Newsome through his lower jaw with a claw before any of them could retaliate. He opened fire along with Specialist Fallon as the beast violently ripped its claw backward, splaying Newsome's helmet and face wide open; it tossed him aside like a ragged piece of meat before turning its attention to Fallon. With blinding speed the beast lashed out again, dodging Fallon's weapon fire in the process. A spray of blood signaled the end of Fallon's life.

Roman opened fire, riddling the beast across its back and forcing it to stumble forward as it savaged Fallon's body, yet it would not fall. Its magical wards carved into the beast's flesh flared as each round failed to pierce their mystical barrier. Infuriated, the beast turned, its silver eyes full of hatred and rage locked onto him. He felt his body go cold and numb, petrified with a primal fear; at that moment he saw his death. His screams of pain echoed through the ruins as his life came to a deliberate and slow end.

Brooks watched as one by one, each of his squad members' life sign indicators turned black until there was only him and his communication trooper Specialist Jackman left. Only years of intense training kept him calm enough to reassure Jackman that remaining where they were was best. Yet, in the back of his mind, he was hoping Sergeant Hierra and his recon troopers would show up soon; he prayed they would be able to turn the tide of this failed ambush before it was too late.

"Hang in there, trooper. We are going to make it out," he said, resting a reassuring hand on Jackman's shoulder, unaware of the presence that now stepped from within the shadow of the room.

Secrets, Lies, and Holo-Vids

THE SENATE LIBRARY WAS ONE of the few places, other than antique shops, that you could still find an old-fashioned paper book. The library was extensive, eight stories tall with over seven hundred thousand books preserved in stasis seals, some dating back as far as the eighteen hundreds. In many aspects, it was more a museum than a library, a tribute to the astonishing literary works of mankind over the centuries. Many came to marvel simply at the history, while others came to enlighten themselves from the minds of times past. Today, however, was different. The library was nearly empty save the few librarians and the occasional visitor.

Sarah stood leaning against the wall in a corner away from the window in silence, flipping through her source notes on Bill 2062, while occasionally looking around and then checking the time on her wrist PDA. She was used to secret meetings; it was common behind the closed doors of the senate for information to be passed in shadows. She had learned that after spending cycles building up a rapport with several key members of the senate and establishing an extensive network of contacts. However, this was different; her contact, simply known as Lighthouse, had contacted her a few days ago wanting a meeting. What was unusual was the time and location. The meeting was to be in the back of the senate library, exactly twenty minutes before Senator Amberman's press conference. It was a very public place by Lighthouse's standards, and such places he normally avoided unless it was to be a simple drop off.

"You know, I had been wondering if we would ever meet face-to-face," a man said, startling Sarah as he approached from around a nearby bookshelf. "Forgive me, I didn't mean to startle you," he said apologetically.

Sarah shifted her stance and stood extra straight, trying not to show how uncomfortable she was at being caught off guard.

She switched off her wrist PDA, surprised to see Senator Amberman standing before her. "Senator, I wasn't expecting…," Sarah started to say before he politely cut her off.

"You weren't expecting to see me, I know. I have always admired your work from afar and how you always report the whole truth, regardless of how ugly it may be. You have a talent for understanding the ebb and flow of the political arena here in the senate and seeking the truth. It is why I have been passing you information for the last few cycles under the alias of Lighthouse," Senator Amberman said, again catching Sarah off guard with his statement. "But that is not important now. I am here personally because I need to ensure you understand the severity of the information, I am about to entrust you with," he said. Sarah tried to activate her wrist PDA to record what he was about to say, but he stopped her. "There is no need for that, and in fact, what I am going to tell you, you will want to ensure you are in no way directly connected to it for some time, Mrs. Hock," Amberman continued with a tone of caution in his voice as he moved closer to her. "I don't have much time, so pay close attention. Bill 2062 is the second step in a plan that will be the undoing of our society as we know it. At the heart of it is Senator Harkus. I know you may believe it is Galum Corp, but they are only a puppet in a much bigger plan."

"Why don't you go public, or address this in your press conferences?" Sarah interrupted.

"Because there are forces at work here that must be exposed properly and at the right time or society as we know, could very well collapse in chaos. Have you ever heard of Project Nephilim?"

Sarah stared with a slightly confused look, trying to recall if she had ever heard of such a project through any of her contacts.

"No, of course, you haven't. What you need to know is that we were sent out here on a mission to survive, giving mankind a fighting chance in the face of extinction, even if it meant doing the unthinkable. Mrs. Hock, I want you to pay close attention to Senator Harkus. I haven't been able to pinpoint his complete involvement but I do know he is the key to what's going on," he whispered softly. "I have to go. My aide will be looking for me if I don't show soon," he said after checking the time on his wrist PDA.

"Senator, I have so many questions. What is Project Nephilim? If Galum Corp is just a puppet, then how much is Logan Summit really involved?" Sarah persisted, moving to step in front of him.

"You're a resourceful woman and I know a reporter of your talent will be able to take the little I have given you and find the truth. Ah, so you know, I have Senator Sullen doing his own investigation. Speak with him when the chance arises. I am sure you will know what to do with it all when the time comes. I only ask that you say nothing of our meeting here, or what I have mentioned thus far, to anyone. There are those who are willing to go to great lengths to see that the path I have set you on never comes to light," he warned before walking around her and heading out.

He paused to look over at a bookshelf nearby. "Mrs. Hock, I would suggest reading the book *The Human Condition* over there on the shelf. It is one of those 'must reads,' if I do say so myself. See you at the press conference, Mrs. Hock." He disappeared among the aisles of bookshelves.

Sarah stood in the back of the library for several minutes after Senator Amberman left before going over to the bookshelf he had indicated and found the book *The Human Condition*. She looked around cautiously, making sure she was alone, before removing the book from stasis and opening it. Inside was a micro data-crystal slid in between the center pages.

Bad Deal

THE SECOND GROUND ASSAULT ROBOT came online as Conrad closed the hatch to its central processing unit. His part of the job was to install a new CPU in the two specifically selected Ground Assault Robots (GARs) One-Nineteen and Ninety-Nine in the storage bay. Every sound had him pressing himself flat against the hull of the robot to avoid detection. He was a nervous wreck and found himself having to stop and take deep breaths to steady his hands as he worked.

He thought back to how he had gotten himself to this point. A mysterious woman had begun approaching him several months ago to do small jobs. He had been hesitant at first, but the jobs were simple and the money being offered was more than worth what was being asked of him, money that helped save him from some soon-to-be unpleasant events had he not been able to pay back the gambling debts he owed. When he was asked to do this job, he wanted to refuse it, but he had already done so much already, as the mysterious woman pointed out (Mill and Winston Tech LLC. was one of the leading manufacturers of military weapons and tampering with their production would earn him more time in prison than he was willing to experience) that he agreed anyway. He climbed down the ladder, watching as Sheldon and Marshall, who had no doubt been put into a similar situation, were loading thousands of rounds into the robots' empty internal ammo bins, along with mortars. He kept telling himself that he was just installing CPUs and that was it. Whatever this was all for was beyond anything he knew or cared to know. By the end of the day he would have an extra two hundred and fifty thousand credits to spend partying and gambling in Kansin; by the end of tomorrow night, he would be so intoxicated with a few of the sexiest high-end hookers he could find that it just wouldn't matter.

He walked around to the front of the two robots, and as the last of the belt-fed ammo was fed into their ammo bins, the robots stood. All three men stepped back in surprise, not sure what to expect, each looking around making sure they were still alone in the storage bay. "I've done what I was told. I am out of he—," Marshall started to say before the robot nearest to him sent him flying across the bay into the wall, crushing his spine on impact.

Sheldon turned to run, but the other robot was upon him with two quick leaps, knocking him to the ground before crushing his upper body under its massive paw. Conrad looked on in terror as both robots turned to face him; the reality that he had been set up quickly set in.

Exactly what was programmed into those damn CPUs I installed? This can't be happening! he thought to himself.

Frantically, he began yelling for help, quickly deciding that going to prison was a far better option than death, but storage bay fourteen was on the far side of the compound, far from earshot, and as a powerful slap crushed his skull, death instantly became his only option.

Not So Friendly Rivalry

"COME ON, YOU GOT THIS, babe, push," Terrance cheered as he watched Ziyi slowly push the barbell all the way up and rack it.

"Not bad, three sets of one-forty-five, seven times," she panted as she stood, wiping the sweat from her face.

"Not at all, another week and you should be up to three sets of ten reps easily, babe," he assured her, reducing the weight on the gravity bar back to zero.

"I'm going swimming to stretch and cool down. You want to come with me?" she playfully said while removing her gloves and wrist wraps.

"No, I'm going to go spar for a little bit. Just come get me when you are ready to go," he replied before kissing her good-bye.

"Save some of that energy for later," she whispered with a suggestive smile, turning to walk away.

The sparring room was unusually packed for this time of day. Despite the climate control, it was much warmer than usual with all the people crowded around the center mat cheering and yelling. Curious, Terrance waded through the crowd to get a better look at what was going on. As he made it to the front, the crowd went into an uproar; all around him people were cheering and cursing as credits were being exchanged.

Looking out onto the mat at the two combatants, he didn't recognize the guy who was slowly getting off the mat, but he did recognize the female who confidently circled him, twirling her signature magenta-colored katana-shaped stun blade—Poison.

"What's going on?" Terrance asked a guy taking bets.

"Wraith is kicking Rivera's ass. She took him down in less than a minute. I just made like a hundred credits!" the man exclaimed, before turning his attention back toward the mat as Rivera stood and readied his stun blade.

Rivera was clearly shaken and still suffering the effects of the last strike from her katana. Holding her katana in a ready position, Angela paused with a cocky smirk, seeing the uneasiness in his eyes.

"You know, Rivera, with all the crap you talked, I would have thought you would be a challenge, but you fight like a schoolgirl. Is that what they teach you in infantry school these days?" she taunted as she continued to circle him before finally stopping directly in front of him.

"Fack you!" he shouted and charged forward, swinging his sword downward.

She countered by spinning to the side, deflecting his swing high and then slashing through his mid-section; he fell to the ground in agonizing pain. The crowd fell silent as her blade vanished; she turned and knelt next to Rivera's head as he still shook from the blade's stunning effect. She grabbed a handful of his hair, lifting his head up as she lowered her head to whisper in his ear.

"Fack me? I don't think so...I prefer men, not girls," she whispered sarcastically, before letting his head fall back to the mat.

The crowd went wild realizing the fight was over; final wagers were being settled. Terrance watched as Angela collected credits in her towel from several people before handing it all to another woman that he didn't recognize.

"How much do I have so far?" Angela asked Mya as she dumped a towel full of credits into her gym bag.

"Well, so far your PDA has received nine hundred and twenty-two credits into your account, plus whatever you just put into the bag. Keep this up and we will have enough to go on a serious shopping spree!" Mya exclaimed.

"Wait a minute...we? Nice, Miss Prissy, I don't see you out there." Angela laughed and walked back to the center of the mat.

"Anybody else wants to try their luck? 'Cause so far you guys have been really lame," Angela shouted, eyeing the crowd as she circled the mat.

Terrance watched as there was a lot of talk among the crowd, but no one stepped forward. He reached into his gym bag, pulling out his double-bladed stun staff hilt, and stepped onto the mat. The crowd quickly fell silent. Angela paused for a moment before turning to see who her new challenger was.

"Well, well, well…if it isn't my old buddy and new squadmate, Terrance…or should I say, Maluss," she sneered.

"I am going to enjoy killing your ego, Poison," he countered, as the glowing blue energy blades extended from the ends of his staff.

"Ah, yes, double-bladed Ju-Tin Kata, right? Very impressive, one that only a truly ambidextrous person can master. It has always been your preferred style, hasn't it?" Angela signaled to Mya to toss her another katana from her gym bag.

"I hope you haven't forgotten that I am ambidextrous too," Angela smirked, nonchalantly catching her second Katana while activating them both as she twirled them around her; she stopped as she brought one to a mid-guard position and the other in a reverse grip behind her.

"Cute," Terrance spat, clearly unimpressed.

All around them, the crowd began shouting bets and chanting. The combatants began slowly circling each other, looking for a weak point in the other's defense as the crowd shouted, "Fight, fight, fight!"

A few tense moments passed, then Angela launched forward with several quick attacks, testing Terrance's defense as he parried each attack and countered. The two quickly became locked in a battle of skill as each strike was skillfully parried and countered with blinding speed.

"I have never seen anyone move that fast!" a bystander exclaimed in total amazement.

"Yeah, some serious skill man, I would have been hit at least ten times in the first—" the bystander's friend began to respond back, freezing mid-sentence as one of Angela's blades stopped millimeters from the tip of his nose after missing Terrance's throat. For the space of several heartbeats he held his breath, feeling the nerves in his face tingling as the blade's disruptive energy threatened to set them on fire in numbing pain.

Angela glanced down at the bystander's crotch and then back into his eyes, smiling with devilishly. "Clean-up on aisle one. This guy just pissed himself," she said sarcastically, turning to parry another of Terrance's attacks.

The roar of the crowd grew louder as the battle became more intense.

"You know, if you want to give up now, I would understand," Terrance sneered as they locked blades.

"I was thinking the same thing," Angela shot back as she countered the lower blade of his staff and then forced him to stumble back with a swift elbow to the chin.

Angela stepped forward to deal the finishing blow, but to her surprise Terrance dropped to one knee, blocking her blow and swiping her off her feet. She hit the ground and quickly rolled away as Terrance brought down his energy blade, intent on burying it in her chest. The two stood up, taking new battle stances before rushing in again. Each strike came faster, with everyone meant to deal the winning blow; their blades were just blurs of light until finally, everything came to a sudden stop. Terrance grinned in satisfaction, staring Angela in the eyes with his blade less than an inch from her neck. The crowd fell into a hushed silence.

"Game over, old friend, time to kill that ego of yours," he sneered. Angela grinned and looked down, his eyes following hers to see her blade a breath away from his groin.

"Is it now…old friend?" Angela sneered back, locking eyes again.

For the space of several moments neither moved. Finally, a man in the crowd walked out onto the mat. "Wow, that was one hell of a bout. Relax though, it's a draw you two."

Suddenly over the intercom, a computerized voice began speaking, "Attention in the gym, all personnel, you are to report immediately to your command. This is not a drill."

Terrance deactivated his staff. "For now," he uttered nonchalantly.

"I don't do draws," Angela fired back, bringing her blade down and through his left thigh. Every nerve ending in his leg was instantly set on fire, forcing Terrance to collapse to the mat.

"I'll let them know you are going to be late. It's going to take you a few minutes to hop over to HQ," she mocked, turning to leave with the rest of the crowd.

Liberation of Chaos

"THIS IS NEW HOPE SECURITY Force, Unit Tango Fifty-Four, in pursuit of rogue GAR's. We are headed north on Highway Sixteen, we currently have visual on one of the targets, request air support immediately," Security Officer Robins reported, trying to determine where the machine was heading next.

"I can't believe this. Military facking robot beasts running wild through the city? What's next? This is exactly why I am voting for the new barrier city!" Robin's partner Nathan said with disbelief as he accelerated and dodged another oncoming hovercar.

"Right now, I'm just concerned with how to stop this facking thing when we do catch up to it," Robins snapped back as he saw the destruction the robot left in its wake.

The highway was quickly becoming chaos as the robot raced into oncoming traffic, running and leaping like some large cat on the hunt, oblivious to the growing number of security vehicles chasing it or the lives that were brought to an end as it crushed and tossed vehicles aside.

Nathan slammed on the brakes, before quickly accelerating, pulling the vehicle into a hard left and swerving to avoid a car landing mere feet from where they had been seconds ago. He pressed down on the accelerator even more as he cleared two burning and overturned cars.

"Try and get right on it! I'm going to try and take a shot at it with the vehicle disruptor!" Robins hollered as he readied the disruptor rifle.

"The disruptor is made to kill power cells on vehicles, not military robots. You think it's gonna work?" Nathan frantically asked, dodging another car.

"I don't know but what other choice do we have? Just keep it steady for a sec," Robins answered, trying to lock onto the GAR.

"That's it…almost got it…," Robins whispered to himself; the target receptacle in his scope turned red as it locked on. Just as he began to squeeze the trigger, the road in front of the patrol car caved in under the force of some unseen object. Neither he nor his partner had a chance to react as the front of the car gave way, folding in under the violent and sudden impact with the object. The last thing Robins saw as his patrol car flipped up and over, semi-visible, flickering humanoid form beneath him; a moment later his car crashed down and exploded into a ball of fire and superheated metal as a barrage of pulse cannon rounds tore through it.

GAR Ninety-Nine stood slowly, its attention focused on the flaming carnage of what was Robin's vehicle; its cam-optics field flickering before finally switching off, making Ninety-Nine completely visible for the first time, as it turned and opened fired on the approaching security force vehicles. The highway became a raging inferno as GAR One-Nineteen transformed into its humanoid form and opened fire, joining its twin. Like mechanical angels of death, their yellow eyes flared behind the tinted slit in their armored faces; they obliterated the unarmored security and civilian vehicles without prejudice in a storm of twenty-millimeter death. Lives were ended in an instant as they were torn apart in explosions, consumed in flames, or shredded in a hail of razor-sharp shrapnel.

In the midst of the relentless devastation, Ninety-Nine shrugged off a burst fired from an approaching security force helicopter. Unmoved, it replied in kind, sending a burst of armor-piercing explosive rounds through the cockpit, turning it into a hailstorm of shrapnel to those below. With the helicopter eliminated Ninety-Nine scanned the surrounding area, indiscriminately killing the few that survived the initial onslaught until the sound of the wounded and dying were silenced.

"All units, fall back to the secondary perimeter. I repeat fall back to the secondary perimeter! We aren't equipped for this Headquarters, for God's sake, where is S-SWAT!" Lieutenant Stevens shouted, in total disbelief at the havoc and destruction, over the com-link as his mobile command helicopter lost both its escorts to incoming fire.

In the midst of the flaming wreckage, both GARs stood motionless, tracking the incoming security command helicopter as it landed, along with a growing mass of security forces attempting to set-up barricades a less than a quarter of a mile away, as their primary objective changed. Ninety-Nine shifted into its quadruped form once again, fading from sight, its cam-optics engaged as it sprinted off for its next objective. One-Nineteen's eyes flashed, verifying its remaining ammo as it began targeting the security forces behind the barricades ahead. Mercilessly, it began to move forward, an angel of death intent on reaping a bountiful harvest.

TWENTY_EIGHTH DROP SHIP

Cav's thoughts reached into his battle-frame's cortex processing unit, pulling up the data and specs of the Type IV Hunter Killer Ground Assault Robot. Immediately, a 3-D image of the robot appeared in his vision. He took a moment to analyze the data. The robot was a giant, standing almost fifteen and a half feet tall. It would tower over his Gallant battle frame by almost six feet and outweigh it by five tons. He rotated the image, studying the robot's humanoid design. The body resembled an armored warrior dressed in an ancient suit of full plate mail, streamlined and modernized by techs who apparently watched more than their fair share of anime. Nevertheless, it was clearly a machine of war and no cartoon. The pulse cannon attached to each arm made that clear. The robot was an old design concept, born of ignorance some ninety-three cycles ago when there was still little known of this world called Tallagen and what was considered its inhabitants.

The dual form concept was to serve the purpose of fear and awe, perhaps even reverence. With the idea that the natives would fear the large wolf-like creature or respect the humanoid shape, the robot would assume the appropriate form for the situation. The concept proved naïve to say the least.

The GARs were kept in service until about forty cycles ago, when Prime Minister Lagaman had created the Co-Exist Act that opened the doors to peace talks with the natives, mainly the Feralan people. Many saw the robots as a reminder of a time when people were close-minded, ignorant, and saw the natives as nothing more than sub-par savages, similar to how many saw African slaves or the Nazis saw the Jewish people in ancient times on Earth. So like so many other symbols of hate and ignorance, they were hidden from sight so not to remind people of a past that everyone was all too eager to separate themselves from. Most of the robots were recycled, but a small number of them were deactivated and locked away in a war reserve despite the protest of many on the Co-Exist Committee.

As the dropship engines powered up, a holographic image of Major Lightfoot appeared in the center of the bay, along with a 3-D image of the type IV Hunter Killer Ground Assault Robot's schematics. "Twenty-Eighth, the situation has gone from bad to worse. There are two type IV Hunter Killer Ground Assault Robots on a rampage through New Hope. Up until a minute ago, both robots were located near highway marker forty-seven on the main highway; however, one of them has since disappeared and its presence is currently unknown. So far, over one hundred and eleven lives have been lost, and I hate to say there may be more before this is all over," Major Lightfoot explained, looking at each squad member seated in their battle-frame, before returning to the center of the bay.

"With up to four inches of duratium alloy armor, those HK's won't go down easy, and I assume the remote CPU kill switch isn't working. So how do you want us to handle this, sir?" Cav asked, examining the technical data in the holographic images.

"Sir, the potential for collateral damage is high once we have engaged them. Getting in close is not the best option with a Type IV HK, especially in beast mode with those phase blade claws," Messenger chimed in.

"Understood, but you need to deal with this as quickly as possible, and as quietly as possible. I don't have to tell you that inside the city's barrier, the jurisdiction belongs to the security forces and S-SWAT. I also don't have to tell you that they just don't have the capabilities to take on one HK much less two. This leaves us, the military, to handle this operation as cleanly as possible. The media fallout from this is already going to be bad enough. That's why your squad is going at this alone. The brass doesn't want to panic the population any more than they already are by turning this into a major military action. In fact, Senator Amberman has refused to cancel his press conference despite what's going on. I am downloading all the current tactical information to you now," Major Lightfoot said before turning his attention back to the holographic display. "ETA, nine minutes," Captain Mathers said over the com-link as the dropship began to rise from the runway.

"Spearheads to Victory!" Major Lightfoot sounded off with the Twenty-Eighth motto as he saluted; the entire squad repeated the motto and returned his salute as his holographic image vanished.

"Type IV's are kitted out mainly for anti-personnel. They aren't really outfitted with heavy anti-armor weapons," Messenger noted.

"Yeah, but those twenty-millimeter pulse cannons will cut through pretty much anything we can deploy safely in the city, including us," Maluss responded.

"True but they are not as heavily armored as the type IIs, so your pulse rifle has a chance of damaging them if you can manage to hit the weak points, Maluss," Messenger replied.

"Shouldn't be too much of a problem for an ace pilot like you," Wraith said nonchalantly, looking at Maluss's pulse rifle in stow across from her. "By the way how's that leg of yours doing?" Wraith asked, faking concern.

Maluss replied, having his battle-frame rub its forehead with its middle finger, clearly flipping her off.

"The way you two go at it, you would think you two facked or something," Siren joked.

Gerald tuned out the chatter of the group as he continued analyzing the situation. One-Nineteen was out in the open, while Ninety-Nine had simply vanished, but to where? Deploying the team to end this as quickly as possible was critical. He looked up at Sergeant Second Class Walt inside his Hades battle-frame before directing his attention back to the 3-D holographic image of the highway. Tactically, the open area would be the best place to deploy Messenger to minimize secondary collateral damage if he decided to deploy Grave Digger. Funny how Hades pilots always gave their railguns a name, sort of a rite of passage once they earned a call-sign. Speaking of call-signs, Gerald made a mental note to ask Walt how he earned the call sign Messenger one day. He was a five-foot-eleven, two hundred and thirty pound, dark-skinned hardcore bodybuilder, and the call-sign Messenger just didn't seem to fit. Sergeant Second Class Tanaka's call-sign Siren fit her; with her exotic look and voice, it was an obvious choice. When she sang her voice had an ethereal haunting sound all its own. He remembered how he heard she had once used her singing to draw the attention of several Feralan warriors so that she could get a clear shot; she put a bullet through the Shaman's hearts they were guarding. Sergeant Second Class Poison's call-sign Wraith fit as well. She moved with such swiftness and agility that her personalized ethereal gray painted battle-frame with crimson eyes was like some ghostly apparition appearing from nowhere to deal death before disappearing again. She was a nightmare on the battlefield, and he was damn glad she was on their side.

"Two minutes to highway marker forty-seven. Cav, how do you want to deploy?" Lieutenant Cosby asked over the internal com-link. "Maluss, Messenger, One-Nineteen is yours. We will keep searching for Ninety-Nine," Cav replied.

"Roger Captain Mathers, can you lay down some covering fire with a low pass and we'll do a low-level rapid insertion?" Maluss asked as he stood up along with Messenger, moving towards the tailgate of the dropship.

"That's an affirmative, stand by," Captain Mathers responded as the tailgate opened and the drop ship began to rapidly descend.

OFFICER SMITH

Colony Security Officer Smith couldn't help but see the irony in all this. Over a hundred cycles ago, the president of the late barrier city Cordon chose to steal control using superior military numbers to drastically reduce food supplies in the hope of forcing the other cities to accept his authority. The rest of the cities suffered for months, but none as much as Batal; at the time it was a new city and relied on the rest of the colonies greatly. As negotiations continued to fail and starvation prospered, Hamina and New Hope attacked with their full military might. War spread across the colonies until victory was achieved at the cost of one hundred seventy thousand lives and the destruction of the largest barrier city, Cordon.

From the ashes of mankind's sin, the Alliance Military was formed. In a unanimous agreement, it was decided that no city would maintain its own standing military. Instead, there would be a single military pooled from each city's resources that would serve the colonies as a whole. The Security Special Weapons and Tactics (S-SWAT) was formed at the same time to handle internal threats that escalated beyond standard security capabilities. Now, the very law designed to bandage the wounds of human greed was becoming a huge burden in a fresh wound. He sighed heavily as he got up into a crouching position, pressing close to the concrete barricade in front of him.

"Where is the S-SWAT at? We are getting slaughtered out here!" Smith shouted into his helmet's com-link as he saw another vehicle explode, killing a squad of security officers nearby before he ducked back down. With a lull of incoming weapon fire, he chanced another look; the robot had stopped about a hundred meters from the barricades and was systematically wiping out all resistance off to his left. He ducked back down as Security Officer Millet threw himself up against the barricade next to him.

"How's your ammo?" Millet asked.

Smith quickly peered down at his ammo counter on his assault rifle. "Thirty rounds remaining and one magazine left. Not like it matters. I might as well be throwing rocks as far as that thing is concerned. Either way, all we are doing is pissing it off," he said with frustration heavy in his voice.

"It's all we got till S-SWAT shows up and deals with this damn robot," Millet said.

Smith turned to put his back against the barricade, taking in the chaos and death all around him. He watched as fellow officers ran for cover while others tried to pull the wounded to safety; vehicles burned while defenses crumbled.

Suddenly, Millet popped up, unleashing a quick burst of fire from his assault rifle along with three other officers nearby. One-Nineteen never gave them a chance to realize their mistake as it instantly returned fire; the concrete barricade exploded into a shower of dust and rubble. Millet and the other officers who were taking cover behind it exploded into a shower of bloody mist. Having hit the ground just as the others opened fire, Smith laid still, hoping the robot would consider him to be among the dead. For a moment, he considered just staying under the debris until he heard the sound of a large vehicle; he pulled his face from the ground, looking up to see an S-SWAT battle frame transport pushing through two burning security vehicles.

"Payback motherfacker!" he sneered defiantly as the vehicle came to a stop and its doors opened. However, his hopes were quickly crushed as he was violently thrown backward by mortars that impacted the first three S-SWAT battle frames, turning them into twisted, burning hulks as they stepped from their transport pods.

Smith tried to call out, but only blood dribbled forth from his lips as he started to suffocate from his own blood; pain wracked his body and everything seemed to be moving in slow motion while the ringing in his ears drowned out the chaos around him. The last thing he saw was another S-SWAT battle frame exploding, showering him in purifying flames.

Nearby Lieutenant Stevens feared the worst as he hid behind a destroyed personnel carrier; all his hopes had been tied to the S-SWAT, yet all but one of their battle-frames now laid in ruin. The cold reality of dying and never seeing his family again made his gut twist. He watched as the remaining S-SWAT battle frame desperately evaded another burst of incoming fire.

With each near miss, the knot in S-SWAT pilot Omar's stomach tightened as he did his best to buy time for the surviving security officers to retreat without being gunned down. He had given up any hope of taking the robot down after repeated direct hits from his assault rifle failed to penetrate the armor. Yet he continued firing, hitting the robot again and again. His options were quickly running out and before long he knew his luck would as well. "LT, I am going to do my best to keep drawing its fire from you and your men, but you need to hurry!" Omar said launching into the air to evading another attack.

For a brief moment, Stevens sat, frozen with fear and overwhelming despair, his mind trying to regain control of reality as three officers nearby were shredded by gunfire. If not for the roar of a dropship racing overhead, followed by its nose-mounted gun firing, he would have remained where he was, lost in hopelessness. He dared a peek in the direction the ship was firing, amazed how agile the robot was. It reacted with inhuman speed and agility to avoid the barrage of heavy-caliber pulse rounds, throwing itself into a diving roll before standing up and breaking into a full sprint. His eyes widened as One-Nineteen transformed in mid-stride to its quadruped form and leaped over the remaining barricades, landing a few feet behind him. The metallic beast began to growl threateningly as it slowly paced back and forth, positioning itself to attack, as Maluss and Messenger landed close by.

The Truth of Lies

SENATOR AMBERMAN STEPPED FROM BEHIND the podium, approaching the edge of the stage, taking the time to observe the thousands of attendees seated and facing the stage. The immense granite stone stage stretched the length of the main senate building behind him. He looked behind to the archway leading from the main building to the stage; six of its great pillars were eloquently carved from Baston Crystal mined from the underwater caverns of Hamina's great lake, Athena, into the image of figures representing justice, law and order, wisdom, integrity, duty, and humanity. The final two pillars near the rear of the stage were of archangels bearing towering shields and spears, representing the stalwart strength of humanity's faith to survive. The senate buildings themselves borrowed their design style from the rest of the city, combining ancient Roman architecture with an ultramodern design with its many pillars and arches. He looked up into the open sky, gathering the last of his thoughts, and once again returning his attention to the audience.

With a firm and sincere tone, Senator Amberman began. "I have devoted over forty cycles of my life, along with many others, to secure and maintain a peaceful coexistence between humanity and the Feralan people. I stress humanity because Bill 2062 would strip us of that. Many who support this bill would say that the Feralans are savages and beyond redemption. They would say that we have the right to subjugate them to satisfy our selfish desires. Yet…I question you, does this bill not reduce us to mere savages? Is it not stripping us of our humanity in the underlying quest to satisfy our own greed? Have we not learned from our own history; from the atrocities we have committed on our own kind throughout the ages for pleasure? For power?" he paused. "Or perhaps for profit, for religion, for civilization, and even from ignorance? It is obvious that for all our advances, our sins continue to rear their heads time and time again. We now stand at a pinnacle moment. Do we cast off our humanity, stepping into darkness to once again become true savages, in essence committing genocide to further corporate profit, or do we take a deep look within ourselves and cast out the darkness and allow the true meaning of humanity to shine through? Know this, those who seek to throw us into war will keep their hands clean of sin, sitting in their seats among the senate and corporate board rooms behind the safety of this barrier while the honorable men and women, who have sworn their lives to our protection and upholding the laws of the senate, bloody themselves and give their lives in an unwarranted war in the name of greed. Do not be fooled. Bill 2062 does not offer a better future or quality of life, but the beginning of a downward spiral. In just our brief history here on Tallagen, we have again relived past sins, failing to heed the lessons of those before us. Forget not the hundreds of thousands that died because of the arrogance of our forefathers in the initial cycles of our landing here on Tallagen. Forget not the barrier city Cordon, which was demolished from a lust for power and the greed of men. Liberty, freedom, and progression are the rights of all beings, human, Vaxian, or not. Yet, these must not come at the cost of the rights and the lives of others, for then liberty becomes oppression. Yes, oppression. The very thing we have fought to abolish throughout the course of our own history. By voting yes to Bill 2062, we would so eagerly cast the very thing we have fought to free ourselves from upon others because they are different, only for our own comfort and profit. So I ask you today, vote no to oppression and greed! Vote yes for humanity!" Amberman concluded, stepping back from the podium and raising his hand in response to the roaring applause of the audience before returning to his seat on the stage.

Senator Harkus stood up, removing his glasses as he approached the podium. He paused to wait for the crowd to settle, making a mental note of the "boos," wondering just how many, if any, of the audience actually knew that war was far closer than the media and Amberman let on.

Solemnly, he began speaking. "Humanity...Let us not forget the very reason Colonization Fleet Epsilon 218 was created almost three hundred cycles ago. Humanity was locked in a losing war, a war that had extinguished over twenty-four billion human and Vaxian lives by the time of our departure. We are a hope made in the desperation to continue our races. To prevent humanity from becoming extinct. We all are *quite* aware that the last contact we had with those left behind was hearing that several of the Core Systems were on the verge of falling to the Demzerai. Due to the jump gate mishap, we are now far beyond the reach of those we left behind. We have no way of knowing if even at this very moment, in which we debate the future of humanity here on this world, if we may be the very last of our kind in the universe.

"With the loss of our terra-forming ship and the loss of a quarter of our food and water supply ships during the jump accident, we had no choice. No choice! We had to settle on the first habitable world we came across in this alien galaxy, or else risk failing in our only mission, to survive! Tallagen and its inhabitants have made it clear. We are not wanted here and given a choice, I, like so many others, would gladly leave. However, choice is an illusion we cannot fool ourselves with. Instead, we have made the best of what we have been given by fate. Inside these barriers, we live in a state of almost perfect utopia but make no mistake. Outside is anything but serenity. The only thing that separates us from the execrable situation of the outside world is a three-meter thick energy bubble. Space is finite within the borders of these barriers. In order to thrive, we must expand. How ironic that the very thing that ensures our survival also inhibits it."

Harkus continued, "We have tried time and time again to reconcile with the Feralan people, stretching out our hand in friendship, only to have a blade maliciously stabbed through it. Surely, all of you remember, just seven cycles ago, the massacre in Gavin's Valley in which sixty families, a total of two hundred and twelve men, women, and children—people, simply trying to start a new life outside the barrier, were murdered, killed for settling in an area considered sacred hunting grounds by one of the Feralan covens. No warning, no chance to relocate. But these are an honorable people?

They are misunderstood? We have not done enough to forge a lasting peace with the Feralan people?"

"My colleague would have you believe we are the cruel and inhuman monsters from a distant time when ignorance and arrogance paved the way for misguided beliefs in racial purity, racial supremacy, religious intolerance, and slavery. That we are simply oppressing the weak, forcing our iron will in an attempt to satisfy our undying greed. Bill 2062 will provide the necessary room for each city to expand and their populations to grow comfortably for decades to come, without extending their barriers. It will provide a safer, better quality of life by removing all the hazardous production and the majority of industrial production to one location."

"I agree the Feralan people have every right to survive, so do we. Yet peace with one coven does not mean peace with them all. The Feralan people have a religious belief system that is open to interpretation by those that practice it. Yet the common denominator among all covens seems to be that we, humans and Vaxian, are an affront to their Great Mother Spirit. I want you to look to your left and to your right for a moment…Now picture those faces along with your family and friends. Now realize this, the only way to appease their Great Mother Spirit is by removing every one of those faces off this planet. Since we all are quite aware that Arcnine crystals, necessary for interstellar travel, are non-existent here on Tallagen, we cannot just pick up and leave. This means that the only other way to appease their Great Mother Spirit is for them to kill each and every one of us…"

Harkus paused, bewildered, trying to decipher what his eyes were seeing as he watched the S-SWAT Battle-Frame that was guarding the upper-level entrance to the coliseum become impaled by an invisible object. His face paled, and the audience's attention turned to the direction of his frightened stare. He gasped in shock as the limp battle-frame was tossed to the side like a rag doll and as a security officer nearby was crushed into a mush of flesh and shattered bones by the unseen force. Screams and panic broke out, heralding the coming of the metal beast; Ninety-nine stepped forward, materializing out of thin air as the cam-optics field disengaged. The audience quickly broke down into full chaos as people frantically tried to get out of the coliseum by pushing, shoving, and trampling those in front of them.

Ignoring the audience's panic, Ninety-Nine began scanning the coliseum, sensors quickly locking on to four S-SWAT battle-frames moving to intercept it, along with two battle-frames and several security officers now moving to protect the stage. Flaring its metallic mane, Ninety-Nine fired several mortars, destroying two of the approaching battle-frames and killing dozens of people within an explosive shower of fire and shrapnel.

TWENTY-EIGHTH DROP SHIP

"Twenty-Eighth, we just located the second HK. It just showed up at Glory Hall Coliseum," the holographic image of Major Lightfoot said, pointing at a highlighted building in the image's background.

"Sarah's there! Are there casualties?" Cav stood up, interjecting with urgent concern.

"There have been casualties, but how many, or who they are, is unknown at this time. All we do know currently is that there are several members of the senate and several hundred civilians in that coliseum. Sergeant, do what you have to do to get them out. Back-up is en route," Major Lightfoot's image disappeared.

Cav stood up, moving toward the rear of the dropship. "Captain Mathers, we are going in hot!"

Moving up to stand near Cav, Siren reached out, placing a cautious hand on his shoulder. "I know your wife is down there, Cav, but we have to play this right. We go in not thinking this out, and this whole thing will blow up in our face."

Cav inclined his head slightly toward Siren's hand, and although she could not see his face, the cold stare of his battle-frame's eyes as they flared behind their protective face shield was all she needed to understand to know that it was best to remove her hand.

"It should identify me as the primary threat. I can use that to draw it away while you get your wife and the other civilians out of harm's way. Wraith interjected, attempting to diffuse Cav's agitation with Siren. "If I can get in close enough to use my knuckle guards, I can take it down and wrap this mess up before anyone else gets hurt."

"One minute to the target area, stand by," Corporal Johnson warned before closing his face shield and signaling Corporal Yu to open the tailgate.

Cav stepped forward onto the tailgate, his nearly two-ton armored body unaffected by the chill of the racing wind. Below him, the city moved in slow motion; his thoughts were consumed by the vision of hopelessness he saw in the beast eye's the night of Hammer's death, and now the feeling haunted him again at his fear of Sarah's fate.

"Thirty seconds to the target area, stand by," Johnson said, signaling the squad to get ready.

"Make sure you check your fire. No grenades or rockets unless you have a good target. Siren, use your heavy armor-piercing rounds. When you have a shot, take it. Either you kill the facking thing or slow it down enough for Wraith to get in close! I'm going to find Sarah and get the civilians out," Cav ordered without looking back, readying his pulse rifle.

"Greenlight, go! Go! Go!" Corporal Johnson shouted, signaling the squad to exit.

Conception

WITHOUT HESITATION CAV LEAPT FROM the tailgate, quickly followed by Wraith and Siren. Within seconds the three battle-frames landed with enough force to shatter the concrete ground into a crater under the sudden impact of their armored bulk; each dropping to one knee dampening the excess force of the landing that the frame's inertial dampers could not dissipate. Their sudden appearance drew Ninety-Nine's attention from its grisly task; ripping its razor barbed tail free of a retreating S-SWAT battle-frame's torso, Ninety-Nine turned to scan the new threats and opened fire immediately. With all the power her mechanized legs could muster, Siren leaped straight up, propelling her armored body thirty feet into the air to avoid the deadly barrage of twenty-millimeter explosive rounds that tore the shattered concert floor asunder where she had knelt mere seconds before. The battle-frame's CPU responded to her brain's neural commands to evade, firing maneuvering jets to aid in skillfully rotating and flipping her sleek armored body in a graceful aerial dance, avoiding several more rapid bursts from Ninety-Nine's pulse cannons as her jump pack pushed her higher and higher into the air before finally landing atop the upper coliseum's wall, some one hundred and eighty feet above the massacre below. She reached over, detaching her sniper rifle from its left thigh mount; a subconscious command sent to the weapon's grip-activated nanites within the weapon to immediately begin extending the barrel and stock to its full operational length as a small armored cable, extending from her wrist, attached itself to the pistol grip. With the connection complete, a small image box appeared in the upper right corner of her vision, displaying the magnified view through the rifle's enhanced scope. She paused before raising the rifle to locate Ninety-Nine among the chaos below. Fires raged out of control, blocking exits from the coliseum, save near the rear of the stage where the senators, along with several security guards, were attempting to move without drawing the machine's attention. The remaining survivors were forced to choose: a fiery death or the machine.

Sarah awoke to the sound of explosions and weapon-fire, choking on ash and sulfur as her lungs burned from the superheated air around her. Struggling to sit up, her head pounded with each slight movement she made. She reached up to touch the source of her pain, gasping at the realization that the warm wetness she felt in her matted hair was blood. Everything began to swirl, consciousness slowly draining away, until another explosion nearby rocked her back to reality. She yelped, trying to force back the scream that wanted to escape her lips as the shockwave washed over her, intensifying the pain of her throbbing headache once again. *Get up, Sarah, please get up*, she thought to herself. With that, she began to slowly stand, fighting back the pain, tears streaming down her ash-covered face.

"God, please be with me," she whispered to herself as she reached out to steady herself on a large piece of concrete. Through the clouds of dust, she could just make out the large form of the robotic beast that had attacked the coliseum as well as two smaller shapes sprinting and jumping around it on the main floor. From what she could tell, the fighting was shifting to the other side of the coliseum for the moment, but the exit nearby was blocked with the burning remains of an S-SWAT battle-frame and rubble. She looked down, toward the stage, noticing that the back exit leading to the main building was not blocked. Yet to get there, she would have to move toward the fighting, something she didn't want to do. With a painful sigh that turned into a choking cough, she whispered one final prayer, "God, please allow me to see my husband again." Cautiously, she began moving toward the main floor, making sure to stay as far as possible from the ongoing battle-frames fighting to destroy the killer robot.

BATTLE

Each swipe of Ninety-Nine's phase bladed claws left trails of shimmering streaks. Ninety-Nine pressed the attack, having determined Wraith's Titan battle-frame to be the primary threat. Forcing her to remain defensive by jumping backward and then quickly to the left to avoid a rapid succession of claw and tail attacks that were determined to rend her apart.

"I got the facking robot's attention. Feel free to give me some help anytime now, Siren," Wraith said with a hint of sarcasm.

Ninety-Nine turned. Aware of Cav's attempt to protect the remaining survivors, it launched several mortars whistling through the air toward him before transforming to its humanoid form. Cav activated his jump pack, pushing himself backward to safety, only to realize that only two mortars were actually meant for him; the other two were intended for the twenty survivors he had found trapped among the rubble. A moment later, the survivors disappeared in a ball of flaming shrapnel. Anger and despair swelled within him at the thought of the senseless loss of life.

Cav pushed the thought aside as a warning chimed, alerted him to being locked onto again. He had just enough time to quickly duck and roll away to avoid a burst from Ninety-Nine's pulse cannon before springing up into a kneeling firing position to quickly retaliate with his pulse rifle. The rounds impacted, exploding across Ninety-Nine's thick shoulder and upper chest armor to no effect. Ninety-Nine fired back in defiance at both Cav and Wraith, forcing them to dodge for cover. Using the distraction, Ninety-Nine turned and leaped toward the stage. High above, seeing an opportunity, Siren quickly zeroed in on Ninety-Nine's semi-vulnerable right shoulder joint as it began to transform yet again into its quadruped form and fired. The heavy round punctured the armor of the momentarily exposed joint, exploding deep within and ripping the limb clean off, forcing Ninety-Nine to drop to the ground, crippled, its balance thrown off as it completed the transformation.

"Now, Wraith, use your boom hammers. Get it while it's down!" Cav shouted.

Wraith immediately jumped skyward, launching two high explosive rockets at the downed robot. With deadly precision, the rockets impacted, and before the fireball of the explosion fully expanded, she activated her jump pack once again, thrusting herself forward and down. Her knuckle guards slid into place, energy arcing across them as they powered up to deliver the killing blow. Suddenly, a warning chime sounded in her mind, the battle frame's CPU-enhanced senses alerting her to a danger her eyes did not see. Reacting to the warning, she shifted her weight, turning mid-air, while quickly countering with a right cross at the last moment to fend off the metal claws that had lashed out through the fire and smoke at her. A loud thunderous boom cascaded through the coliseum, signaling that her punch had connected; as Ninety-Nine's phase bladed claws sliced into her upper torso armor, damage warnings began to flash in her vision.

"Fack, it was playing dead!" Wraith shouted as she landed, instinctively reaching to protect the gaping wound to her battle-frame. She quickly fought off the ghostly sensation in her chest, a side effect of her mind interpreting the damage to her battle-frame as a wound to her actual physical body.

"What's the damage looking like?" Cav asked, moving to put himself between Ninety-Nine and Wraith.

"Not good, the claws severed most of the left side abdominal oblique bio-optic muscles, along with cutting the thoracoepigastric power vein in three places. Repair nanites are working to stabilize the power flux. Frame's efficiency is down to 61 percent. I am going to divert power to increase nanite synthesis, not going to get benched that easy."

"Lookout, it's on the move!" Siren shouted over the com-link. From the slowly dissipating smoke, Ninety-Nine rushed forward, backhanding Cav sending him hurtling through the air into a nearby wall and slamming a still-disoriented Wraith to the ground. Immediately, Wraith reacted, rolling to her left to avoid a ground-shattering stomp aimed for her head. Yet, before she could react again, a swift kick sent her flying across the ground before coming to what would have been a bone-shattering stop if not for her frame. Having triangulated where the sniper round that had taken its arm had come from, Ninety-Nine spun around, raising its remaining pulse cannon and fired. Siren reacted, launching herself into a somersault. Her sudden movement forced her cam-optic field to fail, making her visible once again in mid-air. With Siren now fully visible, Ninety-Nine relentlessly fired seeking to shoot her down. Siren twisted and rolled her armored body with the skill of a gymnast, evading each pulse cannon bursts, as she descended to the coliseum floor. Some distance away, Cav lifted himself from the ground, shaking off the momentary disorientation of the impact. Thirty feet in front of him, Ninety-Nine stood damaged, yet no less dangerous. He quickly scanned the machine, assessing its capabilities. The robot's right arm and pulse cannon had been blown off by the well-placed shot from Siren. The round had damaged several internal systems when it exploded inside the shoulder as well, destroying the cam-optics field generator, one of the ammo storage bins, and the repair nanite storage system. The robot was down to its last remaining pulse cannon rounds but it continued to fire the weapon aggressively, determined to kill Siren for the damage she had done. Its left arm was now crippled, having been blown open from the mid-forearm downward thanks to Wraith's boom hammer strike. The robot was now left with only the one pulse cannon; it could no longer transform and use its secondary weapon system or mortars.

 Nearby, Wraith stood. That she could even stand after the damage her frame had sustained was a testament to the Titan frame's resilience, as well as her own. Cav's scan showed her frame was at 47 percent efficiency, yet he knew she was far from out of the fight. The stimulants being injected into both of their bloodstreams made sure of that, he could already feel his head clearing as he surveyed the situation. The senators and their small security force had used the distraction to make a run for the main building along with several other survivors, one of whom was Sarah. He zoomed in, quickly locking on to her and performed a medical scan on her. She was hurt and slowly bleeding into her abdomen along with a mild concussion. The joy his heartfelt at seeing her alive dissipated with what his scan revealed next; she was approximately seven weeks pregnant but there were no life signs for the fetus. Suddenly, Siren landed, blocking his view of Sarah and the survivors heading to the main building.

"You okay, Cav?" Siren asked, looking over her shoulder before turning her attention back toward Ninety-Nine.

"I've had better days, but I'm good," he replied, pushing the thoughts of Sarah's pregnancy aside to focus on the battle.

"Wraith, can you still fight?" Cav asked over the com-link. "Oh, I am *so* about to put the hurt on this facking robot,"

Wraith sneered in response.

"Then it's time we end this fight," Cav said, placing a hand on Siren's shoulder.

Siren nodded in silent affirmation as Ninety-nine turned to face them.

Amidst the chaos, an exhausted Sarah was relieved to see the Security Force Troopers with a group of survivors, along with the familiar face of Senator Amberman, as she climbed through the debris onto the stage. There was a growing discomfort in her stomach along with the returning feeling of becoming light-headed. She paused a moment in the hopes of catching a second wind but it didn't come. Exhaustion finally getting the best of her, Sarah collapsed to her knees. "Help me, please!" Sarah cried out, hoping to get the attention of the quickly distancing group.

Senator Amberman stopped, turning at the sound of Sarah's plea for help.

"Senator, please come with us, sir. The Alliance will secure the situation. We have to get you and the other senate members to safety now," the trailing security trooper said, trying to respectfully guide Amberman along with the rest of the group.

"Trooper, if you haven't noticed, the fight is moving closer to the stage and she is obviously injured and not going to make it to safety on her own," Amberman protested.

"Sir, please. I have my orders," Trooper Daniels said, blocking Amberman's path.

"I am not going to risk leaving one of the senate's leading correspondents, or anyone else for that matter, to possibly get killed.

So either you help me or by God get out of my damn way son!" Amberman shot back, pushing his way past security officer Daniels.

Daniels hesitated, just long enough to ponder losing his job and the charge of dereliction of duty, before racing ahead of Amberman to help Sarah. In the short time, it took to reach her, Sarah had fully collapsed and was now sprawled across the floor like a lifeless doll. Daniels knelt down, taking her wrist into his hand to check for a pulse. Her pulse was weak and her breathing shallow; she was dying fast, and as another explosive shockwave washed over them, he was tempted to tell the senator she was dead so they could head toward the main senate building to safety as fast as they could. But after hearing the determination in Amberman's voice, he knew it would not be that simple.

"She's lost a lot of blood and her pulse is getting weak, Senator," Daniels said as he continued to examine Sarah, keeping one cautious eye on the closing battle.

"Do what you can and let's get her to safety."

Daniels reached into his small med-kit, which was strapped to his left thigh, pulling out a small aerosol vial. Moving her hair, matted and stuck to the gash in her head, earned a low groan of protest as he sprayed the wound with bio-foam, sterilizing the wound and staunching the bleeding as the foam filled the gash. Next, he reached into the med-kit and pulled out a medical nanite injector along with a small holographic medical scanner. He began scanning Sarah's head and over her body down to her feet, mapping all the injuries to her body in the process. Once the scan was complete, he surveyed the list of injuries, prioritized by severity, and the number of medical nanites it would take to stabilize or repair the injuries. With a heavy exhale, he reached into the med-kit once more, pulling out a second nanite injector while selecting the first injury on the list, and waited until a small blue circle appeared, confirming the medical nanites sync with the medical scanner and program was complete.

"Senator, I don't have enough medical nanites in these two injectors for what she and her baby need. I'm not sure if I can save either one of them, much less both of them," Daniels said as he injected Sarah with the nanites.

"This is where faith comes in, son. God's will be done," Amberman replied confidently, as Ninety-Nine leaped onto the stage fifty feet away.

Cav and Siren leaped onto the stage, positioning themselves defiantly between Ninety-Nine and the survivors. Finally, out of ammunition, Ninety-Nine grabbed a piece of broken concrete as a make-shift war hammer, quickly closing the distance, and in one fluid motion swung the make-shift weapon in a huge arc, attempting to crush Cav's and Siren's heads in the process. Cav and Siren easily evaded the attack and countered, Siren landing a powerful kick to Ninety-Nine's face, crushing one of the robot's eyes in the process as she flipped backward while Cav ducked and leaped forward, slicing deep into Ninety-Nine's right knee with his phase blade and forcing the machine to its knees. Cav's attack was quickly followed by an unexpected thunderous boom, signifying Wraith's knuckle guard delivering her vengeance. He jumped back to see Ninety-Nine's remaining arm and shoulder blown free from the body, sending the robot spinning to the ground face up. Without hesitation, Wraith pounced onto the downed machine, punching down and through Ninety-Nine's thick chest plate to grab the main power regulator buried deep within.

"I wish you could feel this," Wraith said, staring into Ninety-Nine's remaining eye with contempt before ripping the power regulator free and crushing it.

Gladiator

UNLIKE THE REST OF NEW Hope, the industrial district was an area designed for functionality with no thoughts as to the aesthetic. The district was a mixture of various factories, processing plants, recycling centers, power plants, and waste disposal facilities divided into zones; it was a direct contrast to the sprawling parks, crystal clear lakes, and majestic statues surrounded by stylish architecture throughout the rest of the city. The constant sound of thousands of workers and machines working to ensure that the city needs were met seemed to be organized chaos to those unfamiliar with the district. But now, for the first time, the district fell silent except for the sounds of weapon fire and explosions.

The ground exploded behind One-Nineteen as it raced around the corner of a storage tank, evading another burst from Messenger's assault pulse rifle. With cat-like grace, One-Nineteen slid, spinning itself and transforming into its humanoid form. Stepping out from cover, the deadly machine fired a barrage of twenty-millimeter rounds in retaliation, forcing Maluss and Messenger to take cover in opposite directions.

"It's playing cat and mouse with us, leading us deeper into the industrial zone," Messenger said through clenched teeth, ducking down to shield himself from a nearby truck exploding which showered him in a plume of flames and black smoke.

"Yeah, I know. We're the facking mice and it's getting old. We need to end this," Maluss replied, peering from around the corner from a side street.

Messenger watched Maluss take aim, hitting the robot several times, but One-Nineteen's armor refused to give way. Messenger moved to stand, lifting his assault pulse rifle to aid Maluss in his renewed offense. His target acquisition locked on, yet he hesitated, noticing several of the storage tanks around them and behind One-Nineteen were painted with red hazmat warning symbols. Scanning the tank nearest to him, the words "Enriched Nulonium" clearly flashed in an overlay of the storage tanks along with the warning that they were highly explosive.

"Maluss! Hold your fire. All these storage tanks are full of enriched nulonium!" Messenger shouted at the realization of the situation.

Looking to take advantage of One-Nineteen's momentary pause, Maluss snapped back sarcastically, "Yeah, and?" It took a moment before it dawned on him, his nonchalant attitude abruptly fading as he suddenly understood the reason for the warning. "Oh fack!" He lowered his pulse rifle.

"We are sitting in the middle of a damn bomb just waiting to happen," Messenger said, confirming Maluss's conclusion.

Going on a hunch, Messenger scanned the GAR to confirm his suspicion. He sighed with disgust. "Maluss, the robot's fusion power cells are beginning to overload. It's why the machine has been trying to evade us this whole time. It needed the time to jury rig itself. It is going to self-destruct, and with these tanks, it'll take a quarter of the city with it!"

"The fack it will. I got plans tonight!" Maluss responded, ducking back into cover to scan the surrounding buildings' structural integrity; his frame's sensors identified a viable three-story building not far from his current location. "Messenger, give me a distraction as best as you can on the count of three," Maluss directed, relaying a graphical image to Messenger's HUD in the direction that he would be moving.

"Somehow I don't think that's going to be a problem," Messenger replied, his sensors detecting that One-Nineteen was now locking onto him.

"Raven One, I need an immediate weapon loadout drop at the coordinates I am sending you now, configuration Gladiator."

"Roger that, Maluss, package ETA forty-five seconds!" Captain Mathers responded.

"Okay, Messenger, on three…" "Maluss, what are you going to do?"

"Take it out the only way we can without going up in a blaze of glory in the process, up close and personal."

"You're going to do what? It's a Type IV HK, designed for close combat, remember? That's damn near impossible *and* suicidal without a Titan battle frame's boom hammers to take it down quickly if you're lucky enough before it rips you to pieces!" Messenger protested in disbelief.

"Yeah, well watch me make the impossible, possible!" Maluss confidently replied. "One…two…three!" Maluss shouted over the com-link.

Messenger opened up a steady stream of explosive shells, pouring them across One-Nineteen's heavily armored torso, forcing the deadly robot to throw up its arms and turn away to protect the weaker armor of its head from the rounds of Messenger's assault pulse rifle. With One-Nineteen distracted, Maluss rushed from cover at top speed toward the target building, leaping up and out of sight to the rooftops above.

One-Nineteen fell back into cover as a round grazed its right leg and exploded, rending a jagged wound in its armor. The GAR paused momentarily, reassessing its mission priorities, calculating that Messenger's threat priority was now level one and needed to be eliminated prior to completion of its other objective. Rerouting the majority of power back to its primary combat systems, it left just enough power to the secondary systems to continue the restructuring of its fusion cells for self-destruction. One-Nineteen renewed its offense, releasing a full barrage from both pulse cannons in Messenger's direction. Barely reacting in time, Messenger turned to run down the side street, away from the volatile tanks. The wall he was near exploded outward; round after round sheared through the building mere inches behind him as he ran. He turned to go down another street, taking cover behind a maintenance garage as the two buildings that had absorbed the majority of One-Nineteen's fire during his dash to avoid the relentless barrage came crashing down, earning him a moment of reprise. Or so he thought. One-Nineteen came crashing through a nearby wall, greeting him with a devastating punch to the head that sent him reeling backward, only to be seized by the arm and flung through the garage wall into a store across the street.

Upon the rooftop, Maluss watched the large almond-shaped cargo pod deploy its anti-gravity chutes to slow its rapid descent before landing heavily upon the building's rooftop in front of him. The cargo pod's sides folded down with a hiss, opening like a metallic blossom to reveal its instruments of destruction as he transmitted the access codes. Dropping his pulse rifle, Maluss secured a large round shield to his left arm and, with a slight hum, teal energy rippled across the shield's surface as its protective power field activated. Next, he armed himself with two gladius-styled swords, securing one to the inside of the shield and readying the other, testing it for weight and balance before activating the sword's destructive phase field. "I know you would try and talk me out of this if you were here, Acalia. I can hear you calling me reckless, even now. But this time, I have no choice. So put in a good word with God for me, sis," Maluss whispered. He instinctively reached for the religious medallion he wore around his neck. "Now, the game changes." With his frame's eyes flaring, Maluss turned, breaking into a full sprint before leaping off the rooftop with a battle cry fueled by pure fury.

In the street below, One-Nineteen began a slow trot toward the collapsed shop as Messenger surfaced, frantically pushing aside rubble and attempting to free himself from the waist-deep prison of debris. Like a predatory cat, One-Nineteen slowly moved in, anticipating the kill. Messenger stopped struggling to free his body; there was no time and he knew it. With his pulse rifle buried at his feet and his railgun offline, he drew his combat blade in one last act of defiance.

"Bring it!" he shouted.

One-Nineteen burst into a full sprint, leaping forward with a shattering roar, claws outstretched for the kill. Messenger threw up an arm in a last attempt to shield himself. A furious battle cry, amplified by a frame's external voice emitter, forced him to look up just in time enough to see Maluss descend from above like an avenging angel to intercept the charging mechanical beast. Sensing the new threat, One-Nineteen reacted, transforming in mid-air to its humanoid form, to intercept the attacking battle-frame. The two collided, One-Nineteen bearing the brunt of the impact, as the two metal warriors slammed into the street. Unhindered by the weakness of flesh, One-Nineteen immediately turned the force of the impact into a rolling kick, launching Maluss away, before transforming back into its quadruped form. Fueled by adrenaline, Maluss tucked, rolling with the impact to spring to his feet, shield held high and sword ready.

One-Nineteen paced back and forth, scanning and analyzing Maluss; the phase charged claws sliced effortlessly into the concrete with each step. Eyes flaring, Maluss slowly began circling the mechanized beast, his mind going through dozens of scenarios on how each move could play out. For the space of several breaths, each of the armored combatants searched for a weakness to exploit in the other's defenses. The robot analyzed multiple scenarios: 75 percent probability of success destroying target with range weaponry, ammo depleted; 91 percent probability of success destroying target in close combat. Self-destruction reconfiguration and alignment at 94 percent completion. Analyses complete…

"Maluss, time is running out!" Messenger warned over the com-link.

"Okay then, this ends now!" Maluss spat, charging forward.

One-Nineteen lashed out, attempting to slice Maluss's head and sword arm off in one blow. Anticipating the attack, Maluss threw up his shield to ward off the attack, dropping to one knee under the impact before thrusting upward with his sword. One-Nineteen pulled back to avoid the thrust and immediately countered with another slashing attack. In the back of his mind, Maluss imagined this was how it must be to get hit by a Rocape. The giant beasts that dwelled in the Soman desert were unique in that they ingested rock which their body metabolized into their bones; it eventually created hardened bone protrusions along the hands, dorsal area, shoulders, and head. The rocky bone growths continued to expand throughout the creature's life span, giving them considerable mass. He recalled seeing the damage done to a survey team's armored personnel carrier; it wasn't pretty. Each of the creature's fists weighed in at over a thousand pounds. Another blow suddenly impacted his shield, sending structural integrity warning messages down the left side of his vision. *The pounding that APC took had to feel similar to this*, he thought.

Maluss jumped back, watching the missed attack crater the street. "This damn thing hits like a Rocape."

"I warned you about taking it on up close for a reason." Pushing aside the last of the rubble, Messenger lifted his rifle free; even without the technical data of its condition, he could see it was damaged beyond use. "My rifle's useless. It's too badly damaged."

Maluss grunted under the impact of another blow to his shield. Although the shield's power field prevented One-Nineteen's phase-powered claws from slicing him to pieces, the force of each blow was taking its toll. Warning signs of structural integrity failure in the shield, as well as his shoulder, began to appear across his vision as his protective force field flickered.

"Target it with your rail gun!"

Messenger took a quick look around. "I can't take the chance…"

"Just do it! I'll take care of the rest," Maluss lashed out, his sword making a sweeping upstroke, forcing One-Nineteen to relinquish its assault to avoid the attack.

Messenger's rail gun extended and lowered onto his right shoulder. "I hope you know what you're doing, Maluss."

"Don't I always?"

"I'll let you know…if I'm still in one piece after this is over." Detecting the target lock of the rail gun, One-Nineteen immediately jumped back to give itself a wide berth from Maluss; its attention was now drawn toward Messenger.

Seizing the moment, Maluss charged forward, sword at the ready, moving fast, even for the abilities of a battle-frame. Caught off guard at the speed of the attack, One-Nineteen reacted a second too late; the phase-powered sword sheared through its right leg, severing it just below the knee. One-Nineteen staggered sideways, crushing a nearby car and creating a shower of sparks. Driven by anger and adrenaline, Maluss drew his other sword from its sheath within the shield and then discarded the shield as he twirled the dual weapons in unison.

Its beast form crippled beyond use, One-Nineteen transformed into its humanoid form, taking a knee to steady itself. With a cold metallic voice, One-Nineteen spoke, "Combat capabilities reduced to 32 percent, all remaining power diverted to the primary objective."

"Sounds like things aren't going according to plan," Maluss taunted it.

"We got about fifteen seconds, Maluss. You've got to sever the HK's main power cell now!"

One-Nineteen stood, turning to face Messenger while slinging the crushed car at its side toward Maluss.

Reacting even before Messenger could yell a warning, Maluss leaped into the air, pushing off the car as it passed beneath him, holding both swords high. With the full might of his armored body, he brought the swords downward as he landed. A moment later, One-Nineteen collapsed into three pieces in front of Maluss. Without looking down, Maluss stood, crushing the disconnected main power cell, his frame's eyes flaring in response to the smug smirk impulse his CPU interpreted for his face. "I told you I could make the impossible, possible."

Point of View

WITH HIS COMBAT BLADE SKILLFULLY angled in between its vertebrae, the Feralan died almost instantly. Hopefully, painlessly as well, Master Sergeant Mahoma Hierra liked to believe. With a quick survey of his surroundings to ensure his deed went unnoticed, Hierra began concealing the body beneath nearby foliage to avoid detection by any of its clansmen. He was sure that they were nearby. He paused to examine the body as his combat armor's cam-optics field reinitialized, bending the visual spectrum of light and helping him quickly become invisible once again. Moments ago, he had gotten a distress call from Sergeant Brook's communication trooper requesting immediate support. More troubling was Specialist Jackman's video feed that was relayed with the message; in it was one of the beasts, dubbed "Chindi" by the troops in the field, which had recently been classified by command as threat level Alpha Mike, which meant the beast possessed mystical abilities and was extremely dangerous. The transmission had ended as abruptly as it began, leaving him with no time to get further details; he had ordered his squad to return to the ruin's eastern end as fast as possible.

The beautifully crafted armor the dead Feralan wore resembled ancient samurai armor, providing excellent protection to the vital areas of her body in addition to her forearms and shins. He knelt down to remove the Feralan's helmet, exposing the face and letting her burnt-sienna hair fall free. Her delicate features were so beautiful yet alien to him. He watched as a stream of dark blood trickled from the corner of her mouth down into her pointed ear before being swallowed by the hungry ground. She was young, at least by the alien standard. It was believed that Feralans lived to be at least six hundred cycles old, if not more, and judging by her youthful appearance he assumed she could not have been more than a hundred seventy-five cycles old.

The small piece of his mind that felt pity seemed to anguish at the sight before him. Her skin was silky to the touch, which deceptively hid the resiliency of her flesh. *They were so different…yet similar to us in many aspects*, he thought. Humanoid, comparative in size and physical shape, with clear physical distinctions between male and female like humans, but the similarities ended there. Their four-toed taloned feet were a tell-tale sign. Upon closer inspection, their light brown skin tone contrasted sharply with bright white almond-shaped eyes; her emerald vertical slit irises were another clear indication that they were far from human.

Hierra said a silent prayer as he finished concealing the dead Feralan. The looming shadow of war was becoming increasingly evident as the media portrayed it, but the truth was that they had already been at war for some time now, Hierra thought. He had taken more lives in the last two cycles, since joining the ranks of special operations as a Recon Patrol Trooper, than he had in his entire eleven cycles of military service.

"Didn't know you had taken up nature watching as a hobby?" Preacher asked cynically. "There are two more bush babies about thirty meters that way for you to admire, but I didn't put them down as nicely as you did," Preacher sarcastically whispered, taking a kneeling defensive position near Heirra.

Inside his helmet, Heirra grimaced. Normally recon squads were a tightly knit group considering that all they had was each other when outside the barrier for extended periods of time. However, out of the six-man team, only one squad member really got along with Sergeant First Class Preacher and it definitely wasn't Heirra. It wasn't because he wasn't a good trooper—he was. But he had a twisted and negative view about non-humans and took perverse pleasure in killing them; somehow the shrinks hadn't noticed his deviance in any of the routine mental evaluations.

"We discovered this land and have the right to it. These savages need to respect that and us," Preacher would often say when the subject of the Feralan people came up.

How you could discover a world that already had an indigenous population and claims that you had the right to sweep them aside was beyond him. Heirra realized a long time ago that conversations that weren't tactical in nature were pointless to have with Preacher. Preacher was the type of guy that a few centuries ago would have been wearing a white hood and burning crosses; it was why deep down Heirra despised him.

"Keep it moving, get into position," Heirra snapped icily.

He quickly pushed aside his annoyance with Preacher and refocused on the task at hand, ensuring that all enemy activity was neutralized, as they converged back on the ruins to support the squad. He scanned the dense rainforest, taking in every detail of his surroundings as well as the potential danger it held. Cycles of training and experience, along with almost losing his life on more than one occasion to the indigenous fauna, had taught him to always be on his guard. Yet he couldn't resist noticing the natural beauty of it all as he moved toward the ruins.

Ankor Trees dominated a large portion of the forest in this area. The largest of these trees grew upward of forty feet, their trunks twice as wide. Many of the forest animals called them home, especially when their branches were covered with large white blossoms that were full of sweet nectar and even sweeter fist-size orange berries like they were now. Beneath the cover of the canoe-sized leaves, it was like another world.

Harmless Lirds caught his attention as they fluttered about, feeding on insects and berries lured by the Ankor Trees; the Lirds were Tallagen's unique version of a hummingbird, he thought. The four-winged reptilian birds were highly prized as pets in the barrier cities for their intelligence, but even more so for the iridescent colors their wing feathers displayed in rich contrast to their bluish-gold scales. Nearby, several Tonchs were eating the berries that had fallen to the ground close to a grazing herd of wild Kiyaks. The elephantine-sized mollusks were twice the size of the largest Kiyak bull, but despite their size, they were harmless, spending most of their time foraging for vegetation, ready to quickly withdraw into their massive cone-shaped shells at the first hint of danger.

The Kiyaks closely resembled a moose-like buffalo and were a different story; during mating season the males became very aggressive and territorial. He was glad that mating season was still several months away considering he had almost lost his life to a territorial bull a few cycles back. For now, though, the Kiyaks held no risk for him so long as he steered clear of the calves within the herd.

Despite the tranquility, Heirra was well aware of the dangers such a setting hid. Wherever there were prey animals, there were bound to be predators. Tallagen had far too many creatures that could easily kill a fully armored trooper for his comfort. Even more disheartening was the fact that there were creatures that could even take down a battle-frame if given the chance. He looked down at his rifle and arms; the engaged cam-optics field activated a spectrum filter within his visor, turning it opaque silver. The invisibility it afforded gave him some comfort, but being invisible was a minor defense in a world so adept at dealing death.

He spied the thin tripwire-like webbing of a Lurker. They were aggressive but inactive hunters. These insidious arthropods resembled a giant spider that had bred with a lobster; they grew up to fifteen feet in length and could easily reach eleven hundred pounds or more. They preferred to wait inside burrows concealed with a camouflaged trapdoor with several tripwires extending from the hidden entrance. The moment a tripwire was triggered, the Lurker would launch forward, seizing its prey in it pinchers and delivering a neurotoxin with its five-inch fangs before dragging the paralyzed prey back to its hidden lair to be devoured alive.

However, the predator Heirra feared the most in Calspan Rainforest was the Thyras, more commonly called a Corso Dragon since it so closely resembled a combination of a Cane Corso hound and a Komodo dragon. An apex predator at the top of the food chain, it could stand over eight feet tall at the shoulders and it was large and powerful enough to take down whatever it chose. The perfect predator, with jet black and remorseless eyes sitting forward in its head, giving it excellent depth perception; it had an additional eye on either side of its head which afforded it an almost three hundred and sixty-degree view of its surroundings, day or night. Massive vice-like jaws with oversized canines and thick razor claws capable of tearing through armor with ease made them extremely fearsome. Hardened bony plates, capable of stopping small arms fire, shielded its head, shoulders, back, and haunches; thick and densely packed muscles made it extremely resilient and hard to kill without heavy weapon fire, which made his assault rifle almost pointless. With an above-average animal intelligence, it was eerily cunning for a beast. Its dark scales helped it blend into the surrounding rainforest, making it difficult to spot until it was often too late. Interestingly, the Feralans used them as mounts, though how they tamed such a deadly beast was beyond his understanding.

A screech from above drew his attention to a pair of Gray Sky Raptors soaring high above. One of the largest of the Sky Raptors species, these majestic four-winged reptilian birds were giants among their kind, dwarfing their distant cousins, the Lirds. It was not uncommon to see them this time of the cycle, hunting in mated pairs, until the end of spring when nesting season began and one parent would stay with the egg. Like all Sky Raptors, evolution had honed them into perfect aerial predators; despite having an enormous wingspan that could exceed sixteen feet, their wing, and body design made them agile and fast enough to maneuver within the confines of the rainforest almost as easily as in the open sky in the pursuit of prey. Luckily, they didn't normally consider humans to be prey. Still, Hierra looked at his outstretched hand, taking comfort in his invisibility.

The silence of the com-link was broken by the chatter of his squadmates, confirming they were almost into their designated positions along the tree line on the eastern end of the ruins; "awaiting orders" reminded him that the greatest danger to be concerned with was in the ruins.

Slowly, Sergeant Second Class Barr knelt within the tree line, pushing his cloaked rifle through the underbrush of the clearing's edge. "Ten o'clock position, I have eyes on six targets, east side of the ruins. Appears to be one friendly laid out in the middle of them."

"Roger that, I am moving into the six o'clock position now. The rest of you sound off when set and stand by." Heirra quickened his pace, making sure not to make any sound that would alert the forest to his presence.

In a hushed whisper, each team member sounded off one by one over the com-link. "Reynolds, eleven o'clock position, standing by. Hemp, eight o'clock position, standing by. Smith, nine o'clock position, standing by."

Staring down the length of his barrel, Preacher smirked in anticipation. "Preacher, seven o'clock position, on hold status with one of the bush babies in my sight." A moment later, his smirk became a wicked smile when his target acquisition indictor locked on to the Feralan's head.

The Feralan Jogol had grown up learning the skills of a wood crafter; it was to be his purpose within the coven as it had been for his father before him. Since he was young, he had held a fascination and admiration for warriors. He would marvel at the warriors during the coven gatherings. Each dressed in their armor, with unique clan designs and full-face helms. The greater the status and deeds, the more personalized the armor became. He dreamed of wearing his own armor one day, armor worthy to rival even that of the legendary warriors Hallen or Jarsha. Yet among his coven, there had been very few allowed to travel that path. For as long as he could remember, it had been the will of the coven veil-seer that they follow the Great Mother Spirit's path of knowledge. The day the veil-seer Asla came to his coven was the day his dreams became a reality. To be accepted and trained by one of the mightiest warrior covens was a high honor; when he made the careless mistake of losing his helmet during the ride to the ruins, he felt a mountain of shame fall upon him when the other warriors glanced at him with hushed whispers.

TREELINE

Sergeant Second Class Hemp never took his eyes off Brooks, half-dead, bound, and helpless at the feet of his captors, as he diligently keyed programming codes into his armor's wrist-mounted computer. He had done this many times, both in practice and in the field; it was his specialty, electronic warfare. He considered it a game of sorts, watching programming code flow past his view. The challenge to outdo his last time was always his motivation. Even before he received the warning "ACCESS DENIED" flashing in bold red letters, he was already creating new access subroutine and within a (personal best) time of 4.3 seconds, the message "ACCESS GRANTED" flashed in bold green letters before him, remotely linking him to Brooks's computer system. There was a momentary flicker in the left side of his vision before information from Brooks's computer began to display. "I'm in Brooks's systems. It's not good. All the others are dead. Accessing his mission video feed…"

Heirra, sensing something bad in Hemp's pause, looked up from his scope. "What is it?"

"Chindis, the Feralans, they trans-form…into them…," Hemp replied, his voice a combination of astonishment and worry.

"This just got really interesting," Smith chimed in.

"So the bush babies turn into big bad monsters. Guess we're going to have to kill them real quick-like, before they get the chance," Preacher mocked.

"What about the scientific team members?" Heirra pressed. "Dead, except Dr. Hollis and Dr. Merces. I'm still picking up their life sign readings from inside the main tomb." Hemp killed the link to Brooks.

"Okay, we secure Brooks, then the scientists. Reynolds hit them with a disruptor grenade first. We don't need any magical surprises." Heirra made one last scan of the area. "Go!"

Like the other Feralans, Jogol's hands tightened around his sword at the sound of the burst overhead. He watched with childlike amazement at the shower of chartreuse green particles drifting slowly down from above, like illuminated snowflakes. Never had he seen such a thing. He could only reason it to be magic in his young mind; he watched as each particle flared briefly into a ghostly white wisp of smoke upon contact with Gelgon, the only one who stood among them that had the wards of protection carved into his flesh, before vanishing from existence.

His hearts raced and muscles tightened with the anticipation of battle. His thoughts filled with his potential glory; he would be the one to kill the defiler's shaman and present the head to Katya personally. Gelgon would no doubt summon the predator spirit within him, transforming into his Cainanite form. He would have to act fast to seize the kill or he would lose it to the Cainanite.

It was the last thought he had as Preacher's round exploded inside his head, annihilating his skull and brains into a shower of gore.

Old Wounds

GERALD STARED OUT THE WINDOW of the hospital room. The heavy rains that passed through the barrier made it next to impossible to see much other than the blurry city lights. It didn't matter; he wasn't looking to see anything, in particular, just to try to make sense of his thoughts. He looked down at the streets below, a man raced from the cover of the transit shelter for a bus that had just arrived. Several people had gotten off, forcing him to stand exposed to the pouring rain longer than he had hoped. The wind shifted the direction of the rain, obscuring what little he could see. Leaning against the window frame, he let the steady patter of rain upon the glass push him further into his thoughts and into the events four days ago.

It was a terrible night, raining just like tonight he remembered. That night, sitting in the waiting room with the rest of the team, as Sarah and Wraith went through emergency surgeries. The doctor came to tell him that they couldn't save the baby, but that Sarah would recover. He knew he would have to be strong for her when the time came. He was relieved that Sarah would live, yet the loss of his unborn child struck deep; he was thankful for the comfort of his closest friends as the tears fell that day.

The wait for news of Wraith was no easier. It was a reminder of Acalia, like déjà vu. He had said it out loud, in a hushed whisper to himself. That was when Terrance lashed out.

He flew into a rage, "She is nothing like Acalia! Don't you ever facking compare her to Acalia again!" before storming out of the waiting room, knocking an orderly to the floor in the process.

Terrance's sudden outburst had taken everyone off guard. To the others in the waiting room, he had just seemed overwhelmed from the day's events. Yet Terrance had dealt with far worse with nothing more than a sarcastic one-liner or a joke. Gerald could sense the true anger that bordered on hatred within his words; this was different. At first, he tried to call him back; when it didn't work, he chased after him, catching up to him outside. He had reached out to catch Terrance by the arm, trying to stop him long enough to give him a moment to say something, to apologize. Instead, he found himself slammed into the hospital wall with an arm twisted painfully behind his back.

Terrance spat coldly into his ear, "Only because you are family to me; otherwise, I would snap your facking arm right now." With that, he forcefully pushed away from Gerald.

Gerald turned, massaging his aching shoulder, to watch Terrance storm off into the rainy night. "This is deeper than what you're letting on! What is it, really, between you two?" he called out.

"Karma!"

Gerald stood there for a minute or two; he wasn't sure of anything at that moment. Sarah, the baby, Wraith, and now his best friend turning on him felt unreal; only the warm raindrops colliding with his face felt genuine.

A flash of lighting drew him from the memories of that night. Behind him, Wraith stirred. She had collapsed after finishing off the HK Ninety-Nine in the coliseum. After he found out how bad her injuries were, he was amazed that she was able to fight with such intensity for so long. The doctor's exact words to him were "She should have been dead a long time ago even with that medical suite in those frames of yours. I am not a god-fearing man, Sergeant, but there is no other way to explain how she made it to my operating table alive other than a miracle." She had been put into a medically induced coma for three days after the surgery; since she had awakened from it a day ago, she had spent most of her time sleeping from the effects of the regenerative medical nanites still inside her.

"How long you been here, Cav?" Angela whispered weakly as she woke up, seeing Gerald standing by the window.

Gerald turned to look at the bed. "Call me Gerald. We're off duty. I've been here for about forty-five minutes and I think…I think I need to ask you something."

"I'm thirsty. Do you mind pouring me a glass of water?"

Gerald walked over to the nightstand near the bed, picking up a small plastic pitcher and pink cup decorated with tiny fairies. "This may not be the best time for this, but I really need to know."

Angela did her best to sit up before taking the cup. She couldn't help but notice the humor in Gerald's face as she took a sip from the cup. "My mother brought it to me earlier when she came to visit with my dad. A gift, from my grandmother, when I was sick with the Corellian Flu when I was two cycles old. She said it was magical and would help me get better. So every time I got sick, it was the only cup I would drink from as a child. I didn't know my mom still had it." They both smiled. "Have a seat," she said, taking a small sip and pausing to allow the cool water to soothe her parched throat. "I think I already know what this is about," she said, taking another sip of water.

"I don't think so. It isn't about work," Gerald looked down at the floor, searching for the words.

"It's about Terrance, right?" she said, handing the cup back to Gerald.

Gerald looked up, astonished. "How did you know? I haven't spoken to anyone about this."

"I kind of just got that feeling, you know?"

For a few moments, nothing was said, the awkward silence only broken by the rain coming down outside. For a moment, Gerald thought about leaving and not asking the question after all, but the way Terrance reacted that night demanded that he ask. With a deep sigh, he looked back at the floor. "What is it between you and him? Why does he despise you?"

"What did he tell you?" Angela asked uncomfortably.

Standing up, Gerald moved to the side of the bed once again. "Karma. That's all he said."

"Karma is it…He's still hurting after all this time," Angela reached over taking Gerald's hand in hers. "There is a lot of pain between us. Mainly for two reasons, but it would be easier to explain if I just show you something first." Looking into his eyes she gave a fake half-smile, just enough to raise the left corner of her mouth, her lips parting to reveal the now-extended fang.

Unconsciously, Gerald tightened his grip, squeezing Angela's hand harder than he meant to. A second later he realized and gently released it. "You're a Vaxian," he whispered.

"Yes, although I believe my great-great-grandfather on my dad's side was human," she smiled weakly.

"Does he know?"

"No, when we dated I never told him. We were only sixteen cycles old, just beginning our first cycle at Saints Academy. It was three cycles later when the government officially released the last logs from the mission computer before the accident. There were still quite a few people and hate groups on that anti-alien movement…especially the one about Vaxian colonists taking up seats in the colonization fleet that could have been used for more human beings, leaving their relatives behind to die. I know what it feels like to be discriminated against, simply for being born who you are. So I hid what I was from everyone, except certain faculty members at the academy. I had lost my brother to a hate crime a few cycles before. His only crime was being Vaxian and wanting to tell his girlfriend who he really was. Do you remember the race riots of 2325 in Batal? I had just gotten pregnant earlier that cycle. I was afraid, not for me, but for our child and the world it would grow up in."

"Did he know?"

"At first no, a Vaxian's gestation period is twelve months. That's something they don't teach you in human biology class," she half-joked. "Unlike human females, we don't start showing until around the sixth month, at the end of the second quadmester."

"Wait…how did you hide the…cravings?"

"The Vaxian markets in Batal and Gordia that sell farm-raised Oxcels also sell their fresh blood. My father would bring home some every day and I would always feed before I would see Terrance."

Gerald gently took her hand again. "What happened to the baby?"

Angela looked toward the window and the rain outside for a few seconds before answering. Her voice even softer now trying to hide the pain, her eyes swelling with tears she fought to hold back. "I hadn't had a chance to feed like I was supposed to that day. I had been so busy helping a friend move into her new apartment…I just hadn't had time. On the way home that evening, the craving hit me hard. I couldn't wait until I got home. I had to stop and feed. A couple of 'Right Arm of Humanity' bastards were protesting outside the butcher store I went into. When I came out, they started in on me about being an alien blood-sucking bitch. One was saying how my kind was 'nothing but leeches on humanity' and that my baby was just going to be another 'leech living on the backs and blood of humanity.' Hormones, temper…I don't know…but I blew up. I punched him with everything I had, breaking his nose and fracturing his skull. Before I knew it, someone in the crowd took a signpost to the back of my head. I don't remember much after that. I woke up in the hospital and found out I had lost the baby. The whole time I was in the hospital he didn't know where I was. My parents made sure of it. I saw Terrance once after that, months later, right before my family and I got ready to move to Gordia. I was afraid to tell him what really happened. I loved him too much to take a chance and have to see him look at me with disgust…for him to look at me as anything other than the human girl he thought I was." Unable to hold back the hurt of cycles gone by, the tears finally began to run free down her face. "I didn't want him to have to deal with the pain of losing his child to bigotry and hate. I told him I had an abortion, that I wasn't ready to be a mother. I had no choice back then but to have him believe I didn't want the baby…That was the last time I saw him. I can still remember the hurt in his eyes, his silence. I told him I couldn't do it anymore and got into the car. The next time I saw him, we were assigned to the same Elite Forces training battalion seven cycles later…"

Gerald could see the pain in her eyes. Each teardrop was a fresh reminder of past hurts, love, and loss. Embracing her, Gerald whispered softly, "I am sorry…so sorry. I never would have imagined, but you need to know he would have accepted you for what you are."

"I know that now, but I still can't tell him about the baby. He would still hate me just as much for walking away and not telling him. He loved me and I hurt him, even though I was trying to protect him."

"Times have changed and it wasn't your fault. He wouldn't blame you for the loss of the baby," Gerald said reassuringly.

"Please don't tell him."

"Shhh, don't worry I won't. Sometimes there are secrets even best friends can't share." This night had opened wounds that were far deeper and more painful than any Gerald could have imagined. All he could do was hold Angela while she cried out cycles of pain into his shoulder in silence.

Raging River

THE MASTERS OF THE HUNT'S Throne Chamber, the final resting place of the most honored Feralan warriors, lay beneath one of the oldest sacred vessel trees that Asla knew of. Few things outside the spirit realm garnered Asla's curiosity, yet this ancient and sacred place had kindled an interest if only for the power emulating from its walls. It was here in these ancient halls that coven leaders, or Masters of the Hunt as they were called by the warrior covens, were chosen. In these halls, the Masters of the Hunt gathered to speak with their equals, and gladiatorial duels of honor were settled rather than incur open warfare between covens.

She could feel the spirits and the powers resonating around her, the sensation was exhilarating, almost intoxicating. Her green irises glowed behind her closed eyes as she reached out into the spirit realm, allowing the sensation to flow deeper into her. Sensing a familiar presence, Asla pulled back; she opened her eyes to see her twin brother, Arshul, standing in front of her. A rush of embarrassment came over her but she quickly pushed it aside when she realized his thoughts were as empty as his expression. She paused for a moment, staring up into his cold blue eyes. The bond she shared with her twin allowed them to hear each other's thoughts, yet there was nothing but silence.

Arshul had always been a Feralan of few words, rarely speaking without purpose, but she had never known the absence of his thoughts within her mind except for briefest of times as children. He would strain with the effort to hide his thoughts from her as they played hide-and-seek, but the sheer force of will he exerted would always lead her to him. Asla had no such trouble concealing her mind from him when she chose to. In time, he had learned to hide his mind from her for short periods, but it had never been more than that. Yet here he stood, without the slightest expression of effort, and she could hear nothing. In fact, the few times she had sought the comfort of his thoughts during the journey here, his mind had been silent as well.

She started to question his silence when Darshul entered the chamber, interrupting her before she could speak. Dipping his head in respect, he said, "The other Masters of the Hunt await you, Master."

Arshul turned, extending an arm in the direction of the door. "Come, sister, it is time to convince the war council of our cause."

In the main chamber, Broas, Master of the Hunt of the northern Coven Hamll, stood in the center of the room. Boasting, he re-enacted the final moments of a recent Diamamoth hunt; it ended with them killing not one but two of the great beasts. Positioned around the center chamber were ten of the most powerful and influential Masters of the Hunt. Cael of Coven Arthen, Morda of Coven Zabin, Biztha of Coven Fathen, Zeresh of Coven Lamare, Teresh of Coven Voidolen, Harbona of Coven Gasthia, Jaal of Coven Nar, Navayha of Coven Kaliss, Gayloem of Coven Hasebi, and Fokarl of Coven Darmor. Each was seated upon a throne made of stones, gold, bone, and lined with various furs, listening to the impressive feat.

Diamamoths, intelligent elephantine animals similar to the triceratops of Earth's past, were not easy prey, often traveling in herds of up to thirty or more. While normally docile, the ten and a half-ton males were extremely aggressive when protecting their herd from danger, making such hunts extremely dangerous; it required impressive skill, teamwork, and nerves of steel to make a kill and live to tell the tale. Yet such hunts were beneficial when successful, especially to the covens in the north where food was scarce during the long winter months.

Asla moved to take her place at her brother's left side, waiting patiently for Broas to finish his tale. While she waited, she took the time to gather her thoughts. Again, she reached into her mind to the place where her brother's presence dwelled, and again she was met with cold silence. Pushing her thoughts outward to refocus on the task at hand, she glanced at the audience, weighing their value to her cause. Though each of the Masters of the Hunt and their resources were key to her plans, there were three whose value outweighed the others—Jaal of Coven Nar, Harbona of Coven Gasthia, and Teresh of Coven Voidolen.

Asla's eyes were met by Teresh's piercing gaze, his eyes locking with hers as if he could sense her. No doubt he had watched and studied her from the moment she entered the chamber. Whether his own stare was of curiosity, or simply the instinctive behavior of a predator watching any potential prey that wandered into its territory, he studied her. For a moment, she felt as if he was looking into her rather than at her. She gave a slight bow of her head, more to hide the slight discomfort of his gaze rather than respect. His stare was cold. Nevertheless, she allowed her gaze to linger on his.

Unlike his counterparts, Teresh was not ceremonially dressed in appearance. He could easily have been mistaken for another of his warriors but for the sigil of his coven tattooed between his eyebrows. Teresh was a master in the art of dealing death. His deeds were legendary; among his people, this was held in higher regard than any elaborate dress could express.

Asla reasoned that for one who often struck from the shadows it made sense as not to dress to draw attention to oneself. With his cowl pulled back, she could only see the upper portion of his face and took note of how his light green eyes stood out against his dark bronze complexion. His head was shaved bald except for his warrior's braid, which was cut short for one of such renown, hanging just above his lower jaw from the right side of his head.

The lower portion of his face was hidden behind an armored mask that gave him the visage of a fanged remorseless killer—a death mask. The death mask was worn only by the Saktesh, or Death Caller, and Asla had never actually seen one. For a moment, Asla considered what powers a veil-seer would need to call upon, but then recalled the tales of Death Callers told to her as a child. The creation of the death mask was a carefully guarded secret of Coven Voidolen's veil-seers. Only the foolish tried to uncover the secret of the creation of the death mask; they learned the error of their pursuit from the caress of a cold blade from the shadows.

The mask was an intriguing artifact of power; Asla could barely sense the Great Mother Spirit's power emanating within. It was designed to render all but the most gifted of veil-seers from sensing its power and detecting the wearer until it was too late. It was this same power that enhanced the Death Caller's senses so greatly that it became impossible for prey, man or beast, to escape the Death Caller. The mask was also the source of power that allowed a Death Caller to admit a spirit stunning howl, paralyzing the hunted with overwhelming fear.

Intrigued, Asla continued to study Teresh; his attention had once again turned to Broas. The armor Teresh wore was dark and tarnished, appearing ancient, and was only slightly more elaborate than the armor of the two Death Callers that stood to either side behind him. Clearly designed for speed and consisting of only a cuirass, pauldrons, vambraces, gauntlets, and greaves worn over dark leather, it was the Armor of Ever-night, worn by all Death Callers. The armor gifted those who wore it with the ability to merge with the darkness of the shadows. Teresh's right gauntlet, The Predator's Embrace, was crafted with wickedly barbed talons. While his left gauntlet was absent of such vicious design, his left vambrace extended into a deadly two-edged blade past his armored fist. All this came together to create a deadly stalker of the shadows. Teresh, a worshipper of the predator aspect of the Great Mother Spirit, would be extremely valuable when the time came. Asla turned her attention next toward Jaal.

Jaal of Coven Nar, the Mountain, as he was also known, was the opposite of Teresh. Where Teresh was a master assassin, Jaal was a master tactician, whose strategy and abilities to master the ebb and flow of the open battlefield were the tales of legend. He was a large, heavily muscular Feralan, a stature quite common among his coven, especially within the ranks of the elite warriors that bore the armor and title of Bashstation. Where Teresh's face hid the truth of his many cycles, Jaal's did not. His stern face revealed his many cycles of battle and carried the mark of one of his greatest battles, a scar angling down from his forehead, across his left eye to his lower cheek. It was a wound long healed, earned over three hundred and seventy cycles ago at the hands of the Blood Witch Na'gatish's champion.

His cadre was slain during the height of the battle to storm Na'gatish's keep at the Cove of Tears. Jaal refused to give ground, even against impossible odds, as is the way of the Bashstation. Every step, every swing of his blade was a testament to his skill and determination as each foe fell before him until at last, he faced her champion, known simply as the Devourer. The Devourer fought with such savagery and skill that the blood of over a hundred warriors, including Jaal's eldest son Jal, dripped from its bone sword. In the end, the Devourer's body laid in ruin, and Jaal personally removed Na'gatish's head. It was one of the few times so many covens had come together under one banner, and Jaal had led them.

Another tell-tale sign of Jaal's many cycles upon Tallagen was his head of thick silver-gray hair, pulled back in a warrior's braid that hung past his waist. Its length was proof that even now he remained a powerful warrior to be reckoned with. He was a true Bashstation, a disciplined warrior of iron resolve, fearless and unbreakable.

A great leader, Jaal had a commanding presence, which inspired loyalty and obedience. He sat upon his throne with an air of nobility about him adorned in the heavy slate gray ornamental armor of the Bashstation, with its signature oversized pauldrons. Despite his physical stature, the armor's bulk seemed impossible to bear for long periods. But Asla knew the metal used was unique, harvested by magma spirits guided by Coven Nar's Shruids from the fiery heart of Tallagen that flowed deep below the Mountain of Dormor at the heart of Coven Nar's territory. The metal known as Ethril naturally bore the essence of the Great Mother Spirit within it, making it stronger than steel while weighing far less.

Every suit of Bashstation's armor was a work of art trimmed in silver with various runes engraved along the edges. The right pauldron bore the sigil of Coven Nar, set in gold. The left pauldron bore the sigil of the Bashstation, the head of a male Drax, in platinum. The Drax was a fitting symbol for the Bashstation; the powerful ram-like beasts were admired for their tenacity and stubborn resolve, refusing to give ground in battle. During the mating season, male

Draxes formed small pods and descended down to the plains to select a territory to attract females. The male Draxes would then defend their territory against intruders, fighting as one. In this same way, the Bashstations fought with coordinated unity, discipline, and tenacity that rivaled insanity, refusing to give ground.

At Jaal's side stood his youngest son Jahal, looking just as imposing as his father in his Bashstation armor. One day, he would make a formidable leader in his own right and would be far easier to control than Jaal Asla noted. Asla's attention was drawn back to the center by Arshul carefully probing her thoughts. She had been so deep in thought that she hadn't noticed Broas finishing his tale of his hunt. She reached back, but Arshul's mind was silent again. Arshul turned his head slightly toward Darshul, giving him a small nod of confirmation to begin.

Stepping into the center, Darshul bowed his head slightly while simultaneously raising his arms; his palms facing up, giving the customary greeting and respect of the warrior's code. "Masters of the Hunt, my master and coven's veil-seer have come to address the war council. I now introduce to you my mistress, the veil-seer Asla of Coven Auralla," Darshul announced before bowing to Asla and stepping to the side.

With confidence Asla stepped into the center, each step measured to hide the fire building within her. "I have come to you this day to speak on behalf of Coven Auralla, but more importantly, on the will of the Great Mother."

Navayha shifted in her throne and leaned back. "Do you, veil-seer?"

Asla felt a surge of anger rush through her at Navayha's challenge, but she pushed it aside as quickly as it had come. Navayha was Master of the Hunt of Coven Kaliss, the warriors of the eastern cliffs. Her coven lived high among the cliffs, having long ago been blessed by the Great Mother with the gift of taming the Great Rawks as war mounts, along with other great beasts of the air. No other coven was blessed with such a gift. The Great Rawks were fearsome hawk-like reptilian raptors with wingspans over thirty-two feet. Powerful and graceful fliers, they preyed on all that were unfortunate enough to fall beneath the shadow of their four wings and deadly talons.

Just like her coven's war steeds, Navayha was a fierce warrior who prided herself on grace and skill in battle, as well as her legendary beauty. Navayha's dark auburn hair was cut short in the front and angled, giving the appearance of wings whose tips reached down to either side of her lower jaw. The back was pulled into a thick warrior's braid that fell to her waist when she stood. Her sky-blue eyes, beautiful and deadly, held the coldness of a raptor and the softness of a woman; they were surely the reason that more than one had succumbed to her master crafted sword-spear, "Sky Slayer." Her leaden blue-banded armor accented her feminine form, decorated with several runes surrounding her family sigil and the head of a Great Rawk with wings outstretched adorned her breast and neck in gold. A cloak made of pure ghostly blue-colored feathers draped from her shoulders.

Asla had to remind herself that here, among the Masters of the Hunt, she was not considered an equal. She paused to turn and face Navayha, making sure to dip her head in respect. "I do, Master of the Hunt of Coven Kaliss."

"Continue, veil-seer. Explain that we might weigh the worth of your words," Biztha said dismissively.

Again, Asla fought back the surge of anger that threatened to overcome her. The anger was not completely her own, yet she sensed nothing of her brother. She stopped to consider another veil-seer. Perhaps one of the Masters of the Hunt had brought their own veil-seer, in hopes of sabotaging the meeting. However, she could sense no other. For now, she needed to concentrate on maintaining control, despite the fact that she was not used to such disrespect. It had to be endured until she was done.

The fact that someone was manipulating her infuriated her. Everything about this chamber and the men and women that sat upon their thrones was a reminder as to why she had taken the life of her father during a hunting trip. It was the first time she had merged with the spirit of the predator to become a Cainanite. Her father's stubbornness to hold to the traditional ways blinded him to the true threat of the defilers, even after her mother's death at their hands; it was why she savored the terror she invoked from him before ripping him to pieces.

Asla took a deep breath, focusing to control her anger before continuing. "Masters of the Hunt, Coven Auralla, like you, is powerful. Yet we are only one of the Great Mother Spirit's covens among many that stand divided. The defilers are but a few standing united, and with each cycle, they reach out ever further across Tallagen. Each cycle they wound the Great Mother evermore.

"Thus, Coven Auralla strikes to cull the infection of the defilers. With each attack, we reap a bountiful harvest of blood, but it is not enough. We, alone, cannot wipe their taint from Tallagen. Nor can we reduce their numbers enough to prevent further harm to the Great Mother. It is like killing a few ranknids without burning the nest. What ranknids that remain soon breed, to replace those killed, and they are once again overrunning your home and food stores. It is why your presence was requested this day, Masters of the Hunt."

Gayloem interjected, "Do you perceive us as misinformed of your coven's deeds? You speak of doing the Great Mother's will by killing the defilers. Yet you speak nothing of things forbidden things that Coven Auralla now practices. Is not, the ritual of merging with the predator spirit to become a Cainanite forbidden by death, Veil-Seer? Are you not yourself defiled for using forbidden rituals? Tell me, how can we know that you and your coven are not simply maddened with the predator's blood lust? There are reasons such rituals have been forbidden, veil-seer."

For a brief moment, Asla couldn't decide on which would be more satisfying, sinking her twin daggers into Gayloem's hearts slowly to watch him suffer, or ripping out one of his hearts and devouring it as he watched before tearing out his throat with her fangs in her Cainanite form.

Asla felt the beginning of the transformation but pushed it back. "We do what we must in order to serve the Great Mother Spirit. The ritual of the predator is forbidden...because those who deem it so have not the gift to fully complete the fusion. The Council of the Veil fears what they cannot control. I have been gifted far beyond them, and they fear me as well. It is why they have not moved to attempt retribution for transgressing their law. We cannot allow fear to keep us from our divine purpose to protect the Great Mother Spirit." Asla's eyes flared slightly. It was taking everything now to maintain her composure. The more she spoke, the more she began to despise those that sat upon their thrones as heretics.

"You speak with arrogance, veil-seer. Tread lightly for the Council of the Veil will not allow you to simply break the law and go unpunished. If what you say is true of the Great Mother Spirit's will, then perhaps now is not the time to pass judgment, but rest assured, judgment will come upon you and Coven Auralla," Cael warned.

"So then it shall be, Master of the Hunt. The council may come to pass judgment only to find themselves being judged, for the Great Mother Spirit protects those who honor her," Asla responded, her tone cold and daring.

Deciding to bring the discussion back to why she had come, Asla paused for a brief moment, allowing the fire burning in her to die down. She moved to take a sip of wine from a chalice held by a chamber attendant standing nearby, before returning to the center of the chamber to continue. "Zeresh, Master of the Hunt of Coven Lamare, were not your ancestral hunting grounds within the Emerald Bay ripped from you? Taken by force in the middle of Klamon spawning from your coven during the new sun harvest season eleven cycles ago? Now, the defiler's barrier has forced you to hunt and fish past the safety of the bay, out into the treacherous waters of the deep void and into the territory of the Blood Witches. How many of your coven's people have suffered and starved during the harsh winters that first cycle? This was but one offense of many by the defilers."

"Masters of the Hunt, I will not offer you the untruth of an easy path. Much of our own blood will be spilled in battle. But it must be done. It is our sacred duty to the Great Mother Spirit. We cannot continue to allow her to suffer the pain and indignity of the defilers trespassing upon her sacred ground. We are the guardians, entrusted to safeguard Tallagen. I implore you to join with Coven Auralla this day to serve the will of the Great Mother Spirit and nourish the ground with the blood of every defiler upon Tallagen," Asla urged.

"Our blades taste their flesh in the fields and forest, yet within their cities they are safe. A benefit we do not share. Let us not forget the lesson the defilers taught us in the destruction of Coven Emiret. In order to vanquish your enemy, you must be able to strike at your enemy's heart, which is something we cannot do. The defiler's cities are protected by the walls of light, veil-seer," Morda said.

"Coven Emiret was led to its death by a Master of the Hunt whose pride—"

Gayloem leaned forward, cutting Asla off before she could say another word. "Do not forget the council you stand before, veil-seer! Choose carefully the words that fall from your mouth next. Master of the Hunt Fokrom is enshrined in these very halls."

Without hesitation, Asla turned to face Gayloem, the burning fury within her bursting forth and washing away any pretense of humbleness from her demeanor. Asla fired back, each word laced with venomous contempt. "My words? My words are not chosen for fear of offense, or in simple defiance! My words are the necessary truth of the Great Mother Spirit's will, and not to please the pride of those that would hide behind a title. I offer no apologies, Masters of the Hunt. Fokrom's pride would not allow him to see the threat that entered through his front door. His death should be more than a warning. It should also be a lesson to you all."

"Prepare yourself, sister. Fokarl will make his move now," Arshul warned, breaking his silence toward her in their shared mental connection.

Immediately, Asla looked toward Fokarl, tensing, readying herself for the unexpected.

"Enough!" Fokarl threatened.

The chamber fell quiet; all eyes were now upon Fokarl as he stood up. "Still your tongue, veil-seer, or see it stilled with the spilling of your life's blood upon this honored ground." Fokarl moved to the center of the chamber, approaching Asla as he spoke. "You are in the Hall of the Masters of the Hunt. Your voice carries no weight here, save what we give it. This is a meeting of warriors, yet the Master of Hunt of your coven remains silent," Fokarl said degradingly.

Asla confidently stood, refusing to back down or give Fokarl any indication that he could intimidate her. Towering over Asla by at least a foot, he looked down to stare directly into her eyes with a challenging smirk. "Such a brave little girl, you seem to have more courage than your sibling," Fokarl said, letting out a dismissive laugh before taking a step back to create half an arm's length distance between them. "Perhaps he has lost his courage and no longer has the heart to stand as one of us. Perhaps he hides in the shadow of his sister now," Fokarl scoffed without lifting his head toward Arshul as he continued to lock eyes with Asla.

They had come here to gather the support of the other warrior covens, not turn them against her, but Asla found herself having been provoked into giving Fokarl a reason to draw his blade. Asla did not fear Fokarl. Another time and place she would have welcomed the challenge. She wanted nothing more right then than to see the fear and disbelief in Fokarl's eyes as his life slipped away at her hands. However, recalling the teaching of the warrior's code of Horkari, she knew killing him would destroy any chance of an alliance if she attacked first. He was a Master of the Hunt, and here, she was not his equal. Fokarl had to draw first blood for her to kill him without reprisal.

She allowed no expression to mar her face. She simply stared in silence, her eyes never leaving Fokarl's gaze. However, inside she was becoming furious, and Arshul's silence felt like a betrayal. Every word of disrespect Fokarl spoke, every breath he took, and every beat of his hearts, it all stoked the flames of her anger even more.

"Perhaps he never had his own voice. Perhaps he is just a puppet for his sister's amusement?" Fokarl said with disgust, drawing his sword. Asla watched as the blade slid from its scabbard. It was a finely crafted blade with an oxidized copper tarnish. Along the blade's center, runes etched into it began to glow white. Asla felt a slight tingle as Fokarl held the blade up near her. The ancient blade was known as Ward-Breaker. It had been forged over three hundred cycles ago, specifically for the purpose of fighting against the powers of the veil and those who wielded such power.

"You and your brother are nothing more than insolent children to me, grasping for power, veil-seer. The 'Great Mother Spirit's will' you speak of is nothing but your own dreams of ruling. I am not so easily manipulated, nor are the rest of us! Neither of you is fit to lead your coven; therefore, I will take claim of it, adding it into Coven Darmor…by force, if need be," Fokarl declared, bringing his blade to Asla's throat and then pointing it toward Arshul, issuing a challenge.

Fokarl's insolence had come to full term and Asla was infuriated. He would pay for his disrespect with his life, and then she would deal with Arshul's betrayal, she told herself. But before her thoughts could become action, she felt Arshul's mind-meld with hers. The torrent waves of his rage washed over her, along with all that he had kept hidden from her.

Arshul leaned forward in his throne, his hands clasped, with a look that could only mean death would soon follow. "I promise you death this day, Fokarl," Arshul said with a sardonic tone, drawing Fokarl's full attention along with the eyes of the other members of the chamber to him.

"Step aside, my dawn. The fool has revealed his intentions as I have foreseen," Arshul spoke into her mind as he stood. At that moment, it became clear why Arshul had remained silent. He had proven to be far more devious than she had expected. Asla knew that referring to her by the childhood name of affection he had given her was Arshul's way of asking forgiveness. She allowed the anger she felt at his mental abandonment to fade away, but she would still punish him for manipulating her. She would deny him the satisfaction of killing Fokarl as penance and claim the Ward-Breaker blade herself.

"Aw, perhaps the son of Ruhallen may have some of his father's warrior blood within him after all. Come, boy. Let me spill it and take a closer look at it," Fokarl taunted.

Arshul dropped his sword-spear. "This day, you will lay broken by your own blade. Your death will not be quick or merciful. The marrow of your bones will be sweetmeat to the scavengers. You shall know no peace beyond the veil, for your body will not rest in these honored halls with your ancestors. Your eyes will be plucked from your skull and your head displayed before your coven as a testament to your weakness. Your sons will know your shame before they join you in death!" Arshul proclaimed with vengeful spite to all within the chamber.

"No, he is mine, brother. Blood has already been drawn," Asla urged with her mind.

Fokarl turned to look at each of the Masters of the Hunt with a laugh of disbelief. "A mighty boast, boy, to believe you could slay me with my own blade!" Turning to once again face Arshul, he readied his sword. "Come, see it made false, child," Fokarl spat.

"Your death stands before you already. Blood has been drawn," Arshul said dismissively, moving to take his seat upon his throne.

In his arrogance, Fokarl had paid no heed to Asla. He looked down to find her staring back at him. She held his gaze before looking down, drawing Fokarl's attention to the dark stain of blood pooling at her neckline. A devilish grin of satisfaction formed across her face as she stared back into his eyes.

"You dare play games with me, veil-seer?" Fokarl roared in frustration, swinging his sword in an upward arc meant to cleave Asla in half. Anticipating his attack, Asla effortlessly sidestepped, taking advantage of the momentary opening in Fokarl's guard. She drove her foot into the side of his left knee with all the rage and strength she could muster from the predator spirit within her. There was a resounding crack within the chamber as Fokarl's knee gave way to the force of the blow. It bent inward at an impossible angle, freeing his shinbone from the confinement of his flesh. With a cry of pain, Fokarl collapsed to his remaining good knee.

Fokarl retaliated lashing out, maddened with pain, swinging his sword at Asla's mid-section, hoping for a killing blow or to force her back. Asla leaped back, avoiding the wildly unbalanced swing, and countered with her own attack. She swiftly darted in to smash her armored knee into his unprotected chin. The brutal attack forced a spray of broken teeth and blood into the air as Fokarl's head and body were violently thrown backward, sending his sword across the floor. Unrelenting, Asla used the momentum of her attack to pounce, slamming the full weight of her body onto his lower chest and snapping several of Fokarl's ribs in the process, forcing another cry of pain from his lips. With lighting speed, Asla reached down, snatching both of Fokarl's daggers from their scabbards and drove the blades down through his right hand and left forearm into the stone floor beneath. Fokarl tried to scream but only a muffled gurgle escaped his lips. Slowly Asla stood, staring down into Fokarl's fear-filled eyes with a taunting smile of disgust. "You are a fool, Fokarl. The kind of weak fool that would allow the Great Mother Spirit to suffer at the hands of the defilers."

Defeated, his honor and pride stripped from him by a child, a veil-seer, humiliated as if he were but a novice in the training arena, the agonizing thought struck home. Fokarl closed his eyes, unable to bear the overwhelming shame now weighing upon him. He prayed for death. His broken ribs forced him to take shallow breaths in an effort to ease the pain. His lungs filling with his own blood. He felt his life slipping away slowly.

He watched as Asla moved to pick up his sword, the runes flaring brightly at her touch. Turning, she slowly walked back to him with pure hatred in her eyes. She was enjoying this, of that there was no doubt. She was savoring every moment, just as he would have done.

Standing over him, Asla raised the sword high, her face emotionless. She let the blade linger above him, intent on dragging out what Fokarl hoped to be a swift end to his suffering and humiliation. She watched him close his eyes, accepting his fate. A moment later pain exploded through his abdomen forcing his eyes open as Asla drove his own sword through him and into the floor, intentionally angling the blade to miss his spine and not end his life. She began to toy with the sword, slowly twisting it to watch him squirm.

"He is defeated. Either grant him mercy or a swift death, veil-seer," Gayleom demanded.

"The law is the law. This was no honor duel, but a duel of blood. She owes him neither the honor of a swift death nor mercy!" Arshul rebuked.

With a look of compassion, Asla knelt down near Fokarl's head. "Do you see it, Master of the Hunt? Do you see the veil? Do you long for its embrace to end your suffering?" Asla asked in a soft tone.

Fokarl's mouth, a ruined mass of shattered bone and mangled flesh, could offer nothing more than a weak gurgling moan of acknowledgment and a grimace of pain. Staring into her eyes, he saw warmth and mercy. He saw the comforting peace of death finally being offered. Asla could see the pleading in his eyes to end it, and her eyes flared with an iridescent glow as her mouth twisted cruelly. "You will never know the embrace of the veil, for you are a heretic!" Asla sneered, spitting into his face as she stood, ripping the sword from his abdomen.

The last thing Fokarl felt of the physical world was his own blade upon his neck. There was a sensation of pressure followed by a sharp pain as muscle, tendons, nerves, and bone were severed. Then for the briefest of moments, the chamber spiraled upside down and then nothing.

The chamber sat in silence; all eyes were intently focused on Asla as she stood over Fokarl's headless body. She had secured the respect of the Masters of the Hunt now, of this there was no doubt. She stood, allowing the silence to magnify her victory. She was now an equal and they would listen to her words. She turned to look at each Master of the Hunt directly; they each dipped their head in respect. Finally, she faced Arshul. He too dipped his head in approval but also allowed his pride in her to flow into her thoughts. With a sense of gratification, Asla returned a mental expression of satisfaction, before turning to face the center once more.

"Coven Auralla offers you the chance for glory in victory or glory in a warrior's death. Is this not the warrior's way? Together, we will strike the defilers where they feel most secure…for I shall soon have a way to pass through their barriers. We shall strike at their heart where they are most vulnerable. Their blood shall soon flow like a raging river, nourishing the Great Mother!" Asla declared, staring directly at Gayloem.

False Beginning

SARAH SPENT MOST OF THE afternoon organizing her home office. There was still some soreness in her abdomen after leaving the hospital a few days ago, but she was tired of lying down. With Gerald gone, she finally could get up without his constant protests to rest. Plus, it helped free her mind of the constant thoughts of the miscarriage. That part was far worse than anything her body felt physically. She pushed the thought of the baby to the back of her mind as best she could and continued on. She was glad that Gerald and Terrance were talking again. In the ten cycles, she had known Terrance, never had she seen those two truly argue or get angry with each other. They were so much like brothers at times; if it weren't for the fact that Terrance had a different complexion they could be mistaken as such.

She picked up the last of the books and data pads scattered on the floor near the couch, stopping to look at the titles of each book before placing it in its proper location, in alphabetical order. "*The Human Condition*," Sarah read aloud, recalling the data crystal Senator Amberman had hidden within it.

She turned, looking at the door, half-expecting to see Gerald standing there, ready to escort her back to bed. Moving toward her desk she sat down, activating the holographic screens and keyboard. Opening the book, she removed the data crystal. Making sure the system was disconnected from the colonial data-net, Sarah inserted the data crystal. The typical governmental warning message appeared, followed by the message, "Theta Sierra Prime Classification—Input Password." Sarah reclined in her high-back office chair, its gel padding forming to her body as she moved. It had been a birthday gift from Gerald two cycles ago. She had fallen asleep in it on many occasions, especially late nights when she would activate the heating gel as she worked. *A password*, she thought. *Amberman had given me the data crystal but no password. Surely, he would have known I would need one... Or did he?* She picked up the book the data crystal had been hidden in and carefully flipped through the pages. After a few minutes she closed the book, nothing had stood out to her. Then a thought struck her, and she put the book down and quickly typed in the title. Another security message, followed by a new screen with the title "Project 676 (Code Name: Nephilim)." Sarah selected the file icon and data started to scroll onto the screen:

- Project 676-Code Name: Nephilim—Classification Clearance: Theta Sierra Prime (TSP) ^ACCESS GRANTED^—RESTRICTION: Project Inclusion Only
  - Authorization: Project developed and funded by Colonial Security Section (CSS) by Senate Approval.
  - Oversight: Restricted to: Prime Minister Fred Strasse—Senator Leader Dorman Artres—Senator Tariq Imam—Senator Burt Sonny—Senator Gardina Gossline—Senator Nathan Amberman—Senator Glendon Harkus—CSS Chief Director Bill DonwallCSS Research Director Jill Casland –
  - Project Lead Specialist: Dr. Irene Godfrey Dr. Norman Hendrix *(removed from project as of 2302)***(clearance revoked immediately as of 2302)**
- Data Entry-1A-2294-Project 676 was intended to develop an ^Elite Class of Troopers^ that would be capable of performing as highly efficient strike teams, affording the colony the tactical ability to combat ^Demzerai^ pursuit forces in addition to any potential alien threats to include countering and combating the ^unidentified mystical abilities^ used by Tallagen native races, primarily the Feralan. Research was initiated in 2294 under the Guidance of Dr. Norman Hendrix.
- Data Entry-96A-2297—After three years of computer modeling and research it was determined that exposing human

subjects on a genetic level to the element ^Nulonium^ at age 10 would lead to the highest probability of success.
- Data Entry-99G-2298—Initial test subjects are collected from Hochspey Orphanage—Samaria Orphanage—Valiant Orphanage—Great Hope Orphanage—by adoption.
- Data Entry-101E-2298—Initial trial test on first 7 subjects ^5 males^ ^2 females^, resulted in failure. *(4 died during implantation)*—**(3 died within three hours of surgical implantation)**
- Data Entry-153Z-2300—Under the guidance of Dr. Norman Hendrix, project 676 has continually been set back with failure. 33 tests resulted in unacceptable various mutations in subjects followed by their termination. 45 tests resulted in the immediate death of subjects. 22 subjects died within twenty-four days of surgical modification. Currently, cycle-to-date 107 test subjects have died since live test began.
- Data Entry-187R-2302—CSS Research Director Jill Casland *removes* ^Dr. Norman Hendrix^ from program after ^closed^ door hearing *(Classification Clearance: Theta Sierra Prime (TSP)* of Project 676 progress with Senatorial Oversight members: Senator Leader Dorman Artres—Senator Nathan Amberman—Senator Gardina Gossline.
- Data Entry-187S-2302—^Dr. Irene Godfrey^ is *instated* as the new head of scientific development for Project 676.
- Data Entry-189A-2302—Dr. Irene Godfrey, after assessment of notes on Project 676 has decided to scrap all research and begin anew with her own theory of genetic modification and research.
- Data Entry-215T-2306—Dr. Irene Godfrey presents research data to Oversight members in ^closed door hearing^ *(Classification Clearance: Theta Sierra Prime (TSP)*. Dr. Irene Godfrey research has determined that subjects would first require extensive physiological modification

through genetic restructuring prior to ^nulonium^ integration. Physiological modification would take place over 4 stages spanning 15 cycles, beginning with subjects no older than 6 months. *(Cloning would not be acceptable due to DNA degradation)* Success rate of transformation would be 38.7899% with optimal conditions met within-subject.—Oversight members approve to extend Project 676 after consideration of Dr. Irene Godfrey research.

- Data Entry-217A-2306—Genetic testing begins on all eligible candidates throughout colony under the guise of ^Xetis-Neopneumonia^ inoculation.
- Data Entry-217J-2306-846 viable candidates chosen from a total of 28,200 screened.
- Data Entry-218C-2306-846 viable candidates reduced to 68 candidates by additional ^unsanctioned^ genetic restriction and requirements imposed by Dr. Irene Godfrey. According to Dr. Irene Godfrey *(Research data not located in official log)* additional genetic stipulations will increase survival rate to 49.4368%.
- Data Entry-218E-2306—Despite objection to Dr. Irene Godfrey additional ^stipulations^ by Oversight members *(Senator Burt Sonny—Senator Glendon Harkus)* ^approval^ is given to allow Dr. Irene Godfrey the leeway to begin genetic modification as she sees fit by ^Prime Minister Fred Strasse^ on the recommendations of Senator Nathan Amberman—CSS Chief Director Bill Donwall—CSS Research Director Jill Casland.
- Data Entry-218H-2306—Operation Genesis—Classification Clearance: Theta Sierra Prime (TSP)—^enacted^ candidates are given activator to genetic marker virus *(designed by Dr. Irene Godfrey)* induced during ^Xetis-Neopneumonia^ inoculation. All 68 candidates 43 ^males^—25 ^females^ retrieved within 96 hours of ^simulated death^. Explanation of illness and death of candidates is reported to general populace by various media control reports.

- Data Entry-218Y-2306—Phase 1 *(DNA conditioning & Psychological conditioning)*-- ^begins^—Candidates are renamed under direction of CSS Chief Director Bill Donwall directive.
- Data Entry-220B-2307—Phase 2 *(Initial Genetic restructuring)*—^initiated^—Candidate ^M27^ dies from unforeseen complications—Body incinerated—
- Data Entry-421F-2308—Phase 3 *(Secondary Genetic restructuring)*—^initiated^—Candidates are placed in embryonic chambers after completion of Phase 3, duration 6 months.
- ---- DATA ENTRY REMOVED ----
- Data Entry-732E-2310—Phase 6 *(Hypothalamus modification and enhancement)* ^initiated^—Implantation of hypothalamus is unsuccessful in 9 candidates F4—F7—F17—F20—M13—M15—M22– M29—M31—Bodies incinerated—
- ---- DATA ENTRY REMOVED ----
- Data Entry-001-2311—Major Johnathan Vanes --*(Internal Assessment)*—Classification Clearance: Theta Sierra Prime Alpha (TSPA) ^ACCESS GRANTED^ --^enacted^—Under the direction of DATA ENTRY REMOVED I have been assigned to Dr. Irene Godfrey scientific team, to maintain oversight of Project 676.
- Data Entry-1410C-2313—Phase 8 *(Physical assessment)* ^initiated^ --Candidates continue to develop at an accelerated rate. Age 8—candidates show astonishingly above normal physical attributes. ^Average male^ candidate is capable of lifting four times body weight. ^Average female^ candidate is capable of lifting three- and one-half times body weight. ^Average reaction speed^ of male and female candidates is between .005 and .010. Coordination and dexterity are far superior to normal human standards in all candidates. Endurance capability: male and female candidates on average can perform at peak physical capacity for up to 63 minutes before signs of fatigue set in.—*(Can-

didates require only ^6 hours^ of sleep every ^70 hours^ of activity to maintain peak efficiency without degradation of capabilities.)*

- Data Entry-1411H-2313 –Phase 9 *(Mental evaluation and Direct Neural Interface integration)* ^initiated^—Direct Neural Interface test—^100% acceptance^. Mentally candidates are equivalent to maturity level of late adolescents. ^Average I.Q.^between^110^and^115^.---*(Candidates are showing remarkable results in both ^conventional^ and ^unconventional ^military training and tactics.)*
- ---- DATA ENTRY REMOVED ----
- ---- DATA ENTRY REMOVED ----
- ---- DATA ENTRY REMOVED ----
- Data Entry-201-2313—Major Johnathan Vanes --*(Internal Assessment)*—Classification Clearance: Theta Sierra Prime Alpha (TSPA) ^ACCESS GRANTED^-- ^enacted^—After a thorough investigation into Dr. Irene Godfrey ^secure^ data files, I have discovered that *(unknown stem cells)* were introduced into candidates during ^Phase 3^. This was not made part of ^official data logs^. Applying ** (unknown stem cells) ** was never authorized by Senatorial Oversight members nor CSS. In addition, I also found references to a project known as ***Project 217—Code Name: Archangel***. ****No official data**** available on ^Project 217^.
- Data Entry-1580B-2314—Phase 14 *(Operational integration)* ^initiated^—Candidates induction— Remaining *(surviving)*^candidates^ 32 total, 20 ^males^, 12 ^females^ reached full maturity. ^Candidates^ show no visual signs of genetic manipulation although ^candidates^ are now far superior to normal humans. ^Project 676^ is considered a **Success**. ^Candidates^ are given final memory implantation and integrated into populace.
- Data Entry-213-2314—Major Johnathan Vanes --*(Internal Assessment)*—Classification Clearance: Theta

Sierra Prime Alpha (TSPA) ^ACCESS GRANTED^ --^enacted^—After further investigation into Dr. Irene Godfrey ^secure^ data files it has been determined that *(unknown stem cells)* are in fact ^alien^ in origin.)*— Classification Clearance: Theta Sierra Prime Omega (TSPO) ^ACCESS GRANTED^—^enacted^—The ^alien^ ** (stem cells) ** were harvested from ^Demzerai^ subjects held at Norvalex research center- Dr. Irene Godfrey's former assigned research laboratory.

- ---- DATA ENTRY REMOVED ----
- ---- DATA ENTRY REMOVED ----
- ---- DATA ENTRY REMOVED ----
- Data Entry-1580L-2314 —Candidates Alias— Classification Clearance: Theta Sierra Prime Alpha (TSPA) ^ACCESS GRANTED^—^enacted^— *(^F1^:Genesis ^F2^:Natalia ^F3^:Gianna ^F5^:Aria ^F6^:Ximena ^F10^:Luna ^F15^:Athena ^F16^:Trinity ^F19^:Skylar ^F21^:Raina ^F24^:Nadia ^F25^:Soraya)* **(^M2^:Ryan ^M4^:Lucas ^M7^:Dominic ^M8^: Santiago ^M11^:Xavier ^M12^:Mateo ^M14^:Roman ^M17^:Jaxson ^M18^:Maximus ^M21^:Lorenzo ^M24^:Cash ^M26^:Silas ^M28^:Ryker ^M30^:Malaci ^M32^:Nico ^M33^:Cyrus ^M35^:Ronan ^M40^:Gerald ^M41^:Terrance)**
- ---- DATA ENTRY REMOVED ----
- ---- DATA ENTRY REMOVED ----
- Data Entry-242-2314—Major Johnathan Vanes— *(Internal Assessment)*—Classification Clearance: Theta Sierra Prime Omega (TSPO) ^ACCESS GRANTED^— ^enacted^—Dr. Irene Godfrey genetically modified ** two **^Demzerai zygotes ^introducing ^Human stem cells^ into ^Demzerai zygotes^ as well. I cannot determine if this was a sanctioned experiment or project at this time. The majority of her research data files are heavily encrypted. What I have decrypted and viewed without her knowl-

edge are mostly data files she has accessed at ***Norvalex Research Center*** through a ^back door program^.

- Data Entry-245-2314—Major Johnathan Vanes—*(Internal Assessment)*—Classification Clearance: Theta Sierra Prime Omega (TSPO) ^ACCESS GRANTED^—^enacted^—The extent of modifications to ^Demzerai zygotes^ is unknown. I have been able to determine that the * zygotes * were brought to ** full-term **. I believe they were introduced into ^project 676^ at some point. I recommend ^Dr. Irene Godfrey^ be taken into custody for questioning and genetic testing be conducted on all remaining candidates.
- ---- DATA ENTRY REMOVED ----
- ---- DATA ENTRY REMOVED ----
- ---- DATA ENTRY REMOVED ----
- ---- DATA ENTRY REMOVED ----
- Project 676-Code Name: Nephilim Classification Clearance: Theta Sierra Prime (TSP) ^ACCESS GRANTED^—RESTRICTION: Project Inclusion Only—-Project 676 ^Reinitiated^. *Contact established*
- [---- ---- ---- ---- ---- ---- END OF DATA FILES ---- ---- ---- ---- ---- ---- ----]

Sarah sat back in her chair. She was trying desperately to wrap her mind around the depth of it all—Nephilim, kidnapping, experimenting on children? Project 217, integration into the population. Contact with who? There was so much, and yet there was far more to still uncover in all of this. She knew she would have to handle this cleverly; any of this handled incorrectly would have severe repercussions. Worse yet was the realization that there were Demzerai somewhere in the colonies, the very beings that were responsible for the possible eradication of the USC. That alone was enough to bring about colony-wide panic.

She went through her mental rolodex of contacts. Who could she reach out to? Who could she trust with pieces of the puzzle? At the heart of this, all was Senator Amberman. He had knowledge of it, even condoned this. He wanted her to know, to expose the truth, but why? The information contained on the data crystal was clearly far from complete. So much had been removed; was it by his design? She would have to talk to him again, and soon. In the meantime, there were more than enough questions for a reporter of her talent to begin unraveling. She just had to be extremely cautious in who she involved. Information such as this would be closely guarded, hard to get to, and no doubt those involved would do whatever was necessary to ensure its secrecy. Speaking to Senator Sullen would be her first priority as soon as she could leave the apartment.

She quickly downloaded the files onto her secure datapad before removing the data crystal and secreting it away once again within the pages. She tucked the book into the shelf behind her, along with the hundreds of other books, making sure to place it among books that held no interest to Gerald, rather than in alphabetical order like the rest.

She froze; she heard the front door to the apartment slide open. She held her breath for fear it would give her away. She felt like a child that had snuck out of bed to steal cookies while her parents slept.

"Sweetheart, I'm home," Gerald called out, loud enough to hear if she was awake but not loud enough to wake her if she wasn't. He was so thoughtful.

Sarah didn't respond; she moved quietly across the office, stopping at the door to peep out, hoping Gerald wasn't coming toward her. Not realizing she had still been holding her breath the whole time, Sarah let it go with a hushed exhale when she noticed that Gerald had gone into the kitchen first. She moved to sneak back into the bedroom and stopped.

A thought popped into her mind. Gerald, one of the candidates was named Gerald. Was it possible? Could it be? Could he be one of them? Or could he be something far worse and alien? No, there were thousands of Geralds throughout the colony. What were the chances? "Keep it together, Sarah. Don't let your mind wander into unfounded conspiracy theories like some shoddy rookie trying to make a name for themselves. Stick to the facts, girl," she told herself before continuing down the hall toward the bedroom, hoping to make it before Gerald caught her out of bed.

Turning Point

SAMANTHA JUMPED, CLUTCHING A NEARBY scalpel from the dissection table as the lab door slid open. She was relieved to see an Alliance Trooper in full combat armor step through. His face was hidden behind his helmet's visor but she knew it was Dimples, even before she took notice of his name on the right breastplate of his armor. "What's going on out there, Dimples?" Samantha nervously asked, doing her best to not be drowned out by the warning sirens. "The base is under attack. Hostile forces are in the perimeter, Doc. We are moving all the civilians to the main operation building while the Quick Reactionary Forces deal with the intruders," Dimples replied with urgency.

Samantha knew Dimples was eager to join the fight. In their many conversations, she had come to learn that he was a trooper at heart; it was all he had ever dreamed about as a young boy. Throughout the years, he had managed to maintain his childlike innocence, one of his qualities that had made them such good friends in the several months she had known him. It was a friendship they both had come to value and the reason he was here now to see her to safety personally.

"Hostile forces?"

"Feralans, at least twenty of them if not more, Doc." "But the barrier? How? Why?"

"Look, we don't have time for this! We need to get moving and every facking second you waste asking unnecessary questions you're risking our lives and the rest of your lab coat buddies' lives. So shut up and get moving, Doctor Stello," Sergeant Second Class Tracey Ford obnoxiously demanded, stepping into the doorway.

Sergeant Ford was one of two remaining troopers that had initially deployed with the expeditions. The rest of her squad had already redeployed as part of the normal rotation for recon troopers a few weeks ago when Sergeant First Class Heirra's team arrived as their replacement. Tracey and Sergeant Second Class Graham had stayed behind a few additional weeks as part of the tactical changeover.

Samantha was more than ready to see her leave and Tracey was more than happy to give up dealing with Samantha. The animosity between them was clearly evident to everyone. Initially, they had started out as friends when the expedition began. However, the more Samantha learned about Tracey, the less she liked her. Tracey's views when it came to the Feralan people were insensitive and harsh; Samantha saw her as cold and distant. After a few months, conversations turned to a cordial hello in passing. Finally, they stopped speaking at all after an incident in which Tracey shot a fleeing Feralan, whom she said was responsible for scouting for an ambush on a survey team Samantha had been a part of the day before. Things between them erupted over the shooting and since then the two avoided each other whenever possible.

Samantha wanted to fire back, but no matter how much she disliked Tracey, she was right. Now wasn't the time; she could hear gunfire and shouting coming from somewhere down the hall.

"They're inside the lab building!" Dimples said, readying his assault rifle.

"Sergeants Graham, Reedy, and Pikes move to secure the western junction. Sergeants Brown, Tucker, and Dance move to secure the south side exit. We will be right behind you with these lab coats. Dawkins, you're with me," Tracey ordered, stepping back into the hallway. "Oh, feel free to join us, Doctor Stello," Tracey said, waiting for Samantha to follow Dawkins out of the lab.

STRIKE TEAM

Gliding over the terrain at two hundred and thirty-five miles an hour, the Saber armored infantry fighting vehicle resembled a metal hawk with wings outstretched, descending and ascending with the terrain. Lieutenant Captain Malcom Turner looked out of the viewport of his command station, watching the surrounding plains and forests race by as he listened to the current SITREP coming from Echo Four Fourteen exploration team commander. He had hoped today would be a quiet day and that he'd get home before the Hamina Hammers played the New Hope Hurricanes in the first round of the finals. His buddies Jake, Mitch, Daryl, and Ross would be showing up with beer and food at his brother, George's place. The pre-game crap-talking would begin soon thereafter. Daryl was a die-hard Hurricanes fan even more so than Mitch or himself, and the moment he saw all the Hammer's banners and jerseys hanging on display, it would be on. George and Jake would start with stats, and, after half a case of beer, it would just be straight dumping on each other's teams.

Fun times, but with the information coming in over the com-channel and the data flowing across his main screen, he didn't see it happening. However, as he switched one of his view screens to view the troop bay and Master Sergeant Chelsea Tucson and her Strike Troopers seated within, getting home by half-time seemed like a possibility. Short of battle-frames, if anyone could get in and clean this mess up quickly, it was Strike Troopers.

Of all the Alliance troopers, Strike Troopers were the elite of the elite. Receiving the most diverse training in various forms of advanced close combat, weapons, demolitions, squad tactics, and unconventional warfare, they were a complete package, all wrapped up in a suit of SK-029 power armor. Very few made it through the grueling assessment phase and intense training to be inducted into the ranks of the Elite Forces as Strike Troopers. The armor was intimidating. It was covered in a layer of composite diatitanium mesh under a quarter-inch of reinforced plastatium alloy armor plating with a bio-optic muscular bundle system to amplify the wearer's physical attributes by five times normal. Not to mention, it has a built-in jump pack that allowed them to make superhuman leaps and even fly for limited periods. He had always thought that the design aesthetics of the overall armor was impressive too. The angular wedge-like helmet with its thin Y-shaped visor added to their already alien appearance. It was no wonder the Feralan referred to them as Sakket Gurrel, Sky Devils.

"Malcom, ETA, eighteen minutes," Lieutenant Captain Davis announced from the pilot seat.

"Okay, I will let Sergeant Tucson know." Turner keyed the companel to a direct link with the Strike Trooper Commander. "Sergeant Tucson, we are about seventeen minutes out from the expedition compound. The commander on ground just gave us an update of their situation. It's not looking good. I am transferring current SITREP to you now," Turner relayed.

"Got it, give me a few minutes to access the information," Tucson replied, studying the data and images now flowing across her HUD.

From what she could see, the compound was being overrun quickly. This attack had been well planned. The Feralans had managed to hit the compound when only a handful of troopers were available to defend it. The barrier was functioning, which meant someone must have given the Feralans access. Possibly an inside job, but such expeditions had the members screened for world peace sympathizers. Even still, world peace members were not into selling out people for slaughter. Also, all of the security sensors had been destroyed in one section of the compound, rendering the base defenders blind to what was going on in sector three, near the labs. This wasn't just an ordinary raid; the Feralans were attacking with a purpose, forcing the base's QRF to leave parts of the compound undefended in the process.

"They're after something," Tucson said out loud, not speaking to anyone in particular.

"Who is after what?" Sergeant First Class Mason asked from his seat across the troop bay.

Tucson reached over, opening the top of her left forearm's armor to expose a PDA. She keyed in a sequence of code, transferring all the data she had received to the rest of the squad.

"You see, the Feralans, they're after something in the compound. They aren't just attacking. Whatever it is, I am willing to bet it's somewhere in the labs."

"Well, let's make sure they don't get whatever they're going through all this trouble to find," Sergeant First Class Rush said, leaning forward in his seat.

"We're about to," Tucson said as she stood, removing her helmet and locking it onto her hip.

The rest of the squad started preparing except for Sergeant First Class Griffin who sat quietly, almost lovingly sharpening one of his several bayonets. He hadn't said a word, but that was how he was. He rarely said much once he put on his grim, skull-painted helmet. Any other type of unit and that would have been a serious uniform infraction; among Strike Troopers, it was an accepted violation for those that received the silver star of valor, and Griffin had earned two.

Sergeant Mitchell was sitting back in his seat with his helmet off, eyes closed, and listening to music with his earphones. Tucson could hear the steady pounding beat. How he could sleep with music blaring in his ears like that was beyond her. She gave him a swift nudge with her boot.

Startled, Mitchell sat up, removing his earphones. "I was just checking my eyelids for holes." He grinned.

Tucson began, "Okay, listen up. Sensor scans show that there are currently roughly eighteen hostiles within the compound. Twelve of those are Feralans, one is a Mantis Viper, and the other five are an unknown species of insect humanoids, code-named Scarab Brutes. The Feralans seem to be a mix of your standard warrior class; however, there is at least one shaman and two Chindis as well. The shaman and the Chindis are our main threats and primary targets. The Mantis Viper…you already know the deal. It's fast, it's nasty, and if it grabs hold of you with those spiked graspers, chances are not even your suit will protect you from what comes next. If the bite doesn't kill you, the neurotoxin in its venom will. So take it down at range, if at all possible. There is nothing in the database on these Scarab Brutes. We just know what the troopers on the ground have reported. They seem to be pretty strong and hard to take down, no doubt because of the heavy chitinous plating on their bodies. There is no one shot, one kill with these things. With standard rounds, they have only been able to take them with mass sustained fire. So use either heavy explosive or incendiary armor-piercing rounds when engaging them."

"Currently, the majority of the expedition members are in the main building located in sector two. The main attack force is moving toward it. The expedition commander has one full squad fully engaged in defending the base and another squad, down by two, rounding up the last of the non-combatants. The rest of the troopers went MIA over a week ago while providing security for an expedition to explore nearby ruins."

"No one reported it or thought to figure out what happened to them?" Mitchell questioned.

"Apparently they have been having some really bad atmospheric ionization lately with the weather in that sector. It's not uncommon to go radio dark for weeks at a time, I am told," Rush responded.

Tucson continued, "That means there are only fourteen troopers, and recent reports are showing they have already taken three casualties. They are being overwhelmed. It is up to us to get in and put this assault to rest as quickly as possible. We need to secure the compound. You should also know that Command wants us to go on the offensive as soon as possible so we don't rest once the compound is secure. There are three other strike teams en route to a nearby Feralan village where we believe the attackers originated."

Mitchell raised his hand, drawing a "here we go" look from Rush.

"You know, you aren't in kindergarten anymore, Mitch. Just go in your suit. It'll recycle it for you," Mason mocked.

"That would mean he actually remembered his training," Rush chimed in, laughing.

"Yeah, yeah, you two can go fack yourselves."

"What is it, Mitch?" Tucson snickered, trying to suppress a grin in the process.

"So, can I use the C.A.C.T.U.S. this time?"

"Yes, we could use Mordecai on this one…Any more questions?"

There was a brief silence as glances were exchanged between the squad members, but no questions came.

"Negative, Sergeant," Mason answered.

Mitchell stood up, pulling a large seamless metal box from the overhead stowage above his seat labeled "Combat Assistant Canine Tactical Unit Slave."

"Time to go to work, Mordecai," he said, connecting a cable from the box to his forearm mounted PDA. A holographic display appeared, asking for a six-digit code. Mitchell keyed the command code and stood up, detaching the cable as he watched ripples form across the surface of the metallic box. Within seconds, the box had morphed into a sleek, gun-metal colored, one-eyed German shepherd-sized cybernetic dog.

"Sergeant Tucson, five minutes out," Turner announced. "Roger, sir, we will deploy in three teams. Griffin and Mason in sector one, to secure the admin building. Mitchell and Rush along with Mordecai in sector two to help the quick reactionary force deal with pushing back the main Feralan attack force."

"What about you?" Turner asked.

"Sector three. I am going to make sure that they don't get whatever they came for."

Shall We Begin

THE SKY ABOVE HAMINA, EVEN if it was artificial, was still remarkably beautiful, a direct reflection of the true sky above. In a few hours, the beautiful turquoise sky with its twin suns would give way to a kaleidoscope of blue, orange, green, and yellow hues, signaling a heavy rainstorm in the distance. Senator Sullen sat, with his back to the large U-shaped table in the center of the Galum Corp conference room, taking a moment from reading the Colonial Security's investigation report on Conrad Hills, to ponder over it.

He had arrived to the meeting early, with the intention of having some time alone with Senator Jenissa Aubrey. He was hoping to discuss going forward with a new mining reform bill before the rest of the members showed up. Well, that…and it was always nice to see her.

Senator Aubrey was an average height woman, with short blonde hair and soft brown eyes. She had a wit and ambitious drive that let you know she was quite capable of handling herself, all wrapped up in a nicely toned and fair-skinned body. It was a body he had taken notice of in various evening gowns at several fundraisers. She was a breath of fresh air within the senate. The weight of it all had yet to take its toll on her despite her several cycles within it. She still always had a genuine smile on her face when she spoke with him, even though they found themselves at odds on various issues from time to time. Perhaps it was just in his head, but he was starting to think it was her way of flirting with him. For some time now, he had been trying to get up the nerve to find out but the thought of embarrassing rejection had so far suppressed any attempt to do so.

Sullen had considered inviting her to the launch ceremony of the *Nautilus*, the first manned exploration submarine. The launching ceremony was to take place in Batal two days from now. It was a momentous event, a major step forward in understanding the world they now called home. The enormous submarine would serve as a mobile research station and home to a crew of forty-five sailors and seventy scientists as they spent the next cycle exploring and cataloging Tallagen's oceans. It would be the perfect excuse to ask her to spend time with him. Once he got her there, he could invite her to a late lunch or preferably an early dinner before returning, and he knew the perfect place, Jo-Ann's Crab House, near the pier. Amazing food, with a stunning view of Valhalla Fall's iridescent water flowing into the mesmerizing Turquoise Lagoon. He allowed himself a smile, not only at the brilliance of his plan but also that he had finally worked up the confidence to go through with it, even if it was under the guise of something else.

He took a sip of his still-warm coffee; it was sweet with a slight hint of hazelnut, taking a moment to savor the flavor before swallowing the mocha-colored liquid. His thoughts turned back to news broadcast he had seen that morning as he glanced down at his PDA.

It had come as no surprise to him after the recent rogue robot event almost two weeks ago that support for Bill 2062 had shifted in favor of it. The incident had created widespread panic across the colony, and when people lived in fear, they could easily be swayed. Fear was one of the greatest and purest human motivators. In less than twenty-four hours the fate of Bill 2062 would be decided, and so would the next step in the future of the colonies.

The whole incident had been too neatly wrapped up for his inquisitive mind's taste. The media was quickly given a story of how the "emotionally unstable system programmer, Conrad Hills" had suffered from bouts of manic depression, falling into a final downward spiral of depression over his rising debt due to his gambling addiction and eventually becoming so unstable that he tried to use two Ground Assault Robots (or, as the media had taken to calling the machines, by, Hunter Killers).

There was even a suicide note. It was all just too simple and convenient for him to accept. There were questions that he wanted answers to. Like who were the other two men found dead in the storage area? Why were two machines that had basically been mothballed, loaded with live ammunition? If Conrad wanted to kill himself, then why did he do it with two munitions specialists present?

He thumbed through the report, stopping to read a section on munitions authorization. The investigation report said the two men were loading the machines for weapon testing. He didn't buy it, not at all. This was why he had already started his own unofficial investigation, using his contacts and sources within the media and security forces to gather additional information. If there was more to this like he believed, he would uncover the truth.

Behind him on the far side of the room, he heard the door slide open. Senator Sullen turned around in his chair, hoping to see Senator Joelle coming into the room. He wondered if she would be wearing one of those sexy business skirt suits she often wore. It was a disappointment when he turned to see Logan Summit in an off-white suit, along with an older gentleman and a dark-skinned woman.

Logan Summit broke the silence. "Senator Sullen, I see you are early. Your reputation precedes you. I should expect no less from a man of your caliber and drive."

"I was hoping to admire the view before we got down to business, Mr. Summit. I had been told that you have an amazing view of Hamina from the Galum Corp executive level," Sullen stood, moving to shake hands with Logan.

"And what do you think of the view?" Logan said, directing Senator Sullen's gaze back toward the panoramic windows that made up the far wall.

"Very beautiful indeed, I must say. But I am also curious as to why I am here, and I don't believe I have met your acquaintances."

"I apologize. This is Professor Sven Schmidt, an anthropologist and xenopologist, and Ms. Stoval."

"Ah, so now I can put a name with a face, Professor Schmidt. You're the lead scientist who helped with the expansion study for the impact on building the new city. The very study that was used to push Bill 2062 forward for a vote in the senate," Sullen said, shaking Professor Schmidt's hand and attempting to hide his disapproval.

"I take it then, Senator, that you are not in agreement with my report?"

"I reviewed the report thoroughly, Professor, and I must be honest. I am not in agreement with anything that would bring us to war unnecessarily."

"Senator, I simply made a recommendation based on scientific studies conducted by myself and my fellow colleagues. My report is not advocating war. However, we must be conscious of our own basic needs if we are to thrive here on Tallagen. In fact, I suggested a relocation program for the affected Feralans to minimize the impact."

"Relocation program?" Senator Sullen replied with annoyed disbelief. "You honestly believe the Feralan people will just relocate from the land they consider sacred? Then, Professor, I assume all your studies were purely academic."

"You are seeking to find fault in my report to counter Bill 2062, yet it is clear that the bill will pass," Professor Schmidt pointed out flatly, ignoring the sarcasm.

"Perhaps, but I assure you it will be a long time before the bill is enacted once I am done," Senator Sullen continued, turning to look Professor Schmidt directly in the eyes.

"Senator, please, let us take a seat and discuss this along with Senator Aubrey. She should be here shortly," Logan interjected.

Senator Sullen turned back to face Logan with a perplexed look. "I will not change my stance on this matter."

"Senator Sullen…always burning with the fires of determination and passion, yet without the subtlety of a seasoned politician. The curse and blessing of youth I am afraid," Logan replied just as Senator Joelle entered the room. "But you will be interested in what I have to say nonetheless."

"Greetings, Senator Aubrey, I'm glad you could make it," Logan said, turning to shake her hand.

"Hello, Mr. Summit," Senator Aubrey said, shaking his hand. "Brad, it's nice to see you," she smiled.

What frustration Senator Sullen had with the current conversation faded away at the sight of Senator Aubrey's smile. "Always good to see you as well, Jenissa."

"Please, let us all take a seat so that we may begin," Logan said, moving to the head of the conference table.

"Yes, I'm eager to find out the reason for this meeting, Mr. Summit," Senator Aubrey said while taking her seat.

"First, I'd like to introduce Professor Schmidt to Senator Aubrey. Senator, Professor Schmidt published the new expansion report."

Senator Aubrey and Professor Schmidt exchanged a simple greeting as Logan continued, "And to my right, I'd like to introduce you to Ms. Sophia Stoval. Ms. Stoval is here to share some information, which I hope may prevent any delays once the bill is voted in today…I would have liked Senator Amberman to be here, but business with the president prevents him from being in attendance."

"Mr. Summit, you have such a way with words. If you'd like to know what Senator Amberman is up to, I would suggest contacting his aide to make an office call," Senator Sullen said with poised calm despite his renewed irritation.

Logan heard Senator Sullen's comment and ignored it. Senator Sullen was too closely attached to Senator Amberman and the rest of the Conservative Party to ever persuade him to change his mind now. Senator Aubrey's ties were with the Progressive Party, however. Although at times she had some fundamentally conservative views on certain subjects, gaining her support was still possible now that he had convinced Senator Harkus, along with several other senators, to support her bill. With their support, her bill to fund the design and production of a new heavy transport aircraft would most likely pass within the senate. She was the real reason for this meeting. Senator Sullen was here to prove a point, nothing more.

Senator Sullen took his seat, seeing that a woman had just entered the room and taken a seat next to Logan. He assumed at first that she was Logan's personal assistant Maxine, but he had heard that Maxine was an overly tanned woman in her forties and not very attractive. This woman, however, was strangely compelling and had to be in her twenties with light brown skin. Whoever she was, she seemed to be a mystery to everyone except Logan and Ms. Stoval.

"Thank you for joining us, Ms. Williams," Logan said, acknowledging her presence. She made no attempt to acknowledge his greeting or anyone else in the room. "Ms. Latoya Williams is a representative for one of my prominent special interest investors."

Ms. Williams glanced around the table but remained silent.

Logan continued, bringing up a holographic map of the area for the new city's construction. "Senator Sullen, I know you have been at the forefront of the efforts to prevent the construction program under Bill 2062, along with Senator Amberman and several other members. I also know that you started to put things in motion two days ago to delay the construction program now that the bill will surely be approved. However, I would ask, Senator Sullen, that you please keep an open mind during this meeting. I would also ask the same of you, Senator Aubrey. I am aware that you now hold a prominent chair on the Colonial Defense board replacing the Minister of Defense, Senator Wayne, after that misplaced Vaxian comment going public."

"Actually, I am only chairing until the president makes a decision on who will replace Senator Wayne," she replied.

"Come now, Senator, you have the support of both the senate leader and the Progressive party, which holds 65 percent of the senate seats. You are young, with fresh progressive ideas, tempered with intelligent conservative views. You have actual field experience. Your time in the army makes you popular with the military, a key voting demographic. The people see you as the balance that is needed within the senate, especially in the stressful times we currently live in. The only other person who could possibly be considered to take the position would be Senator Eldrid. However, he's a leftist member of the conservative party and has often publicly spoken against the president and his policies. I fear the president would find him to be too much of an…antagonist…to put him in such a key position that could affect the president's military policies. The president will make his decision in the coming weeks, prior to mid-term elections to gain support for the Progressive Party and his reelection," Logan smiled confidently, leaning back in his chair. "I assure you, you are only keeping that seat warm for yourself, Senator, and Senator Sullen knows that as well. It is why he is hoping to gain your support now to create a delay by limiting military assets."

Senator Sullen interjected, "That's just it, and you know full well that constructing this city in that location will cause a direct conflict with the Feralan people. If you and the other CEOs had chosen to build in a different sector, then perhaps we would have been willing to support the bill with modifications. But instead, you are looking at profit over lives."

"I personally don't agree with the new city governing body being made up of corporate board members rather than elected government officials. But I'm sure that could have been worked out with far fewer delays and less resistance," Senator Aubrey added.

"We would prefer the term 'annex.' 'City' is a term used by the media to rile the public," Logan stated.

"Senators, would you agree that in order for the colonies to thrive that we require resources?" Ms. Stoval asked simply.

"Yes," Senator Aubrey replied.

"Of course," Senator Sullen responded reluctantly.

"Then why do you wish to stand in opposition to Bill 2062, refusing to see past profit as a byproduct of growth and the security of the colony, Senator Sullen? The annex is a joint venture of over twenty-one corporations working together under one board of directors. The Senate does not sit on corporate boards now, so why should this be any different?" Ms. Stoval said, highlighting the corporate breakdown in the holographic display suspended above the center of the table. "From a political point of view, it will also create over one hundred and eighty-five thousand new jobs within the next five cycles. Both parties stand to gain in both the mid-term elections and primary elections coming up next cycle," Ms. Stoval continued, changing the holographic display to show the current political parties' breakdown in the senate.

"Senators, what would make more sense than to build an annex dedicated to manufacturing and resource acquisition as closely as possible to large sources of various metals and resources? Not to mention the large nulonium deposits, which power the very barriers that protect our cities? This area will be viable for resource extraction for centuries after the annex is 100 percent operational. We would protect the valuable lives of our military men and women by not exposing them to the constant dangers outside the barrier to protect our interests in the area," Logan added.

He continued, "Senators, I would ask you to consider how, in the long-term, the annex will reduce the burden on the military by minimizing exposure to the natives, as Professor Schmitt's report stated. Initially, there will be some conflict but it will be nothing our military is not prepared for or capable of handling."

To Senator Sullen, this was starting to sound like the same debates he had heard before, and it was doing nothing to change his stance on the matter. His interest had waned, and at this point, he was only entertaining this meeting due to Senator Aubrey's presence. He didn't want to take the chance that Summit and Ms. Stoval could persuade her to pull her support. It was the main reason Senator Amberman had convinced him to attend the meeting in the first place.

What did interest him was the strange woman sitting across from him, Ms. Milliams. He assumed she had to share the same interest as Summit, considering he had said she represented a "prominent special interest investor." Yet, she seemed to be far less engaged in what was being said than he himself was. During this entire time, she had said nothing nor showed any indication as to what view she held. Instead, she sat across from Senator Aubrey with an expressionless face, caressing a charm of some kind that hung from a gold necklace around her neck.

For the next few minutes, Senator Sullen half-listened to Professor Schmitt go on about his research with thoughts of his next move. Logan was right about Senator Aubrey being elected to the Minister of Defense seat. He was also right that she was ultimately a Progressive and that her support was not 100 percent guaranteed. If she decided to not back his plan, there were other members on the colonial defense board who could possibly be swayed to his cause. Although their effect would be minimal next to Senator Aubrey's, for his plan. He could convince Senator Brown, as well as Senator Tate, to support him with a little political maneuvering. He had refrained from using such tactics in the past due to Senator Amberman advising to hold such aces until it was necessary. Senator Amberman often reminded him that politics was like a game of Holkem. You never used the ace of diamonds until your opponent played the wild card. He continued for a while longer, planning his next move, until his attention returned to the meeting when he heard Senator Aubrey speak.

"Mr. Summit, currently there is a plan before the colonial defense board to provide two brigade combat teams or BCTs, to support the city, I mean annex, construction. This is to further be augmented with an additional BCT. However, I would be willing to consider a more viable plan such as the one offered by General Stafford."

"Jenissa, you aren't seriously considering this?" Senator Sullen asked in disbelief. "All this talk of expansion, annex, for the greater good of the colonies…It's just to cover the war and atrocities to come by doing this! We are here now because we were once in the shoes of the Feralan people. What gives us the right to come to their world and kill them? This isn't about the greater good of the colonies, this is about—"

"Enough," Ms. Williams said coldly. "I have sat here listening to you babble on like children long enough. It is clear, Logan, that Senator Sullen has no intention in stopping his pursuit to delay the annex construction. While I must say that I have patience, far beyond what your infant minds can conceive, Senator Sullen, there is a matter that requires a more pressing schedule than what you are aiming for. Mr. Summit and Senator Harkus may not be aware that, even without Senator Aubrey's support, you can delay the annex far too long for my interests. It is quite unfortunate for you, as my patience is considerably limited in this matter. However, removing you would be far too problematic at this point."

"Excuse me? Remove him?" Senator Aubrey asked, shocked at what she had just heard. "Are you threatening him?"

"Who the hell is this woman, Summit?" Senator Sullen demanded.

"This meeting is over, Summit, and I will have you know, Ms. Milliams, that threatening a member of the Colonial Senate is a felony offense. I assure you, Summit, you will be held responsible for this. Rest assured, that damn city will not see the light of day when I am done," Senator Sullen declared, standing up.

"Sit down! And be silent," Ms. Milliams demanded. Her voice, while still feminine, had become far deeper. Its tone forcing Senator Sullen to sit despite his desire to do otherwise.

Both Senator Sullen and Senator Aubrey tried to protest, yet their mouths would not open. They were trapped, prisoners within their own bodies, unable to do anything other than to follow Ms. Milliams's commands.

"You feel that you wield power because of your title, Senators? Sitting in your little room, governing the lives of a few million individuals? Dictating laws and policies to maintain control over the masses? You fool them into a false sense of security and hope for their future, allowing them to believe it is for their best interests. You, non-believers, have no idea what true power is. Allow me to show you but a fraction of what true power is, Senators. The power to control the very essence of life and death." Ms. Milliams turned her head to look at Professor Schmitt. There was a frightening gleam in her eyes. A cold, distant look, one that made him cold with fear. His fear rose from him like a sweet aroma; it was almost overpowering, and she had to fight back the urge to take him herself. "Remain seated, my dear professor," she whispered affectionately. "It is time, Stoval," she said without breaking eye contact with Professor Schmitt.

Ms. Stoval's eyes began to glow with an aura of red and black flame; they became stark white in a split second, and at that moment, across the room, a spark of reddish-black energy flickered into existence. The spark quickly expanded to form a large black shimmering pool, framed with flames. A doorway, almost beautiful, like a pool of liquid darkness.

"I really wish it didn't have to come to this, Schmitt, but it's the senators' fault. Consider yourself a martyr," Logan said sympathetically, staring at Professor Schmitt as he stood and moved to the opposite side of the room to face the portal.

The temperature in the room quickly dropped, becoming unpleasantly cold, but Sullen didn't feel it on his skin. The cold seemed to reach into him, chilling his very being with dread. He would have shivered if he could have moved. No, he would have run to hide. The feeling of fear was giving way to pure terror as a giant stepped through the dark portal. The hair on the back of his arms and neck stood on end. His heart pounded so hard in his chest that he was sure the others could hear it within the room. He wanted to shut his eyes, to turn his head away; he didn't want to see the giant, but he couldn't stop. Instead, all he could do was look on with a growing sense of terror.

Next to him, Senator Aubrey had begun to cry, though no sound escaped her mouth. The stream of tears running down her face was clear evidence that she was just as terrified as he was. Professor Schmitt's face had turned ghostly-pale and he was sweating profusely despite the cold.

"Lord Harbinger Thaticus, it is time to convert the non-believers to our Lord's will," Ms. Stoval said, her voice now a multitude of voices, all speaking as one.

Sullen watched as the massive, armored monstrosity known as Lord Harbinger Thaticus stepped fully through the surface of the portal, sending ripples across its surface. Sullen closed his eyes, squeezing them shut as if he could hide behind his eyelids from the Lord Harbinger as he began to approach the table.

"Oh no, look and understand the meaning of real power, Senator," Ms. Milliams tauntingly commanded.

Sullen's eyes sprung open against his will to see Thaticus, who now stood on the other side of the table from him, towering over Professor Schmitt. His mind was forced to take in every terrifying detail of the Lord Harbinger, to forever have them etched into his nightmares. Thaticus stood easily over seven feet tall and his shoulders were twice as broad as any man. He wore a deep purple tunic made of some form of animal skin that draped down to the floor. On top of the tunic, he wore an intricately crafted suit of ancient blackened armor. The armor was adorned with vicious blades and spikes, along with runes that glowed with the same reddish-black energy that surrounded the portal's surface. His helmet hid all but his soulless eyes behind a menacing visor that resembled a skull with horns jutting forth from either side. Around his waist various wickedly shaped blades hung from chains, some which were still caked with what Sullen could only assume was dried blood. In his left hand, he held a large sword-like weapon of blackened metal that could just as easily serve as a battle-ax if he changed his grip upon it. Sullen's attention shifted again to Professor Schmitt when Thaticus reached out with his free hand to lift him from his seat by his throat. It was like a child picking up a doll.

Ms. Millams inhaled deeply through her nose as if savoring a pleasant fragrance in the air. "He is rich with fear. Can you smell it, Lord Harbinger? I give you now his essence to nourish your own."

Professor Schmitt twitched, now free from whatever force that once held him captive. Instinctively, he reached up, gasping for air with both hands, trying to grab Thaticus's wrist as he kicked wildly to break free of his grip, but to no avail. Urine soaked his pants as the professor continued to struggle. Yet despite all his effort, Thaticus remained silent and unmoved.

"P-p-pleaseee, I...don't...want to...die...," Professor Schmitt managed to get out as he gasped for breath.

Ms. Millams smiled, turning in her chair to look Senator Sullen directly in his eyes. With a serene tone she spoke, "My dear professor, every decision Senator Sullen has made, whether on his own accord or Senator Amberman's, has led him down a path to this moment. Your untimely death shall now be a clear message and lesson to the senator. You have been chosen for a higher calling that is far greater than your mortal life. You serve a greater purpose on Senator Sullen's behalf, that he may live to fulfill his purpose. Now, I shall grant you the reward of the path you have chosen, Senator Sullen."

Thaticus gave no reply; instead, his visor slid open to reveal a lipless mouth lined with fangs exposed in a grim smile. With a deep and commanding voice, Thaticus spoke for the first time, "Proceed on your way to oblivion. For all shall serve either in life reborn or in death."

Professor Schmitt replied with a yelp of pain as a tongue-like appendage shot forth from Thaticus's mouth, attaching itself to his chest. The yelp quickly turned to blood-curdling screams as he felt his life being drained from him.

Senators Sullen and Aubrey watched in horror, unable to look away from Professor Schmitt's death as his body began to rapidly age. Little by little, the professor's struggling ceased, his screams transforming into moans. Yet, the terror in his sunken eyes never diminished, which seemed to entice Thaticus to feed even faster until at last Professor Schmitt finally fell silent, the last of his life drained from him.

Done feeding, Thaticus retracted his feeding appendage, dismissively tossing Professor Schmitt's desiccated husk onto the table in front of the senators.

With the gruesome show over, Ms. Milliams swiveled in her chair to once again face both of the senators. Her eyes were now completely black like those of the Lord Harbinger yet within them there was a red glow. With a sadistic smile of satisfaction upon her face she spoke, "You will soon come to learn, Senators, like so many before you have, that all shall serve, either in life reborn or in death."

Logan casually walked back around the table, stopping to pick up the coffee pot from the refreshment table. "Burr-r, I am afraid the climate control can't help that chill you feel. It always gets a little chilly when he's around. No offense, Lord Harbinger," Logan said apologetically pouring hot coffee into the senators' coffee cups before pouring himself one and taking his seat again at the head of the table. Logan took a sip of his coffee, reactivating the holographic display of the construction plans, and with a pleasant smile he simply asked, "Now, shall we begin?"

THE END

About the Author

TERRANCE MOBLEY IS A MIAMI, Florida native who is an avid reader of both science fiction and horror novels. From an early age, he has always had a far-reaching imagination and curiosity for the world around him. As an adult, he got the opportunity to truly travel and experience the world before recently retiring as a US Army veteran with 24 years of service. He now resides in Arizona where he seeks to pursue his lifetime dream of becoming an author as well as a game designer.

CPSIA information can be obtained
at www.ICGtesting.com
Printed in the USA
BVHW050847190922
647388BV00001B/64